THE FOREVER DRUG

. . . is the riveting new novel of interplanetary espionage by acclaimed author Steve Perry. Many readers have already discovered Perry's mastery of alternative futures in the exciting *Matador* series. He plunged even further into the future with *Spindoc*, a powerful thriller that introduced us to Venture Silk, liar-for-hire. Now Silk is back, trapped in a game of cat-and-mouse where the loser dies, and the winner lives forever . . .

PRAISE FOR STEVE PERRY'S *MATADOR* NOVELS . . .

™A crackling good story. I enjoyed it immensely!
— Chris Claremont, author of *FirstFlight*

™Heroic. . Perry builds his protagonist into a mythical Ægure without losing his human dimension. It's refreshing.
— *Newsday*

™Effectiv and logical . . . recommended highly for all who enjoy intelligent, thoughtful outer-space adventure!
— *Science Fiction Review*

™Perry writes thrilling, action-packed, compelling science Æction. His *Matador* series has become a classic . . . Pick up one of Perry's novels. You won't be disappointed. — *VOYA*

PRAISE FOR *SPINDOC* . . .

™Fast-paced. . His future world seems very real. *Spindoc* is a fun read.
— *Analog*

Ace Books by Steve Perry

THE MAN WHO NEVER MISSED
MATADORA
THE MACHIAVELLI INTERFACE
THE OMEGA CAGE*
THE 97TH STEP
THE ALBINO KNIFE
BLACK STEEL
BROTHER DEATH
SPINDOC
THE FOREVER DRUG

And from Berkley Books

HELLSTAR*
DOME*

(*written with Michael Reaves)

THE FOREVER DRUG

STEVE PERRY

ACE BOOKS, NEW YORK

This book is an Ace original edition,
and has never been previously published.

THE FOREVER DRUG

An Ace Book / published by arrangement with
the author

PRINTING HISTORY
Ace edition / February 1995

ISBN: 0-441-00142-4

ACE®
Ace Books are published by The Berkley Publishing Group,
200 Madison Avenue, New York, New York 10016.
ACE and the "A" design are trademarks
belonging to Charter Communications, Inc.

PRINTED IN THE UNITED STATES OF AMERICA

10 9 8 7 6 5 4 3 2 1

This book is for Dianne;
and for the Friday night staff and volunteers at
Greenhouse in the summer of '92:
Celia, Joey, Katherine, Delores,
Scott, Dianne, Donna & Bob

ACKNOWLEDGMENTS

Thanks this time go to Michael Reaves, for all the bat and barbarian support, as well as my not-quite-an-Emmy award; to S. Danelle Perry, for help with certain signs; to Mike Byers, for the space bullets; and Massad Ayoob for assorted pistolcraft. Gracias, folks.

Because I could not stop for Death,
    He kindly stopped for me—
The Carriage held but just Ourselves
    And Immortality . . .

Emily Dickinson

THE
FOREVER
DRUG

ONE

THE AIR WAS cool, dry, and smelled like slightly fermented hay where Silk lay stretched out prone. Alien insects buzzed around him and, despite the morning's chill, the early sun beat at the blocker on the back of his otherwise bare neck, trying to get past to burn his skin. There were a few of those squat and ugly creosote-like bushes scattered here and there but mostly the field was empty all the way to the woods, a good four hundred meters or so.

The target was three hundred and six meters away.

Silk supposed there might be people who could hit it with a crossbow at that range, assuming they had a weapon that would throw a bolt that far, but it was twice as far as the longest shot he had ever made. Of course, that had been on Earth, shooting at a stationary target. This was no crossbow he held. And it wasn't Earth.

Silk flipped the cover on the receiver up and pressed the button underneath it. Inside the weapon's heavy plastic stock a tiny generator whined up to inaudibility so fast all he caught was a faint high-pitched beep. The generator, itself fed by a rubberized lithium-slurry battery, poured high-voltage, medium-amperage power into a kind of supercapacitor that stacked and stored it. Within a second, a tiny orange light lit on the rifle's receiver. *Zap*, that fast, there was now enough juice to cook the water in the holding tank to plasma. All he had to do

1

was pull the trigger. A jet of intensely heated steam would boil out of the nonconducting, wound-fibercarb barrel, spinning the copper-clad lead pellet through the stainless steel liner's rifling so when it left the muzzle, it would be traveling at almost eleven hundred meters a second, three times that of sound in local air.

At three hundred meters, it would take the sound of the round breaking the sonic barrier nearly a second to reach a target. If the heavy 8.5mm boat-tailed bullet hit a man in a vital spot at that distance, it was very likely he would be dead before the noise got there. So his rifle instructor had said.

You don't hear the one that kills you, the instructor had told Silk.

"You going to shoot or what?" Zia said. She lay next to him in the dead brown grass, her own plasma rifle pointed downrange.

"Yeah, keep your pants on."

"That's not what you said earlier."

Despite his attempt at concentration, he grinned. That part was still okay. The rest of it might be fucked, but, well, fucking wasn't.

Not yet, anyway.

Silk glanced at the target through the scope. The range-finder gave him the exact distance, and the ghost-read heads-up told him the image was adjusted for parallax and corrected for bullet drop and windage. Like an automatic camera, the rifle took care of all the real work. All you had to do was put the tiny sighting dot on the target and touch a control. Once the weapon's computer was sure that's what you wanted to hit, it would rejigger the image so that a second sight picture would put the missile dead-on at any range the weapon was capable of reaching, and it would do so in less time than it took a man to blink. It had worked that way on the range. Said the instructor: "At three hundred meters if you can hold the brotherfuckin' rifle steady, it'll put 'em all inside a circle you can make with your thumb and forefinger, sub MOA."

"Silk?"

"Okay."

He took a deep breath, let half of it out, held the rest. He willed his heart to slow, then waited for the stretch between beats. One, two, three . . .

Silk pressed the trigger. The rifle whooshed, spat a missile that shattered the sound barrier with a wet *crack*! The plastic stock kicked his shoulder, jolting him. He fought to hold the sight picture, lost it for a second, then found it again.

Three hundred and six meters away, the deer dropped as if its legs had vanished.

Zia, watching the prey through her own rifle scope, said, "Good shot."

Silk felt a sense of something he couldn't quite define, a kind of regret, a sadness. He'd never killed anything before—

Well. If you didn't count people.

Zia Rélanj watched Silk, a couple of meters behind him as they walked to check the downed deer. She was still amazed at herself for bringing him to E2. It had taken some fancy singing and dancing to pull it off, to make it all right, and she still wasn't sure how much Nessie— New Earth Security—trusted her and her supposed trophy, one Venture Silk, late of Earth. It had taken a lot of favors, those she was owed and those she would have to pay off eventually, to keep the brainbreakers from taking Silk apart like an old watch. So far, at least, he wasn't wiped; that was something.

They reached the deer, and Silk bent to examine it.

"Seems to be dead," he said.

"You have your knife?"

"Yeah."

"You want me to do it?"

"No." He pulled a short curved blade with a sharpened hook on the back edge from the sheath at his belt. As he made the first tentative cut to dress the carcass, spilling innards onto the cool ground in greasy loops, Zia wondered about some of the other problems they were going to be having. She was scheduled for the Treatment soon, part of the reward for the job she'd done on Earth, taking out Spackler. Once the series of injections, hormone-balancing and genetic tinkering were finished, she was going to be one of the first few hundred people who might, in theory, live long beyond the span of normal humans. Three hundred, five hundred, maybe a thousand years would be added to her life. Nobody knew for sure. They called it the Forever Drug as a joke, but it might just be that. It was quite a discovery, and made on this supposedly backward outworld, too.

Unless he did something spectacular to earn it, Silk wasn't going to be getting the Treatment, though. And that could make for a problem. Not now, not when Silk was thirty-something and she was a few years younger than that. But if they stayed together, then in fifty years or so, they'd look like an old man and his great-granddaughter when they passed a mirror, assuming they were still together, of course. There was no guarantee of that—a lot of twosomes split apart after a few years or even a few months—so it could be moot. Nobody could predict the future that far ahead. The best chaos-rectification programs would not even try to do human interactions; they were too complex even without a future tense. So who could say?

The problem was, as hardheaded and cold as she could be in her business, it didn't apply when she looked at Silk. She loved the man. Loved him. That had come hard, admitting that; to even say it aloud scared her. But there it was; she could dance around it all she wanted to and it wouldn't change how she felt.

She could refuse the Treatment, of course. Tell them she wasn't interested.

She smiled to herself. That she would turn down a thousand years because her lover couldn't have it would probably get her time in the psycho wards if she told anybody. She'd played pretty fast and loose with her life at times, but this was a prize she wasn't willing to give up, either. Somehow, they would figure something out.

Something to let Silk win the Treatment, too. Just like being a couple, a lot could happen in ten or twenty or thirty years. Even if he were sixty, that wasn't old, just about middle-aged, and she'd never had a problem with older lovers, as long as they were relatively healthy and vital. The Treatment slowed the aging process considerably, so they said. Nobody knew for sure in humans since nobody had undergone the Treatment long enough to see the full effects of it, but the experts estimated that the ratio could be as high as 50:1. For every fifty years you aged chronologically, you'd age one physically. There were still problems in a couple of systems, skin, some of the ductless glands, but overall, the Treatment was supposed to be almost perfected.

Silk gutted the deer, cleaned it out, finished the field dressing. It had been just like the model the hunting instructor had shown him, maybe even less bloody than the fake animal had been. He didn't bury the entrails; there were small predators here that would clean the remains away in a day or two, so he had been told. He wiped his hands and the knife and looked at Zia. "Done."

She rose from her squat next to the carcass. "Okay, let's get back to the camp. Sooner we get this beast on ice, the better."

He shouldered the dead deer. It was surprisingly light, although a walk of more than three klicks would no doubt make it gain considerable weight. This was his first kill. There was a meat tech with a freezer van and a slicing laser back at the camp. For a small fee, he would butcher, wrap, and freeze the deer into neat plastic packages, all marked with the cut—sirloin, rump roast, whatever—and it would be delivered to Zia's cube in a day or two. All Silk need do then was go to her freezer and select a packet, as often as he wished. If he didn't want to go out and kill it himself, he could buy any one of seven or eight varieties of meat at the nearest market.

It still amazed him, the amount of flesh they ate here. On Earth, he had consumed animal tissue fewer than a score of times in his entire life. What wasn't illegal was too expensive on the salary of a spindoc, and he hadn't been poor. He'd had fish, shrimp, rabbit, chicken, even beef a couple of times, but here on New Earth, he could, in theory, eat meat five times a day if he wished with no more oblation than the Government Dole Assistance. Even without Zia's income.

Fat black flies buzzed around the edges of the bloody gaping wound in the deer's belly, some of the insects bumping into Silk's head and neck in their frantic haste to get to their prey. He waved them off with one hand. They circled around in small flight patterns and quickly returned for another assault.

Just ahead of him, Zia walked, the smooth rolling of her buttocks enticing even under the baggy camouflage of the hunting suit she wore. She was a stunning woman, and even knowing she had been designed that way with surgery, diet, exercise, and hormones didn't make her any less attractive. She was nothing like Mac, who had been attractive enough. Mac, before she was murdered, had been a doctor, a medic, a healer. Zia on the other hand, was something else altogether.

Zia Rélanj was a spy.

That was a big part of her attractiveness, her competence. Her ability to coolly glide through danger without raising a sweat, to change her face, drop an opponent with a fist or a gun, to dance with death, smiling all the while. She was not of his world, figuratively or literally, and unlike any woman he had ever known. He loved her.

He loved her, and it was destroying him.

They wound along a narrow trail through another section of woods, trees that looked familiar but weren't quite the same as those of Earth. This particular forest consisted of aspenlike stems as big around as his leg and rising to a twenty-five-meter height. There were thousand of the trees, or so it seemed, but Zia had told him there was actually only one plant; the forest was linked under the ground and, like aspens on Earth, genetically the same in any one stand. The trees had pale yellow bark, smooth and almost cream-colored, and didn't branch for three meters. The crowns were thick with waxy green hand-sized leaves, and when crushed, those leaves gave off a strong scent much like peppermint. They were evergreens, but they shed leaves year round. There was almost no undergrowth where the leaves fell and turned the ground into a crackly carpet of deep and rich red. It was like a walk in a fantasy forest.

There was an alienness about it all, but on one level, it reminded Silk of entcoms he'd seen of the American frontier: wooded, rugged country, sparsely settled, wild animals running around. There was a brash freshness to it much unlike the stale and too-civilized Earth. And from what he knew and had seen, the whole planet was that way. It *was* the frontier. Oh, there weren't any savage natives lurking in the bushes with arrows or blowguns, ready to kill and eat the unwary hunter, but on a given morning in New York City, there would be more people riding the subways than on this entire *planet*.

The camp was only a kilometer or so away now. Other hunters would be bringing in their trophies or leaving to seek them. Zia had killed her deer the first day of the three-day trip. He hadn't gotten his until the last morning. He hadn't particularly wanted to make the trip, but she had insisted. If you are going to eat it, you should know that it doesn't appear magically in the grocer's cooler all wrapped in see-through. If you are willing to hunt an animal and kill it, gut it, and clean it, then you have earned the right to cook and eat it.

A strange philosophy, but he supposed he could understand it. Especially here on E2, where there was so much more land than there were people to occupy it. True, his idea about the *ausvelt* planets being peopled by inbreds in mud huts was wrong, but there was a lot of space, and still a few places where humans had yet to leave footprints. Couldn't say that about Earth, with the almost

seven billion souls there. Even the wildest areas of the
SoAmer forests were inhabited by someone. He had seen
that on his way offworld. The Amazon rain forest wasn't
New York or New Madrid, but there were men in the
jungle.

He was never going to be one of them again. Earth
was back there, and when he'd left it with Zia, he had
given his home up, forever. It hadn't been his fault, but
if he set foot on the planet again, he would be scooped up
and taken apart by the authorities before he could open
his mouth to ask for mercy.

Well. There was no point in pissing and moaning about
what was history. He had to move on.

He shifted the deer carcass slightly, stirred the flies
that had sneaked onto it from behind him. Another frantic
buzzing ensued, then settled down. Go ahead and eat, he
thought. Fuck it. By the time the tech finished with the
deer, it would be sterilized and bloodless. It had been
grazing on the brown grass when the sun came up and
would be converted into plastic packets in a freezer by
noon. Sorry, pal, that's how life goes. He hoped the deer
had enjoyed living while it had the chance.

That was a good idea in Silk's case, too.

TWO

THE PUBLIC AFFAIRS office of the Lower Island Timber & Paper Company was a three-room suite in the back corner of a complex housing maybe thirty other such businesses. The front room was a small one with a couple of chairs and a limited biopath unit programmed for communications. The biopath had enough brainpower to act as a receptionist, should anybody come through the front door, but the vox on the thing needed tuning; it sounded like a woman who'd left the water running at home and was in a hurry to leave and go shut it off. The unit acknowledged Silk's arrival in a staccato rush:

"M.-Silk-please-sit-M.-Graso-will-see-you-shortly."

Silk sat. For maybe three minutes; then the 'path directed him to proceed down the hall to M. Graso's office.

He passed the middle office, which housed another somewhat more complicated biopath, along with a hardcopy printer and assorted electronic and semimechanical machines that might be found in any small business on any planet. Not that the biopath here was anywhere near the AI complexity of the dislinked system he'd had in Hana, back on Maui. He wondered who was working with Bubbles now. She'd been a good partner, despite her warped sense of humor.

A man about Silk's age, maybe a couple of years younger, thirty, thirty-two T.S., sat in front of a composition holoproj assembling what looked like an interactive house organ. Probably a statsheet for the company's workers. Who retired, who died, who got promoted, shoulder to the wheel kind of thing.

The third office was larger than the first two put together and was furnished mainly with a large, dark wooden desk polished to a satiny sheen, a couple of oil or acrylic landscape paintings, and a very fat man overflowing a chair behind the desk. The man was a sumo cruiserweight, easy, two hundred and fifty kilos if he was a gram. There was also a single wooden chair in front of the desk, the legs of which were short enough so that a visitor in the chair would sit looking up at the fat man—unless the visitor was very long-waisted.

The fat man would be M. Graso, the manager, though there was nothing that said so.

Silk, wearing the new blue one-piece Zia had bought him, entered the office.

"M. Silk. Sit down."

He sat. Looked over the wide desk up at the mountain of frowning blubber.

The obese man touched a control with a hand that looked like a smooth and mutated albino starfish. A built-in holoproj blossomed over the expanse of polished wood and resolved itself into a biograph a quarter meter high. From where he sat the words and pix were backward, but Silk had long ago learned to read that way. It was his credit sheet. It was more or less true, the sheet, though there was no way for anybody to verify it. Unlikely Earth would give out job information on a man wanted for planetary treason, among other crimes.

"You've come about the Public Affairs Officer position."

"Yes." He essayed a brief smile. They didn't call them spindocs or spiders on this planet, but the work had to be similar. On Earth, the idea of applying for a job at a deadwater company like this would have embarrassed him. He had spun the truth for the Maui Port Authority, a major conglom, and he wouldn't have worked at a place like this even if he'd been starving.

But that was Earth. Another life.

The fat man, who had yet to bother to identify himself, waved at the 'proj. Silk found himself fascinated at the way the bloated hand seemed to be not so much a human limb as a cancerous growth on the cuff of the gray-green sleeve of the stretch fabric coat. A man who massed that much ought not to be allowed to wear anything made from flexex. He looked like a sausage about to go nova in a microwave field.

"I must say up front I don't like Terrans," he said. "I don't like Earth or anything about the world. However, we here on E2 are civilized and don't allow job discrimination based on sex, race, or planet of origin, so I am willing to interview you. I don't suppose one can help where one is born." His breath smelled like mint, even across the meter of desk.

"But one can leave, can't one?" Silk offered. The rest of the statement ought to be obvious, simple logic, especially to somebody who was a supervisor of public affairs: *Earth might be awful, but here I am, I've left it, haven't I?*

"I have to say, M. Venture Silk, I don't believe you are right for this job. It's not simply that you're from Earth, it's just that you seem to be . . . well, shall we say . . . overqualified."

He waved at the 'proj and displayed a sudden rictus that Silk supposed was a smile. Great. Another fucking bigot.

Silk wanted this job. He needed it. Not for the money—the GDA covered all his needs, which weren't many since he was living with Zia in her cube. He had only been on this world for six months; he didn't have any credit accounts even close to maxed out. The dole would actually keep him in a style not too much lower than the one he'd lived on Earth. It was a lot cheaper here than there.

But a man on the GDA was a man without any ambition. Government Dole Assistance was the official term. God Damned Asshole was the unofficial acronym for

dolees. He wanted a job, wanted the independence that
the stads he would earn at it would bring. Even a crappy
job was better than spending all your time in classes or
sitting around watching entcoms on the holoproj. Any
job.

He could see he wasn't going to get this one, and if
this had been Earth, he would have stood without another
word and walked out. That he could do this in his sleep,
with half his brain gone, didn't seem to matter to Fatso.
There were a lot of people like Graso—if that was who
this lube drum of a man *was*—on New Earth, at least
according to Silk's experience. Mention where you were
from and they went all snide and shitty. Well, well. A
terry, are you? Then they looked at you as if you were
a dog who'd just crapped on their favorite rug.

From the doorway, the man Silk had seen working on
the newsproj said, "Ah, M. Graso? You've got a call."

Graso looked annoyed. Muscles danced under the thick
sheet of his jowls, enough so Silk could see the lumpy
wiggle. He looked like a glacier about to calve an iceberg.
"I am conducting an interview," he said. "I directed the
'path to cycle my calls."

"Sorry, sir, but it's on your restricted line."

"Ah, well, then. Excuse me a moment, M. Silk." Graso
took a com button from his desk drawer and stuck it into
his left ear so that the caller's end of the conversation
would be confidential. "This is Dika Graso."

Silk glanced at the man in the doorway. He was tall,
a good fifteen centimeters taller than Silk's own 183. He
grinned at Silk, nodded a little, then turned away.

Silk pretended to ignore Graso as he listened to half
of the conversation. "I see. But—no, I didn't mean—of
course I'm a loyal citizen! Yes, yes, I see."

Silk watched him peripherally and his pasty, doughlike
face went even more so. Somebody with a strong hand
was on the other end of the fat man's tether, and they
were jerking the leash. Graso blinked watery blue eyes
rapidly as he listened to the unseen speaker, nodding
in silent agreement with what he was being told. "Yes,

yes, yes, I understand. No, there's no problem. We are in accord. Thank you."

Silk ostensibly looked at one of the paintings, a rendering of a high waterfall cascading down into a frothy pool. He pretended not to notice when Graso finished the com. There was a moment of silence before the fat man spoke to him.

"Ah, M. Silk. The press of business weighs heavily on me these days. I am afraid I may have spoken somewhat hastily with regard to your possible employment." Once more the rictus.

Silk listened. He had been good at his work, and he knew a spin when he heard one. Graso was twisting something here. A few seconds ago he had been about to show Silk the door. Now he was talking as though the interview had just begun and that he was seriously considering the application. Why?

Who had been on the other end of that com?

"The truth is that a man of your experience would be of great benefit to our company in the capacity of a public relations officer. There are no other applicants of your caliber. When can you start?"

Zia stood naked in front of the full-length mirror and examined herself critically. Since her return to E2 she'd been working out regularly, so she was holding at just under 60 kilos, which looked a little thin on her 173 cm. but not too thin. Breasts were a bit large for her frame, but that was part of the hormone augmentation the medics had determined made her more attractive as an op. The fine blonde hair above and below was her own. She did a quarter turn, raised up onto the balls of her feet, observed the play of muscle in her calves. She was athletic-looking but not overdeveloped. She could live with this body for a few hundred years.

The door opened and the doctor came in, carrying a small flatscreen. He nodded at her, then at the table.

Zia ambled to the exam table, unconcerned over her nudity. She'd been naked in front of enough doctors over the years that she'd gotten used to it. She glanced at him to see if he was affected by her downy blonde pubis and firm tits, but if he was, it didn't show.

He lit the table. The ultrasonics and sealed-beam X-rays flashed through her and fed their images into the table's computer. The results showed up on the medic's flatscreen a second later. He looked at the result and nodded. He was one of the older ones, maybe fifty, with thinning brown hair combed straight back and the beginning of a potbelly under his loose whites.

"Everything within normal limits," he said. "Any complaints?"

"No."

"Any unusual symptoms?"

"No."

"Fine. We're done. I'll log your exam into the MR. You're good for another six months."

"Thanks, doc."

"You can get dressed."

He turned and started for the door. Before he reached it, the door slid open on silent rollers to reveal Mintok.

The doctor brushed past Mintok without speaking and Zia got the impression there was no love lost between the two men. Hmm. She ought to look into that. Could be something useful there. A good op never missed a chance to collect ammunition she might need someday.

She slid off the table and looked at her supervisor. He was a big man, wide, built like a weightlifter, thick arms and wrists, with short black hair and thick brows that formed a single furry bar. Hair grew that dark all over him, she knew from experience. He wore a black silk duster over a matching flex unitard and eelskin boots that were blacker still. He carried a lightweight stacked-carbonfiber 6mm Olüm pistol in a small-of-the-back holster under the duster. He smelled like musk-and-pine depil cream, and his beard would need another application of it soon. He had to use it twice a day, as she recalled.

"What?" she asked, as she reached for her clothes.

"What? That's my question, Rélanj. As in, what the fuck are you doing having Pinkie's secretary call some dick-drip manager for a timber company to get your boyfriend a job?"

Zia pulled her panties on, snugged the elastic cloth into place, reached for her bra. "He's qualified for the work and he wants something to do."

"He's a terry."

"Who helped me make sure Spackler didn't shoot his mouth off on Earth and who saved my life a few times in the process. I owe him. And since Nessie owes me, I'm just passing it along."

"He's a Terran. You don't really trust this clown?"

"As much as I trust you, Tave." She smiled, oh so sweetly, as she stepped into her skirtlike synlin pants.

He ground his teeth together. "What about us?"

"Us? There's no 'us.' We had sex together a few times, that was all."

"You liked it."

"Yeah, so?"

"So, what has this terry got? A wart? Or does he do some degenerate shit they like back on Earth? Use his mouth on you?"

"Not your business, *Commander* Mintok."

"I'll bet you get bored with your new toy pretty soon, Zia. You'll want what I can give you."

"Let it go," she said. "It was good, but it's history."

He tried to keep from showing it, but it bit him. Mintok didn't like to lose. He said, "Your terry better watch his step. He's not used to our world. He could get hit by a van or mugged by a stronghand while he's out for a walk or something."

She smiled at him and said, "Remember Stano?"

His frown burned with a mix of sudden anger and surprise.

Stano had been a brute from the hinterlands who had joined New Earth Security because he liked to hurt people and they would allow him to do so legally. He had gotten to FO-2, a second-stage field officer who wasn't ever going to go any higher. He was a flawed thug, but there was a place for big men who didn't mind bonework, and he was perfect as an armbreaker and sometimes disposal technician. He had been a good fifteen kilos heavier than Mintok and much stronger.

Stano had taken it into his head that he wanted Zia. He pursued her and wouldn't take no for an answer. He followed her, watched her, and when it finally dawned on him after two months that she absolutely did not want his attention and had no intention of returning it, he got ugly.

He followed her home one night and flexed his muscles at her.

Here's the deal. You spread 'em, cunt, or I'll hurt you, bad.

Okay, sure, whatever you want.

Afterward, when he was emptied, Zia massaged and stroked his back gently and told him how wonderful he was, how much of a man he was, and how much she had liked it. Lulled by his sexual exhaustion and her tender ministrations, Stano fell smiling into what must have been a blissful sleep, no doubt intending to give her more of the same hard treatment she liked when he awoke.

A couple of days later, a canpicker found a man's naked and blackened body in a recycle bin in the South Beagle warehouse district. His neck was broken, and he'd been doused with high-octane IC engine fuel and set afire. The fuel could have been bought at any pumping station. According to the autopsy, he'd been alive when the fire began, but probably paralyzed from the shoulders down. He would have been unable to move as he lay there and cooked, but could have been conscious and aware of what was happening.

There was not much forensic evidence other than that, except for traces on an unburned patch of the corpse under one armpit and in the oral cavity of what the labbos thought was human urine. Armed with that, the reconstructive techs guessed that somebody had A) broken the man's spine, B) pissed on him, then, C) set him burning.

Dental and bone scans identified the man as New Earth Security Field Officer Grade Two Tedah Stano.

There was a halfhearted investigation by the local police to run down suspects before it was dropped for lack of real interest. Stano hadn't been a likable man on his best day. There were always more like him where he came from, dead was dead and in this case, no great loss. The official report eventually came to say that Stano had probably died in a botched robbery attempt, although nobody in Nessie really believed that. What kind of idiot would try to stronghand Stano? He was built like a gorilla and he carried a pistol in a shoulder holster where it showed, plus everybody with half a brain knew what he was. Beagle was a small city, couple hundred thousand folks was all, and Stano had never been shy about telling people what he did for a living. Most figured he was getting a return on a deposit from somebody whose uncle or brother or father he had taken out. There were hard men and women out in the Badlands who didn't take any shit from anybody. The piss was not something a man wanting a stad credit cube and jewelry was likely to do, was it? And where were his clothes and gun?

Unless somebody came forward and confessed, this killing was going to go into the log and stay there unsolved forever.

Nobody ever asked Zia about Stano's death. Nobody ever suggested she knew anything about it, at least not to her. A few people had known about his pursuit of Zia and that she had warned him off, but there was no reason to assume anything else. People assumed things, though; they sometimes instinctively believed things they had no logical reason to believe. Nobody ever said it to her, but a rumor arose and flowed through Nessie only days after Stano's demise:

Better for your health not to fuck around with Rélanj . . .

Zia smiled at Mintok where he stood gaping at her.

Her supervisor turned and marched out, not speaking.

She continued to smile at Mintok's stiff-back as he left, more for the cam which was no doubt recording her than for how she really felt. Mintok wasn't stupid. His ego might not like the threat, but he understood it well enough. If anything happened to Silk, she was going to hold Mintok responsible.

She didn't like threats, either.

She pulled her shirt on and brushed her hair back. It had grown out some from the butchery she'd had to do to it on Earth, but it still wasn't long enough to ponytail past her shoulders where she liked to wear it. She glanced at the timer over the mirror. She had a workout scheduled in fifteen minutes, and she could make it to the school walking if she hurried. She didn't want to be late. Tanîto had a mean streak and did not like her students to be late for class. She had been known to slap a tardy student unconscious for such a sin.

Mintok was big and strong and carried his gun always, but he didn't frighten her. Tanîto had taught her a great deal about unarmed close combat, and Zia had a lot more respect for the older woman than she did Mintok. Zia would sooner cross a pack of hungry devil dogs than she would Tanîto. Mintok was only a man.

She hurried out of the mediplex and into the afternoon sunshine.

THREE

NAKED, COLBURN ENJOYED the late September sunshine.

He sat in the captain's chair on the aft deck of his fifteen-meter motor yacht just off the coast of San Juan Island near Friday Harbor, Washington. As he sipped beer from a self-chilling pilsner glass, he was well aware of his biopath's polite electronic throat-clearing in the background, but he chose at the moment to ignore the sound. It was warm, the wind was light, gulls chased themselves across a psychedelic blue sky. This was the last of the Hammerhead Ale, and unless he wanted to resort to drinking that pasteurized commercial goat piss most people called beer, he'd have to go ashore soon. Or at least call and hire somebody to make a run to the Portland Metroplex to pick up a barrel or two and deliver it here. Certainly he intended to relish this final glass; never knew but that a big meteor might fall on the planet and make this beer his last one.

"Ahem," the biopath said again.

"All right, Bruce, what is it?"

"You have a com from Leonard Silverman."

Colburn held the glass up so the sun shined through the ale, the light turning the liquid into a honey gold. The chiller was designed to cool goat piss beer and it got the ale too cold, of course, but after the cooling cycle was done, a few moments in the light was enough to warm the malty brew to the correct temperature. He took another sip, savored it. "All right. Put him through."

Another two sips of the liquid passed while the biopath on the other end of the com went to find its master. Meanwhile, Charity Heart came up from below and stretched catlike, blinking against the brightness of the afternoon.

Charity Heart was a glorious vision, forty-three years old, tawny, also naked. She was a full-sized woman, a couple of years younger than Colburn himself. She spent an hour each day doing various exercises to keep herself trim, and she could pass for twenty-five at a distance, thirty up close. She padded across the teak deck and bent to kiss Colburn, her long hair falling down over their faces. She wore colored droptacs this morning, turning her eyes a surreal electric green. She flipped her ash-colored mane back with a sharp twist of her head and smiled at him, then went to the foredeck to do her tai chi. The form took an hour, the way she did it, and soon after she started, small boats would begin arriving in the vicinity to drop anchor where their owners could watch. Nudity was common on the water when the weather permitted, but even so, she was something special. He preferred to sleep with women near his own age when it was possible, so that he could talk to them without having to explain his references. Charity was but a couple of years younger, close enough. Sex was delightful with a skilled partner, but one couldn't spend all of one's time screwing.

Charity Heart was a prostitute, a thousand stads a night, or a flat five thousand a week. She'd been with Colburn for four months at the weekly rate, and he much enjoyed her company. There was also a good possibility that Charity Heart worked for Terran Security as one of Silverman's spies, not that it mattered. Colburn didn't do things in front of people they or anybody else could use to hang him. She was a great companion, and if she happened to be picking up a few more stads from Silverman for reports on him, so what? He had nothing to hide from Silverman—at least nothing Leonard would ever find out.

He had enough money to keep Charity Heart, the boat, good ale, and pretty much anything else he wanted for another seventy or eighty years at the rate he was spending it, probably as long as he would live, which was why he wasn't in any hurry to take the com his biopath offered. He knew what Silverman must want.

"Good evening, Croft." The pause while Silverman's system and then Bruce scrambled and unscrambled the transmission was short enough so Colburn couldn't detect it. The boat's holoproj struggled against the sunshine to present the caller's image but only managed a pale imitation.

"Ah, I see it is still afternoon there."

Colburn smiled and raised his glass to Silverman's doppelgänger, knowing he must look the picture of *carpe diem*, the image of sybaritic self-indulgence. Like Charity, he could pass for younger, especially when he rinsed the natural gray out of his still-thick hair. His body was fit, almost fanatically so, the muscles tight, the skin lightly tanned. He smiled because he knew that Leonard Silverman, even though he was halfway around the planet, was quite aware of the time zone Colburn inhabited and that his small pretense otherwise was just that. One of Silverman's great skills was the affectation of absent-mindedness, even to the point of stupidity at times. There were people who bought into that scenario, but Colburn was not one of them. What he saw was a lean, angular, affable man, sharp planes and an expensive haircut-and-set, dressed in three thousand stads of Little Saigon's best linen tailoring. What he *knew* was that Silverman was one of the smartest, twistiest, deadliest men on Earth. He was the head of Special Projects for Terran Security, an innocuous and euphemistic term that didn't begin to tell anybody exactly what Silverman and his people did.

"And how is the smog in lovely Brisbane?"

"We don't have smog here, Croft, you know that. That would be illegal."

Both men smiled.

"I don't suppose I could convince you to come off hiatus for a little job?"

"Not likely."

"Fate of the planet in the balance?"

"Isn't it always?"

Another pair of matching grins. Silverman stayed in character, but they had known each other too long to play patriotic games.

"Well, it really is, this time. Maybe fate of the galaxy. The most important assignment we've ever been handed."

Colburn set the ale glass down and considered the sun-dimmed image in front of him. "Oh, really?"

"Have you ever known me to be prone to hyperbole?"

"It sounds . . . intriguing. Still and all, I am quite content to sit on my boat and sip at my ale. You have younger, faster, hungrier operatives at your beck."

"But not better ones. I know you have all the money you need, I won't insult you, but there's a prize here worth breaking your retirement for."

"Do tell."

"Double scramble, one time only," Silverman ordered his biopath.

"Bruce? You get that?"

"Certainly, sir," Bruce said.

"Go ahead, we're patent here," Colburn said.

"How would you like to live to be a thousand years old, Croft?"

Colburn blinked at the holoproj. Whatever else was true, Silverman was not, as he had said, prone to hyperbole.

"Perhaps we should meet and talk," he said. "I'm out of beer, anyway."

Silverman smiled.

Colburn didn't much care for Brisbane. It had grown from a nonpretentious working-class city to be like Los Angeles, too big, too dirty, too noisy. But he wouldn't be here long. As the cab wended its way through the clotted traffic—despite the computer control system supposed to keep it flowing—Colburn considered once again the cryptic comments Silverman had made less than twenty-four hours earlier. The head of SP could make funny with the best of them, his timing was superb, but he never joked about the Job. If he said it was possible to live for a thousand years, then he believed it. Whether it was true or not was something Colburn would have to be convinced of, but with the resources Silverman had to call upon, the man ought to know.

Besides, whatever else, they made a couple of passable ales here in the city. At the very least he could have some of it shipped to his boat.

Silk tied the laces of his kung-fu shoes with the double runner's knot he'd been shown and then stood. Shoelaces were long out of style and common usage, but Tanito liked the traditional ways. The locker room was almost empty, most of the students already dressed and on the main floor, stretching. Zia hadn't arrived yet, and the classes were scheduled to begin in ten minutes. Tanito didn't like her students to be late; that was one of the first things he'd learned, and she was not shy in expressing her displeasure. Silk had always thought that martial arts masters were supposed to be reservoirs of calmness and serenity but that's not how it was in this school. Tanito—the word meant "teacher" and if she had a real name he hadn't heard it—would sometimes behave as if she were a hungry animal at the zoo and the students were dinner. If you did something that displeased her, she was apt to deck you without a word. It made for polite behavior and a willingness to do what you were told in a hurry.

Silk went out into the workout room. There were usually two classes going at once, the beginners and the advanced. Tanito taught both of them, though one of the advanced students did most of the scut work with the beginners. There were nine students in the beginners' section and five in the advanced group. Silk had begun training within a couple of weeks of arriving on E2. He had quickly gotten tired of Zia stepping between him and people who wanted to give him a hard time about being a terry. They were quick to raise a fist here on the *ausvelt* world at any real or imagined slight, and Silk didn't intend to hide behind Zia for the rest of his life.

He nodded at Pinter and Gauge, two of the other beginners. Both had already raised a sweat that darkened the armpits of their sand-colored heavy cotton twill uniforms. Silk found an empty spot on the polished wooden floor in front of the mirrors and began a series of stretches. Behind him, the school's door opened and Zia entered and hurried into the locker room. Silk was careful not to acknowledge her as she went past. It might be common knowledge that they were together, but in the training hall, she thought it was wiser to regard each other as they did any other student.

A minute before the class was to start—and Taníto was never late—Zia emerged from the dressing room in her sands and moved to the advanced area. You lined up according to rank when the classes began and Zia was second from the end, next to Bûso, a golden-haired bodybuilder of a man who was the prime student. Although she was pretty sure she could take the man, she told Silk, if push came to shove. She had more practical experience than he did.

Silk had seen Bûso knock an eighty-kilo kick bag off its shock strap with a flat punch. He wasn't the least bit interested in testing himself against the man. He stood at the opposite end of the room from Bûso, since at under six months, Silk was the most junior student.

Precisely as the chronometer over the mirrors flashed on the hour, Taníto strode out onto the floor. She was a short woman, compact and muscular herself, and dressed as everybody else in flat-soled flexall shoes and a two-piece cotton suit. Her head was shaved and there was a small symbol tattooed on her skull, some arcane twisted and interlinked mandala-like design done in shades of green. Without speaking, Tanito moved to the front of the room.

"Line up."

Everybody hurried to obey. The fourteen students stood facing the mirrors and Tanito. She gave them a military bow, a nod, and the class bent at the waist almost as a unit to return the salute. "Neck," she said, and began to roll her head from side to side, stretching the muscles of her neck.

The class copied her.

This part was done by the entire group, the stretches and warmup, and it took about thirty minutes before Tanito was finished. When he'd first started the martial arts training, Silk had thought he was in pretty good shape. Back on Earth, he'd swum regularly, and no small distance, almost daily. The first couple of classes, he barely got through the stretches and warmup, much less the actual fighting techniques that followed. He had gradually gotten more adept. Now he could make it almost to the end of the two-hour class before he was totally exhausted.

Except for an occasional grunt of effort, the class proceeded silently. Tanito did not allow talking while the workout was in progress, save for her instructions and to answer questions she or her assistant instructor might ask. This was not a place where you came to bat the breeze or party, this was serious business.

Although Silk knew little of such things before he started training, he quickly came to realize that there were hundreds—thousands—of fighting styles. Wrestling, boxing, hand-held weapons, almost as many variants as there were cultures. The system that Tanito taught was called *kolo*, and it was a blend of systems, so she said. Once physical conditioning and a few basic stances and moves were taught, the training became individualized. No two people were alike, mentally or physically, she said, and thus it was senseless to try to fit everyone into the same box. Tanito looked at a student, measured his or her abilities in her mind, and tailored the teaching to fit the trainee. A large, muscular man had power, and it was thus utilized. A small, thin woman would not have the same muscular advantages but she might be faster or more flexible, and it was those things that should be turned to her advantage. In *kolo*, you could improve your body to make it more efficient, but you took cognizance of that which could not be altered and learned to use it. And what you were at thirty was not the same as what you were at sixty, so you had to learn how to evolve, too.

Silk was not a small man, but neither was he a giant. He was moderately fast and strong, fairly flexible and while each of those things could be improved, he was never going to be as strong as Bûso nor as fast as Zia. Nor as mean as Tanîto. *Kolo* took that into account. *Kolo* became, as he was learning, an individual art. If he managed to stay in training for two or three more years, he would know some moves that all the students knew, but also techniques that only he would be likely to use.

Coming from a world where cookie-cutter mind-sets were the norm, this idea was fairly radical. Then again, he had been a spider, spinning the truth to fit what was needed, so it wasn't that much of a stretch to understand the concept. At least in theory.

As Tanîto moved down the line of students, slamming her fist into their bellies one at a time to test their muscles, the theory lost ground against the practice. Nothing like a rock-hard fist in the gut to give you the reality.

Two students away from him, Tanîto thumped Pinter's abdomen. The impact caused him to fart loudly.

Next to him, Silk peripherally saw Gauge grin at the sound.

When Tanîto moved in front of Gauge, she returned the woman's grin.

Uh-oh. Gauge's face went blank, but not fast enough.

Tanîto's punch was a few centimeters higher on Gauge, smack under the sternum. The great plexus of nerve there was not adequately protected against such a strike, and she went pale and breathless as Taníto's fist knocked the wind out of her. Gauge managed to hold to her feet but she swayed.

The first time Taníto had punched Silk that way, he had sagged to his knees and vomited. Taníto had not said a word, only waited until he cleaned it up and resumed his stance. It was a tough school. The only reason he'd been accepted was because Zia vouched for him.

Taníto came to stand in front of Silk. Snapped her fist back and into his stomach with a speed he found hard to believe. He was lucky this time; he tightened his muscles at precisely the right instant, not too soon, not too late, and absorbed the force with his entire abdomen.

Taníto didn't say anything, which was how he knew he got it right. When it was wrong, you heard it. Half the block heard it.

After the warmups were done, the class split into sections. Bûso came to take the beginners through a series of one- and two-step attacks and defenses while Taníto led the advanced students in a freestyle multiple attacker defense. Zia was first up for the advanced class. She stood in the middle; the others gathered around and then leaped at her. She danced around, throwing and kicking and punching them, and avoided being taken down. Silk had seen her do this for real, on Earth, and it didn't surprise him that she could manage it here.

Bûso said, "You want to pay attention here, Silk? Are we boring you?"

Silk shook his head. Bûso was almost as hard an instructor as Taníto, but at least he never rode him about being a terry. All he wanted was proper technique, and if you did that, he didn't care if you were from Earth—or from York or Fuji or Ujvaros or any of the eleven planets in the seven systems. If you walked the walk, that was all that counted with Bûso. Silk liked that.

Still, it was hard to watch Zia doing her fighting dance with what seemed such effortless grace when he was as clumsy as a kid with a new pair of skates. This was her planet, her game, and he was playing catch-up. He didn't much like that.

Gauge was angry at the shot to the solar plexus she'd had to eat, and when she and Silk did their two-step dances, she hit him a little harder than necessary. He'd be bruised when he hit the showers. He was tempted to give it right back to her, to slam his knuckles into her head hard enough to make *her* fucking ears ring, too, but he held off. He had sense enough to realize that he wasn't the one she was pissed at and neither was he upset with her.

Silk was waiting at the bus stop when Zia came out of the school, laughing at something Bûso was saying to her. She touched the big man on the shoulder with one hand before they parted and she walked to where Silk sat on the glasfiber bench. Zia had a cart, a little two-seat electric four-wheeler, but she seldom used it in the city.

"What was that all about?"

She looked at him. "Excuse me?"

"You and Bûso."

"Well. He and I were making an appointment to get together to fuck each other's brains out after you fall asleep."

Silk sighed and stared down at the ground between his feet.

"I'm sorry," they both said simultaneously.

"None of my business," he said.

"I'm being snide," she said. "What's the matter, Ven?"

He shook his head. "I don't know. Nothing you did."

No. It was what she *was*.

She slipped her hand under his arm, entwined their fingers. "Let's go home," she said. "I bet I can make you feel better."

FOUR

SILK COULDN'T WAIT. Before they got into her cube, he
started to pull her clothes loose. He slid one hand under
her shirt to feel her breasts, the other hand down into
her pants to seek the warmth and wetness of her mons.
The sexual heat burned bright in him and he wanted to
throw her onto the floor and jam himself into her right
here, in front of the world, to hell with going inside.

She was right there with him, her hands busy, squeez-
ing his groin, sliding along his erection, pulling his shirt
loose to drag her nails down his spine.

They dropped their gym bags with the sweat-soaked
uniforms and half tumbled through the door to her cube.
She kicked her shoes off. He nearly ripped his own shirt
pulling it over his head without undoing the cro-strips
that held it closed. They lunged at each other, almost
like wrestlers, grappled for a better hold, fell on the
floor behind the front door. Silk kissed her, hard, thrust
his tongue into her and in a moment, penetrated her. She
was slick, ready. Lying on top of her, he pumped and
raced toward his orgasm, heedless of anything else. She
urged him onward:

"Yesyesyesyesyes*yes*—!"

He came, and his driving need drained with the fluid
of his ejaculation.

She clutched him, wouldn't let him pull out, until
finally he relaxed. She hugged him tightly.

29

"We'll get stains on the carpet," he said.

"Not if you don't pull the plug."

"Yeah, well, the plug is going to pull itself."

"Doesn't feel like it's shrinking to me."

She was right. He continued to throb erectly.

"Okay, then. Your turn."

He began to move again, slower, with more care. Later, he could use his hands and mouth on her, whatever she needed for her own release. He was usually a good lover, considerate of his partner.

Usually.

But even as they rocked in that oldest of man-and-woman rhythms, Silk knew that what he had just done hadn't been lovemaking. He had wanted to control her, to own her, to dominate her. And she had responded by accepting him, pulling him in tighter, letting him rut like an animal. Absorbing his anger and his seed.

It made him ashamed. He felt bad about his situation? About being a terry on a planet where many people spat when they said the word? About being a tyro, a beginner in her world? Fine—he'd pound her into sexual submission. Now there was a clever idea.

Jesus, Silk. It wasn't her fault.

Well, technically speaking, it was. You'd never have come here if she hadn't dropped into your life after Mac's death and conned you good.

My choice. I could have stopped it at any time.

Sheeit you could have. You were thinking with your dick then, too. Put your spindoc's sharp little brain on hold, didn't you? Went for the package she presented like a fat, dumb lily from a graywater agro-commune just come to town for the first time.

Fuck you.

Oh, that's a good one. Listen, pal, you had a life on Earth and you were doing just fine. Zia here landed on you like a big meteor. You want to fall on her like Pan and screw her brains out once in a while, you're allowed. You paid your admission fee to the house of pleasure, pal, and it wasn't cheap, so enjoy it.

But that first surge into Zia, that careless and urgent slamming into her groin so that it was painful for both of them, hadn't been any kind of pleasure. It had been punishment, and no matter what his little voice said to try to rationalize it, Silk knew the truth. He was sorry. He ought to be better than that. He would make it up to her.

Zia cradled Silk in her arms with her bent knees above his back, her hands on his buttocks, adjusting herself to his moves, calling to him. That she loved him was no longer open to dispute. She couldn't deny that to herself. Even though he had been angry with her, it seemed to be gone now and he was somewhere else. She wanted him here, with her, in the moment. When that happened, when he let himself go into his passion, that was when it was the best for her, for them. Now he was holding back and she didn't want that. Didn't want him to go through the motions without *being* there all the way.

He thrust deeper and she squeezed him internally, trying to add to his sensations, to pull him into the moment. She knew what it was like to hold back; she had held back her true self from every man or woman she had ever been with. Part of that was because of her job. She had to stay in control when she was with a subject. Part of it was because she had never met anybody she could trust with her soul.

Until Silk.

Until that moment in the fresher of the suborbital ship traveling from Hawaii to Seattle when he had knelt in front of her and kissed her and she had blossomed into his lips like a hothouse flower and *surrendered*.

It had been more than a surprise. It had been a high-voltage shock. A major restructuring of who she was, but even as she tried to deny it, she couldn't pretend it hadn't happened, couldn't lay it to her jiggered hormones or the danger they'd just shared. There was a bond between them, a connection that was thicker and deeper than just the physical one. She couldn't explain it rationally, but on some level, she knew Silk was her soulmate, the man who would be there for her in a way no man had ever been.

That had scared the hell out of her . . .

He began to move faster, and she felt her own orgasm flutter and build. She matched his rhythm, sought to pull him to her core. It didn't happen often, a climax this way. He could do it to her with his fingers or tongue every time, but just rocking, that was rare. It was happening now . . .

He sensed it. Tuned in to her and began stroking longer and harder. Like plucked strings on a lute, now they were more than just two notes. Now they were a chord, singing the same song, dancing to the same tune.

Now he was here.

Her thoughts faded and she became a thing of sensation.

The wave curled over them, broke, foam and pleasure fell on them as she reached her peak and soared over it. Even as she felt him join her and shake with his own spasms again.

Yes! *Yes!*

When she was done, limp, satisfied, she hugged him tightly and bit his shoulder lightly. This was how lovemaking was supposed to be. You were supposed to be fulfilled, happy, connected. Not two, but for at least a brief and sparkling moment, one. This was the physical expression of love. He had been angry but he wasn't angry now. He was like a little boy, tired, happy, *hers*.

She didn't see how it could get any better than this.

Colburn rented a hotel suite with a full business comp and sat down in front of the terminal to find his new family. He was adept at playing the nets; as a freelance operative, he had to be. Information was, after all, power. Once Silverman explained the situation, there was never any doubt that Colburn was going to take the job. Silverman had known that, of course.

He logged into Omnicom, the commercial retail sales net of which he was a member in good standing, and keyworded his way into the services section. In these days of instant photographs and gigabyte storage even on the average home comp, there wasn't much call for photographic processing and image storage, but there were still people who had their pictures processed commercially. Anybody who wished could do it at home, what with the idiot-proof programs available, but some people didn't want to spend the time or energy. There were still technophobes and people with too much money. They would upload their camera's files, have the photos cropped or shaded or otherwise enhanced, then download them back into their own systems, either for display on their holoproj units or for hard copy from their home printers.

Once in the system, Colburn used a stolen password to access the files. What he was doing was technically illegal, but from a practical standpoint, nobody would ever do anything about it even if they somehow found out, also unlikely. He paid for his on-line time and what he took would never be missed, since he was only copying files and not stealing or deleting them.

He opened the catalog and began to scan the names. Although most people on Earth were finally nearing Huxley's tea-color, Colburn was still relatively fair-skinned. He skipped names like Mbutu and Sikh and Pranamanjani. He picked six names from the catalog, one each from Europe, Asia, Africa, North & South America, and Antarctica, and copied their files to a transfer program, then logged off the system.

In his room, the copied files trickled into his RAM cache. He opened the first one, saw the pictures were of buildings, closed it.

The second file was of a birthday party, cake and children, and while most of the people present were fair-skinned Europeans, none of them seemed particularly appealing.

The third file was the winner. Here was a family outing to a deeland, looked like one in China or Korea, and the holographs were of a slim and attractive brunette woman of perhaps thirty with two children in the six-to-nine range, a boy and a girl. They all smiled a lot. There were a couple of images of a man, alone and with the others, the four of them smiling into the automatic camera against a backdrop of rides and man-made mountains. Perfect.

Colburn had his printer make hard copy of five of the holographs, none of them with the man in them. Two of them he had made wallet-sized.

The wife, he decided, was Melinda. Graduated from one of the SoCal schools with her masters in what? BusAdmin? Yes. She ran a consulting business out of their home, did fairly well, but the kiddie track had kept her too busy to really get into it. Besides, she didn't want to be a workaholic, the children were too important to neglect—you only got two, you know.

The boy was Brad, he was six, being socialized at one of the new retroschools in Greater Houston where they lived.

The girl was Sheryl, she was almost nine—her birthday would be in August—and a terrific speller and reader. Liked that fantasy stuff, dragons and trolls and all, you know how little girls are.

Their house in Greater Houston was a three-bedroom condo down near the big new golf course on the south end, you know, the one where they played the Invitational Tournament last year? And Colburn himself, well, he was a marketing analyst for Perkins & Parker Pharmaceuticals Group, specializing in the holistic preventative supplements end of the business. Doing very well, if he did say so himself.

That ought to be sufficiently boring so he wouldn't have to talk about it long if anybody asked.

Now he had a family and a job. A few more odds and ends and he'd be well on his way.

He commed the front desk and asked for a bellperson to be sent up, a male.

The guy appeared at the door three minutes later. He was maybe twenty-three or four, tall, good-looking, crisp in his uniform.

"You got a wallet?" Colburn asked.

"Yessir, sure."

"Show it to me, would you?"

The young man shrugged and pulled a beat-up nylon wallet from his uniform's back pocket. It was black, worn, frayed a little at the edges. Perfect.

"I'll give you twenty stads for it. The wallet."

The kid blinked. "Huh?"

"How much cash you have?"

"About twelve, fourteen stads."

"Okay, twenty for the wallet. Twenty for the cash. Any cards or nonessential, nonholoprojic ID?"

A bellboy at a major hotel in Brisbane must have heard some strange requests, but Colburn bet he'd never heard this one before.

"Yeah, I got a union card, no pix."

"Twenty more for the card. Anything else in there you don't need?"

The boy opened the wallet and looked through it. "Got a pass to the Totalmax theaters. A lottery ticket. Uh, a holo of my grammie. Rest of it is ID and stuff, licenses, medical trax, keycard."

"Twenty more for the pass and ticket. Twenty for grammie's pix. That's, what? A hundred stads, right?"

The boy nodded. "Yeah."

Colburn pulled a money clip from his pants pocket and unfolded five crisp, red twenties from it. The boy almost fell over himself to grab the bills. He pulled his ID and keycard from the wallet and passed it to Colburn, who took it and grinned. He tossed the wallet onto the couch behind the computer chair in which he sat. "I guess that'll do it, then."

"That's all? You wanted my wallet and the shit in it?"

"Yep. Thanks. It's a gag I'm playing on my brother."

The bellboy shook his head. "Your money."

"Yours, now."

The boy grinned and left.

An hour's work with an illegal program he'd paid a small fortune for, and Colburn had in the RAM cache a driver's license for the U.S. state of Texas, complete with holoprojic verification, a dole ID, never used once, he would tell if anybody asked, and several business cards. He pulled several sheets of assorted printing plastic from a briefcase, including an official one from the World Dole, also bought at a premium price on the black market. Installed the sheets in his printer and had the machine download and hardcopy his false identifications. A few minutes with scissors and an edge smoother, and he would be one Clete Claibourne, resident of Greater Houston. A little work with an emery board, and the cards would be aged to match the wallet.

The little details were what convinced people you were who you said you were. Colburn had never lived in Texas but he could do a faint southern accent when he spoke American. He had been to the city enough times to describe it and it wasn't likely he was going to run into anybody offworld who'd ever been there, but it was another small detail. Another few days of this kind of thing, and his cover would be thick enough so no sharp edges would show through it. He had learned to be methodical about this part of the business, and because of that he had never been outed from a background while on a caper, not once in twenty-four years.

Croft Colburn was the best there was at what he did. This would probably be the last caper he ever did, and he wasn't going to have it go sour over some niggling bit of business. No way.

He smiled. A few more details and he'd be on his way.

FIVE _____

GETTING INTO THE biomed center was an interesting exercise in security, Zia saw. The building was dogged down tight, armored doors set in carbonex frames, with walls of smooth synstone, probably reinforced plate or barweave under the casting. No windows until the third story, and those looked to be duraflex or denscris, able to resist a high-powered bullet or a small bomb without shattering.

A pair of armed guards sat at the entrance checking IDs even after the reader okayed them. Zia tendered her card, got the nod from the scanner and the guards. They gave her a receipt for her pistol, a little 6mm Risthawk. She looked at the weapons they carried, high-capacity stressed-plastic handguns, Mortons, probably 10mm. They'd be loading fifteen rounds each of low-penetration explosive ammo, a single shot of which would slap a big man flat. The guards, a man and a woman, both looked fit and alert; they weren't low-rent muscle but moved like trained pros.

The lift was operated by a third guard, also armed.

On the fourth floor a short hallway led to a heavy door where yet another guard sat behind a thick clear plate— Zia rapped it lightly with one knuckle and from the deep and almost metallic *clunk!* decided it was denscris. She went through the ID routine again before being admitted. Nobody was going to wander in here by accident. Zia had the impression that if somebody tried to storm the place by force, there would be a sudden wall of security teams to back up the four guards she'd seen. It was a big secret, and it got big protection.

A short woman in medic's whites waited for her just inside the door.

"Zia Rélanj, I'm Dr. Marad, I'll be supervising your Treatment."

"Dr. Marad."

"This way, please."

The woman seemed pleasant enough, if a bit tight, and Zia didn't really care. She didn't want a song-and-dance master pumping potentially lethal chem and hormones and God knew what mutagenic stuff into her body, she wanted somebody who knew what they were doing. The Treatment was supposed to be as top secret as such things got, but she'd heard the rumors. The side effects could be anything from a mild fever and general malaise to a sudden fulminant, foaming-at-the-mouth death. That didn't happen often, so the stories went, but if it was one out of a thousand or one out of a hundred thousand, that probably didn't make the unlucky winner feel any better.

Given that she'd risked her neck often enough against worse odds, she wasn't too worried, but lying on a table while somebody else ran the show wasn't the same as being on your feet with a gun in your hand and a plan of your own to beat the competition.

They went into a surgical theater in which half a dozen people also in whites bustled around under bright overhead lamps. Zia glanced up and saw that one of the bulbs was a polarized UV bug-killer.

"Do I need to get undressed?"

"No, just lie down on the table. We'll go in through your left jugular, just pull your collar down a bit, that ought to do it."

Zia moved to the padded table, sat, then swung her legs up onto it. A smiling man moved in and sprayed her neck with something icy cold and sour-smelling. Another man rolled a plastic bottle mounted on a stand next to her. A long, clear plastic line with a hollow needle on the end of it dangled from the bottle, down past her shoulder. The bottle was marked with the "Danger-Radiation!" glyph. The needle was big, really big; it looked like a chromed drinking straw with a sharply angled tip, and was covered with shrink-wrap plastic stamped "Sterile" over and over in red. There was what looked like a slot in the needle running the entire length of it. How cheery.

Marad moved in, now wearing surgical gloves and holding a small, pointed instrument. She touched Zia's neck with the thing. "Feel that?"

"A slight sense of pressure."

"Any pain?"

"No."

"How about this?"

Zia didn't feel the instrument.

"No."

"Good. We've used a topical antiseptic/anesthetic spray to sterilize and numb your neck over the vein. I'll insert the trocar and cannula—that's the big needle with a tube in it—then remove the needle and leave the tube in place. The infusion will take twenty-two minutes. You can sit up if you want, as long as you don't leave the table. We can bring you a magazine or a music player if you would like."

"No, thanks." She wanted to watch what was going on, to keep as much of a sense of control as she could.

"The table is wired, so Karl will be monitoring your telemetry." She waved at a tall, brown-haired man whose muscular frame strained at his whites. She continued. "We'll have pulse, respiration, cardiographics, myotonics, encephalographics and even a half-assed axial tomo scan if we need it. But if you notice any uncomfortableness, any symptoms at all, please tell us."

"Okay."

Marad moved in. Zia could smell her perfume, a faint hint of spice and musk, as well as the clean scent of her uniform. Reminded her of laundry days when she'd been a girl, when life had been hard but simple.

Marad fiddled with her neck, then stepped back and said, "Insertion complete. Run and meter."

"On the clock," somebody said.

Zia felt a cold rush, said so aloud.

"That's normal."

"Done this a lot?"

"Come, come, Agent Rélanj, you know I'm not allowed to say."

They smiled at each other. "I feel a slight euphoria. Like I could fly."

"We hear that, too. No problem."

"You hear it," Zia said.

"Yes. I wouldn't know, from personal experience."

Ah. So the doctor in charge of administering the Treatment hadn't taken it herself. Was that because she hadn't earned it? Or because she knew something Zia didn't and maybe didn't want to undergo it? Zia would be interested in the answer to that one, but she knew better than to ask. It was not only top secret, it was also a rude question. Like talking about a party to someone who hadn't been invited.

The time went quickly. The medicos moved now and then, but mostly they sat and watched her or their instruments.

"In ten seconds," the one named Karl said. "In nine . . . eight . . . seven . . ."

Marad moved in. As the count went to zero, she clamped the IV line shut and smoothly removed it from Zia's neck. A woman stepped next to her and pressed a plastiflesh bandage over the wound. The bandage hummed electronically and sealed the opening.

"That's it?"

"Almost. We need you to drink this." Marad handed her a throwaway paper cup with a few cc's of brownish liquid in it. She downed the fluid, which was salty and slightly bitter. "Hmm. Tastes familiar. Almost like . . ."

She stopped. It tasted like a man's ejaculate. She didn't want to say that aloud.

She didn't need to say it. Marad grinned. She had heard that one before, too.

"Okay, we'd like to sit in the recovery room for a few minutes to make sure there isn't any anaphylaxis, but I don't expect any. After that, you go home and we'll see you next sixday."

Zia nodded. The full Treatment would take a month, four visits. That seemed fairly incredible, given what it promised. True, it was terribly expensive. If she'd had to pay for it, it would cost half a million stads. But she was being treated by a grateful government. She'd earned it by keeping the secret from falling into the wrong hands.

Well. That wasn't strictly true. There were no doubt people on Earth who suspected, maybe who even knew. Silk's ex-woman had figured it out, but she was dead. And that big man who had chased them all over the planet, he had known. He was dead, too. Spackler's defection had caused a world of problems, but by eliminating *him*, the main portion of the grief had gone away. They might suspect but they couldn't prove it, and more importantly, they didn't have any hard evidence about the Treatment, nothing they could use to duplicate it. New Earth had eclipsed her mother, had come up with the secret of life, or at least a big chunk of it, and there wasn't a thing terry could do about it.

She sat in the recovery room, and every five minutes or so, somebody stuck his head in to check on her. Otherwise, she was alone. Her body was now full of miracles starting to work. Chemicals, hormones, colonies of virally infected and mildly radioactive bacteria, recombinant genetic materials, undoubtedly other things she knew nothing about and couldn't begin to fathom. One quarter of the way to forever, maybe. Perhaps someday everybody would be privy to this, but for now, she was one of the chosen few. And it was a very big deal. The ultimate reward.

It didn't feel like anything at all. She felt the same as when she'd come in.

If it hadn't been so easy, Silk might have taken some enjoyment in the work. As it was, he sat at a desk with the advanced biopath humming in front of him and knew he could do this half-asleep and on heavy drugs.

True, the computer wasn't as slick as Bubbles had been, and he had to do some of the scut work himself. True, the company's mainframe biopath was a robotvox no-nonsense job who didn't try to look like your kindly grandmother and who didn't recite the policy to him every time there was a spin to be done. That was worth something. But the work itself was dull. This was a virgin world, nearly, and only a million or so people on it, lots of room. Couple that with the pioneer mentality, and there wasn't much the timber company could even *do* to irritate people. Want to log ten thousand acres clean to the dirt and plant hemp on the clearcut? Hell, it was out in the middle of nowhere, noplace, who cared? Out of sight, out of mind. Want to throw up a paper plant that barely met industrial pollution standards, that filled the air with noxious vapors and ear-pounding noise? Hey, people needed work; there were twenty small towns out in the woods that would cut each others' throats for the privilege of having the plant, even if they had to build it in the town square.

Want to cut down the planet's largest *Shagaro* spruce tree, along with the heart of the largest known stand of such hundred-meter-high giants, and pound them all into toilet paper? No problem. Well, yes, there were maybe nine environmentalists who wrote angry faxes to the holonews and big print media, but they were such a minority nobody paid them any mind. Christ, it was a spindoc's dream. Or nightmare, depending on what you wanted out of a job.

Still, it took a certain amount of work and it would bring in a paycred. It would give him a certain amount of independence; that *was* important.

"A call from Brian Skribmásìno of *The Daily Fax*," the computer said. Its voice was male, human, neutral, and it didn't seem to have much of a sense of humor.

"Calling in regard to . . . ?"

"The man accused of tree-spiking on the South Island Farm."

"Display that file," Silk said. He leaned back in his chair, a form-fit plastic unit that was comfortable enough.

The holoproj fired up and showed him a holograph of a bearded man being led away in cufftape by a pair of company security men. The story under the pix was fairly simple. The company deputies had caught the malefactor, one Sano Blato, driving tempered ceramic bomb-spikes into the trunks of a stand of fir about to be harvested. The spikes wouldn't hurt the harvesters, who used heavy pincher gear to snip the thick boles at ground level, then expansion grinders to strip the limbs and bark away. Nor would the teamsters in the big logging helicopters be bothered as they hauled the timber from the forest. But when the logs went into the mill for laser planing and slicing into boards, the heat from the cutting light would cook a ceramic spike hot enough so the charge inside it would go off. Depending on where the log was in the process, that could mean anything from a few startled yells to a blown conveyer line to dead bodies. Because the spikes were nonmetallic, the detectors missed them and it took one of the new HO— hard object—scanners to locate them, a time consuming and expensive business.

Silk got all this from the HX sidebar to the company's story floating in the air.

"Put the reporter through," he ordered the biopath.

"Hello, who've I got?"

The man's image flowered in the upper right corner of the 'proj. He was thirty-five, blond, good-looking.

"Hello, Brian," Silk said. His voice was warm, eager to please. They had never met and had spoken but one time a week before, but that gave Silk leave to be buddy-buddy personal. "Venture Silk here."

"Ah, yes, I see. M. Silk, I was wondering about the company's stance on the upcoming trial for M. Blato."

Off camera Silk waved at the 'proj, using the hand signal that commanded the biopath to call up the relevant file. It was color-coded in blue print so he wouldn't get confused. To the reporter he said, "Call me Ven, Brian; we're not much on formality here." He read the new file and spoke at the same time, a skill any good spider had to have. *Nail the sucker's ass to the floor and pour acid on him.* seemed to be the gist of the company's internal memo on the tree-spiker. *Then scatter the ashes over the deepest part of the ocean.*

They did not like M. Blato uplevels at LIT&P, no sah, not in the least.

"Well, we at Lower Island T&P do not wish to be vindictive. We recognize that the unfortunate M. Blato's efforts to impede our lawful business were born out of a sense of sincere, if misguided, idealism."

"So you are going to drop the charges?"

Silk's professional smile lit up. "Well, Brian, I'm afraid not. While we sympathize with M. Blato's sincerity, we cannot in good conscience allow people to spike trees and get away with it. Even if we were to feel otherwise, Blato's acts were criminal and potentially deadly. We value our employees very highly, and an explosion in one of our plants would certainly endanger their welfare."

As he scanned the story, Silk saw the spin that would best serve the company. He smiled again and put it forth.

"Our plants are all unionized, as you probably know, Brian. Can you imagine what the unions would think, were we in management to turn our back on such acts as these?" There. That was subtle but also obvious enough so anybody with half a brain couldn't miss it.

"So the company doesn't want to prosecute this wooble but the unions are leaning on you, right?"

"Well. I wouldn't put it that way. But as you know, the union contract expires in just under a month, and we wouldn't want to do anything that might be perceived as being unfair to our workers."

"Did they threaten a strike unless you melt this guy?"

Silk shrugged, his hands upraised. "Hey, *I* didn't say that. In a perfect world we wouldn't have these problems, people in the woods spiking trees that we own, that we planted ourselves, a second-generation forest grown from seedlings. But it's not a perfect world. We must try to protect as much of it as we can. M. Blato chose to break the rules. We didn't make them, but we are willing to live with them."

"Got it," the reporter said. "Thanks, M. Silk. Ah . . . Ven. Talk to you later."

Silk grinned at the man's image as it vanished. He could almost read the story. *A company spokesman refused to confirm rumors that the union was demanding the spiker's head on a platter or they'd stage a walkout.*

Perfect. The company could stomp the spiker flat using the full weight of the law and with any luck at all, come off as nice guys just trying to protect their workers. And the message to any hairy-assed brother radicals M. Blato might have skulking out in the woods was: Hey, fire-bomb the union rep's house, if you please, it's the *union* who wants to squash your little friend, not us.

Probably wouldn't do much good in that arena, kooks and dingloos being less than amenable to such things as reason and even misdirection, but the public at large ought to go along with the spin. And that's what they paid Silk for, the perception, not the reality. The truth was what you made it. Like gold, you could hammer it into thin sheets, draw it into fine thread and spin it into cloth, if you were sufficiently skillful. Silk was that. Maybe his talent would out. Maybe he would rise up to take over an important position. The opportunities were less here on this backrocket planet, to be sure, but then again, so was the competition. Hell, he might just be the best spindoc on the planet. That ought to be worth something.

SIX

COLBURN, IN HIS guise of Clete Claibourne, logged passage on the starship *Pride of Mchanga*, a wallowing ocean liner of a vessel that plied the vacuum seas between the stars. The ship, as all starships did, used the somewhat enigmatic Rhomberg-Morrison Pull Through FTL Drive, a miraculous engine that ate light-years and shat mere hours. The *Mchanga* had never been a top-of-the-line vessel even in its heyday, but it had decent accommodations. It was the kind of ship that Clete Claibourne would fly, not the best but not the worst. Since the crossing of Deep Space to New Earth would only take a few days, Colburn could stand it, even though he knew the beer would be awful. Save for the luxury liners, it always seemed to be that ubiquitous pasteurized goat piss that he hated. You would think that a barrel or two of good beer would be easy enough to obtain and that certainly there would be call for it, but no. Maybe that was tradition. Bad beer and lousy food were expected on a starship.

He took the riser from Dallas-Fort Worth, so as to stay in character. Terran Security had provided him with a reason to be traveling to New Earth: One of its front companies there was a pharmaceutical manufacturing concern. Old Clete was just the guy to advise them about how to up their share of the vitamin supplement market. This drug company was located in Beagle, the second largest city on the planet, if a town of two hundred thousand people might be truly called a city. It had been nine years since he'd visited New Earth, and his features had been surgically altered twice since. Plus the local TS agents had arranged to wipe his retinal scan and fingerprints from the security computers after he'd left last time, so nobody would recognize him, from his face or his prints. In theory. He had checked to see if The Scats onworld had wiped his files, and as far as he could tell, they had, but you never knew for sure. The top level of players in the spy game were devious rascals, and he didn't trust them as far as he could pitch a mountain, even a small mountain. His last assignment on E2 had caused him to kill several people, and they never closed a file on murder, especially a high-visibility assassination as one of the hits had been. He had no intentions of homicide this time, which was too bad. Killing somebody was easy.

There was nothing in his baggage not in keeping with his disguise, no reason for the port scanner on E2 to think anything about him other than that he was just another money-grubbing terry come to sully their planet for a while before he went back to his own regulated, crowded, and xenophobic world. On E2, all he would have to do was pass a scan at the port; then he would be free to roam anywhere he wished. A visitor from New Earth to the motherworld had a month of enforced quarantine to look forward to; indeed, anybody from any of the *ausvelt* worlds got the same treatment. The offworld plague that killed so many people and most of the world's cattle was old news, a cure for it developed decades past, but the quarantine remained in effect. The powers-that-were on Earth had realized what a wonderful tool it was and had left it in place. Control of the *ausvelters* was important. Colburn understood why they had done it, although he didn't agree with it. Sooner or later the *ausvelters* were going to outstrip the homeworld; that was generally the way of bustling, active frontier societies. They were the children who would grow up and look askance at the rigid ways of their parents, children who would then refuse to be thought of, or treated like, second-class citizens. The quarantine was just one more large drop in the bucket that would eventually slosh over. It might be helpful in the short run, but in the long view, Colburn figured it was going to be a costly mistake. The powers-that-were on Earth seldom took the long view. And now, it seemed, those on New Earth would be able to do just that.

As the riser mated with the giant starship docking port in orbit between Earth and Luna, Colburn put the eventual revolution out of his mind. That wasn't his worry. His job, while not easy, was simple enough. If he pulled it off, he would have a long time to ponder the problems of interstellar relationships.

Silk tugged at his sweaty workout clothes, pulled the shirt back into place from the disarray in which Bûso had left it. They didn't do a lot of tumbling on the hardwood, fortunately; they practiced on padded mats most of the time. Now and then somebody would get thrown, just to see if they knew how to fall right. Today had been Silk's turn. He'd attacked Bûso as instructed, a straight punch to the face. Instead of the parry and ridge cut he'd been expecting, Bûso, the bastard, had ducked, grabbed Silk's wrist and shirt, and sent him on a short flight.

The landing was more or less flat on his back. Fortunately, Silk remembered to slap and yell as he'd been taught. His palms stung and it knocked the wind out of him for a second, but basically he was unhurt. He got up, bowed, and Bûso moved to torture the next student in line. Silk wondered if this was all worth it. Yeah, he didn't like feeling powerless, but then again, he got kicked around as much in class as he was likely to get kicked around on the street.

He was distracted. Zia hadn't come to class; he hadn't seen or heard from her all day. When he'd logged off his shift at work and gone home, there was no sign she'd been there since they'd left together that morning. That wasn't like her, to take off without telling him. Of course, in her line of work, such things might be expected; still, she hadn't been given any lengthy assignments since they'd arrived on E2, and Silk had come to expect to see her when the day ran down—

"Yiiee!"

He looked up, startled, saw Bûso charging him. The big man stepped in and swung a looping roundhouse right at his head—

He stepped into the punch, right leg leading. Brought both hands up, fingers open and pointed at the ceiling, palms parallel. Like a braggart demonstrating his dick size, Taníto had told them. He snapped his wrists out sharply and made a half circle, caught Bûso's forearm with the edges of his hands and blocked it, then continued the technique with a right hammer fist to the groin that bounced off Bûso's protective cup and back up into the elbow-pivot backfist to Bûso's nose.

Missed the nose. Felt the knuckles of his right fist slam right between the attacker's eyes, couple centimeters too high.

Watched in horror as Bûso's head snapped back and he went down, stretched out. Heard the thump of his head as it hit the wooden floor.

Oh, *shit*!

The class froze as if suddenly plunked into a swimming pool full of liquid nitrogen.

He'd *decked* Bûso.

Not for long. The big man rolled to one side quickly and came up, dropped into a defensive stance, shook his head and regarded Silk.

Dead. He was dead. Bûso would pound him into jelly. Silk figured he had maybe five seconds to live. He was so scared he couldn't even turn and run—

"Bûso," a woman's voice said.

The big man gathered himself. Silk saw him focus, watched him lash an imaginary tail like a giant cat about to leap on his dinner.

Going to die, Silk . . .

"Bûso!" That was sharp, a command.

Silk risked a look and saw Taníto moving toward them.

Bûso sighed and came up from his killing crouch.

Silk thought he might lose control of his bladder but managed to avoid embarrassing himself.

Taníto arrived at where Silk and Bûso stood, two meters apart.

"Explain," she said.

"I had just demonstrated the wrist-chest throw to Silk and was about to take the waza attack from Gauge. Silk lost his focus. His attention wandered. I sought to regain it. I threw a slow roundhouse to wake him up."

Taníto nodded. Looked at Silk. "And you. What did you do?"

Silk, who was as used to spinning facts into variations as he was dressing himself, was still too rattled to think straight. So instead of coming up with some clever bit to make him look as if he had half a brain, he told the absolute truth: "I have no idea. He came at me and the next thing I knew, he was on the floor."

Taníto nodded again. Turned to Gauge. "What did Silk do?"

Gauge swallowed. Silk could read Gauge's face, and she didn't want to be dragged into this. She said, "Waza Six. Double outward circle block, hammerfist to the groin, backfist to the nose."

"And did he do it correctly?"

"He was high on the nose strike."

Taníto nodded. Turned to take in the entire class. "He was high on the nose strike; nonetheless, the technique was correct." She turned back to Silk. "Do you know why?"

"No, Taníto."

"Because you don't remember what you did. Because you didn't think about it while you did it. That's why."

She turned and walked back to the advanced end of the class.

Silk regarded Bûso. The bigger man smiled. "Nice shot," he said. "You got promise."

Silk's relief was immense. He wasn't going to die after all. Amazing.

Zia slouched in the chair across from Mintok's desk. He sat behind it in his form-chair, pretending to be busy with his computer console. She waited, unperturbed. If he wanted to play big busy boss, that wasn't her concern. He wasn't going to impress her. She knew him too well.

"Store that file," he told the computer. "Stand by."

He looked at Zia. "So, are you tired of clitting around yet? Ready to get back to work?"

"I've been ready since I got back."

"Yeah, well, uplevels was a little perturbed about you bringing your stray home. They didn't know if you were altogether trustworthy. I'm still not sure you are, myself."

"Fortunately you don't run things," she said. She smiled.

"For you. Uplevels is going to put you back in the hopper, but you won't be getting any offworld plums just yet. First you have to do a few toilets to show you haven't lost your edge." He returned the grin. It was a nasty expression. She didn't much like it.

He said, "We've got us a spy in Touchdown. He's working for the port, we've caught him copying lift codes and schedules, low-level tech stuff. He works as a freight router in the private sector, onplanet line called Global Parcel Delivery."

"Who does he belong to?"

"If we knew that, we wouldn't need you, would we?" Again the nasty smile. "His file is under your code access, GPD-3."

"Three. What about the other two?"

"Not your concern. You are to find out who he works for, what he knows, what he *wants* to know, and do it without him figuring it out. He's a big, husky guy, likes women, according to our reports. He ought to keep you wet until you can worm it out of him."

Zia returned the grin. She would cut out her tongue before she would give him the satisfaction of seeing her squirm.

It was a problem, though. Before she'd met Silk, she'd have laughed at the assignment. She'd have the spy in a sexual clutch before he knew what hit him. His pillow talk would give her what she wanted to know and she'd be home, her report done, and if it took more than three days, she'd resign from Nessie. She was very good at her job.

Now, though, there was a complication. The sex wouldn't mean anything, it never had, not since she'd been fourteen and her uncle had introduced her to her power over men. But now there was the relationship with Silk to consider. *She* could keep them separate— work was work, what she had with Silk was something else—but Silk was a question mark. He was terran and thus used to all manner of perversion. Open relationships were common on Earth. But something was going on with him, and she didn't have a handle on it. Some of it was because he was dropped into an essentially alien society and he hadn't found his place in it. Some of it had to do with her being more competent than he on a basic survival level. Some of it she didn't have a clue about.

If Silk knew she was going to leave town to spend a few days in another man's bed in order to do her job, how would he react to that? Would it dent his ego, even though it didn't mean anything to her? Would he shrug and laugh it off?

Not knowing bothered her. Risking his disapproval bothered her, too.

She stood. "I'll read the file," she told Mintok.

"Do that."

She left his office, angry with him. And with Silk. What business of his was it how she did her job? To hell with him. She could march home and toss it in his lap and if he didn't like it, he could bark at the stars. She didn't belong to him, she was her own person.

Then again, she loved him. No getting around that. He made her feel whole in a way she'd never felt before. She was grateful for that. She hadn't gotten all the sharp edges of the relationship worn off yet, she cut him, got cut herself now and then, but it was worth working to keep. He loved her, she loved him. Enough so she didn't want to cause him any deliberate pain.

Maybe she could just not tell him and avoid the problem altogether. That would be the easiest way to handle it, wouldn't it? What he didn't know wouldn't hurt him. Or them.

Well. That decision had been easy enough to make.

SEVEN

COLBURN EXAMINED HIS quarters. The one thing they had plenty of on the *ausvelt* planets was breathing space. The cube he'd been given was huge, six compartments—living room, bedroom, kitchen, two freshers, even a dining room—and would have cost a fortune in any decent neighborhood in a large terran city. There were trees growing in the surrounding yard, itself big enough to build another cube this size on it. But even with the air conditioners on, the place had that funny, alien-world smell. He'd been to most of the *ausvelts* and each had a distinct and different feel to it. The gravity was never quite the same, the intrinsic odors weren't those of Earth, the light never quite looked right. E2 had a yeasty, bread-dough scent in the air he would notice until he got acclimated to it. The light from the local primary gave everything a slightly bluer tinge, the pull wasn't quite a full gee. The oxy was up a hair. He felt physically more powerful here than on Earth, though he knew that was an illusion.

He tossed his luggage onto the couch in the living room, did a quick tour of the cube, then went to the kitchen. He opened the food cooler's freezer section and removed a plastic carton of chopped, frozen spinach. He tore the plastic cover off to reveal the moxbox hidden under the wrapping. Set it on the counter. The moxbox was the size of a personal reader. A small input mike was inset into the upper left corner. Colburn leaned down and spoke directly into the input chip.

"Open," he said.

There was a mechanical *click!* and the moxbox's lid clamshelled up. If the unit hadn't recognized Colburn's voice patterns, instead of opening, the moxbox would have triggered a thick nest of thermel wire wound through out the plastic—just as it would had anybody tried to pry it open. The activated thermel would take maybe three seconds to go from the 0° of the freezer to about 1000°. Anybody holding the box or even standing too close would want to leave in a hurry. If the box itself didn't cook some portion of them, the likelihood of a subsequent fire would hustle them along. When the thermel combustion ended, the box and whatever had been inside it would be slag, if not vaporized. It was one of Terran Security's favorite ways to protect hard copy or small items they didn't want to fall into the wrong hands.

In this case, the moxbox contained three items. The first was a tiny ROM chip that ought to contain all Colburn needed to know about his quarry, including the name of the highly paid informant inside New Earth Security who would offer help, for a stiff price.

The second item was a small pistol. The third, a loaded spare magazine.

He pulled the pistol out and examined it. It was a local product; he didn't recognize the maker's name. The little gun had a stacked-spuncarb frame and slide in mat-black, was about ten or eleven centimeters long, and had a catch on the magazine's butt. Colburn thumbed the latch and ejected the magazine. It held seven rounds of 6mm caseless, silvery truncated-cone bullets each set in a gray cylinder of propellent. To operate the weapon, you racked the slide and chambered a round. You aimed, using the floating red dot sight activated when you squeezed the grip. Put the dot on the target, press the trigger—electronic, set at a kilo and a half, according to the inset scale—and a piezoelectric spark would ignite the propellent, kick the bullet out at supersonic speed, shove the slide back and strip the next round from the magazine. A semiautomatic. Each time you pulled the trigger it would repeat the sequence until it ran out of ammunition. Simple: Point it and shoot.

He thumbed one of the rounds from the magazine and examined the bullet. The slug was a Silver Talon, designed for soft targets. The missile's outer coat was aluminum, the inside of the bullet a soft alloy. Inside the hollow point were flutes, so that when it struck a target it would peel back like a mushroom, allowing the sharp edges of the flutes to cut into tissue as the round essentially doubled in size from 6mm to 12mm. It would hit hard and expend most or even all of its energy in the target. It was police ammo, sales limited to official peacekeepers.

He replaced the bullet and magazine, hefted the pistol. A little less than a kilo in weight, he would guess. Easy to conceal, probably accurate at short range, out to a hundred meters or so. Later he would buy more ammunition and find a secluded place to practice with the weapon. He was an excellent pistol shot generally, but it paid to be adept with the specific gun you were going to carry. A killing weapon such as this one would be very hard to come by for an ordinary citizen on Earth; here on E2, he guessed that this was a common ordnance—otherwise they would have put something else in the box.

He replaced the chip in the moxbox, rewrapped it in its chopped spinach disguise, and stuck it back into the freezer. In theory, nobody had any reason to suspect him of anything and thus no reason to be poking around in his kitchen. Until he was ready to access the chip and download the information, however, he would prefer to keep it safe. The pistol he stuck into the back pocket of his pants, where it was small and light enough to be unnoticed. With a thin pad of cloth folded between the gun and anybody who might fancy looking closely at his butt, it ought to seem nothing more than a fat wallet. It would do until he could get a holster.

Well. He was here. He was armed. He was in control.
Exactly what he wanted.

Somebody stole a truck from the timber division. Whoever it was fanned along for a few klicks, then crossed
over to the wrong side of the road and smashed into a
bus on its way to pick up a group of children. Nobody
was hurt; the driver's automatic restraints popped open
and cushioned his body, not a scratch. There weren't any
children on the bus yet. The thief or thieves escaped on
foot without being seen.

The company wanted Silk to spin it. A stolen *truck*.

He laughed when the call came through, laughed while
his biopath laid it out, laughed again when he thought of
how easy this job was. Spin it? Whatever *for*? It was
open and shut; cut and dried; game, set, and match. No
blame attached to the company at all. The truck, a beat-up
quint-fan utility vehicle, had been triple-secured—engine
ignition keycard pulled, doors locked, stored inside a
padlocked expanded metal fence. The thieves, probably
teeners out looking for trouble to get into, cut through the
fence, broke the truck's door lock and used a counterfeit
keycard to get the van off the ground. The company's
insurance would pay for the damage, both to the truck
and the bus. The worst thing that happened was that
the bus driver had been rattled, but he was fine. A few
children had to wait half an hour until a second bus was
dispatched to fetch them. Big fucking deal.

But the company wanted it spun. His was not to reason
why.

The best thing to do was to lay it out as it happened,
punch up the security precautions, talk about how determined the thieves were, like that. The whole process took
Silk maybe fifteen minutes. He had his biopath squirt it to
the newscom—as if anybody really gave a snake's ass—
and that was it. Fifteen minutes.

And *that* was the high point of his work day.

He did a little research to keep himself occupied, had
his computer run down the history of the company, then

the history of the planet. It had been the first of the *ausvelt* planets settled. New Earth, people called it formally; E2 when in a hurry. There had been a sizable faction of residents trying to get the name changed for the sixty-odd years people had been on E2, to sever any relationship to the mother planet, at least insofar as similarities in names went. That faction had increased in size after the quarantine was left in place on Earth after the pandemic of 2060 that killed six million terrans and most of the larger livestock, cattle in particular. There were huge cattle ranches on many of the *ausvelt* planets but through mutual agreement, the *ausvelters* kept those beeves to themselves—Earth had become largely a meatless society. Unless you were very well off, you couldn't afford fish, rabbit, chicken or some of the more esoteric flesh-foods that were still available. Given the efficiency of soy and pseudopro, animals were not a good return. For what it took to make a kilo of pork, you could make twenty kilos of pseudopro that looked, smelled and tasted almost as good. Almost.

But that was Earth, and this was not.

That done, Silk was through for the day. He took his portable com and left, waved at the empty office as he did so. His boss seldom bothered to come in at all, unless there was a specific reason he needed to be here. If the company wanted him, they would com, and Silk's portable was set to collect any such calls.

When he got to her cube, Zia was packing.

"Going somewhere?"

"Yes. I have an assignment in Touchdown. Probably be there for a week, maybe five days. Counterespionage. That's all I can say about it."

"Ah. And if I hadn't gotten off work early, would I have seen you before you left?"

"You see me now, don't you?" She continued to put clothes into a small bag. "I would have called you."

She was hiding something. Silk could smell it. When they'd first met, she'd spun some fairly incredible stuff and he'd swallowed it, but he'd been off-balanced by

Mac's recent death. It had taken him a while to catch on. Now he knew her better, much better, and as good an operative—as good a liar—as she was, he could feel the unseen truth. Something else was going on.

"Well. Have a nice trip." He could have rented his voice as a meat freezer.

She stopped packing, stared at him. "Don't be that way, Silk."

"Which way is that?" He smiled at her. It was a professional expression. A buttery, teeth-and-lips smile, crinkles at the corners of his eyes. A mask. And she knew it, too, because she knew him a lot better than she had.

"*You* went out and got a job. I have mine, too."

"I didn't say a word."

"Look, let's talk about it when I get back."

"Fine." He tried to look innocuous.

"Dammit, why do you take everything so damned personal?"

"Do I? I'm sorry, I didn't mean to."

She resumed packing, only now she stuffed the clothes into the cheap synlon bag instead of folding them. She was angry.

Good.

He turned and walked out of the bedroom. Went into the kitchen, opened the cooler, found a plastic can of fruit wine, unsealed it. Took a few sips. Nasty stuff.

She came out of the bedroom with the bag slung over her shoulder, her body tense, stiff, her cheeks flushed. He looked at her over the top of the wine. For a moment, neither of them spoke. Then they both tried to talk at the same time:

"I'm sorry—" each of them said. Stopped.

"All right," he said. "I'm working some stuff out, I know it isn't your fault. I didn't mean to take it out on you."

She sighed. "Me, too. I love you. Can I get a hug before I go?"

He put the can down, went to her. The hug was warm, could have gotten hot if she hadn't had a train to catch.

When he released her, he said, "Be safe."

"You, too. I'll com you when I can."

She left.

The anger wasn't entirely dissipated on either side, he knew that, but it had been blunted. He had been angry, but he didn't want her to go away upset with him. He was still bent a little that she would just leave without telling him; he wanted to mean more to her than that. She said she loved him. He wasn't certain about that. He knew he loved *her*. Loving somebody, really loving them was like a cage, one you'd put yourself into. You were in it and you couldn't get out. Worse, you didn't *want* to get out, you liked it, but it did put limits on you. Silk had never dealt with those limits before, and he was unsure about the whole situation. What could he do about it?

He took the wine into the living room and sat on the leather couch. Well. One thing he could do was establish his own independence. He had a job; that was a start. He would start looking around for a place of his own, now that he had stads to rent a cube. Something a cut up from the doleplexes. As it stood now, Zia was not only the center of his life, he was sitting in her cube, wearing clothes she had bought him, drinking her wine. She didn't begrudge him any of it, he knew that, but he needed to be dealing from a position of strength, and being kept by his lover didn't relieve his stranger-on-a-strange-world sense of low self-esteem. Maybe he would find a place while she was gone. Show her that he was not a man without resources. He would feel better about himself, and that had to be good for the relationship, right?

Right.

Waiting to board the maglev train for Touchdown, Zia shifted back and forth on the platform, working her calves a little. Silk had known there was something about this assignment she wasn't telling him. Damn, when somebody got that close, it was almost like telepathy, empathic at the least. It was no big deal. She had slept with scores of lovers, men and women, once even a true hermaphrodite, many of them work assignments. The way to a man's heart was not through his stomach, it was through his penis. Pillow talk was a major source of information in the spy business, and Zia had always been proud of her record. There wasn't anybody any better at the job than she was, not on this planet.

If it was no big deal, then, Zia, why didn't you just tell him and let him chew on it? If he chokes, that's his problem, isn't it?

Well, yes and no. Because I don't want to lose him.

So you lied to him.

Yes.

And the end justifies it?

In this case, yes. Yes, it does.

Ah, I see—

Shut up, she told the nagging voice. Just shut up. I'll finish this job and I'll tell him about it when I get back.

Loud as it was, the sound of the maglev's engines coming on line did not drown out the small chuckle from her alter ego. And the last word it had to have:

Right.

EIGHT

SILK WALKED IN the Pearl District, an area to the north of the city's center. Once upon a time the district had been mostly warehouses and light industry, but many of the warehouses had been cleaned up and converted to loft-style cubicles. Because it was close to the center of town, the rents were higher than they should be; because the district was still not completely morphed and much of it was run-down, the rents were lower than they might be. On balance, Silk could afford a cube in this area—if he found a small one and if he didn't mind a view of dirty sunsucker plastic rooftops and narrow, dark alleys.

He didn't mind. He'd looked at several rental units, a couple of which were within his price range and not too bad. Nothing to compare to Zia's cube, of course, but still some place he could call his own.

He walked back toward the bus stop a block or so from the last unit he'd checked out. The street was just ahead, through an L-shaped alley banked with refuse bins and fifty years of industrial dross. It was almost noon but the overhangs from the alley's buildings cast enough hard shade so the alley was dim. One of the first items on his wish list was a bike or trike; all this walking was hard on the feet.

Halfway through the alley, Silk felt somebody watching him.

When he flicked a quick look back to see who it was,

the dim tunnel was empty. Must be his imagination. But he increased his pace a hair, unable to shake the sensation of being followed.

Just before he reached the bend in the alley, he stopped. Turned.

Nobody. Unless someone was wearing electronic camouflage or burrowing under the plastcrete, neither of which were likely, there couldn't be anybody within twenty meters. He supposed somebody could be crouched behind one of the refuse bins farther back, but who? And why? A strong-armer, looking for a quick score? He'd have a hell of a time catching silk with his twenty-meter head start—there weren't any hiding spots between that last bin and where Silk now stood, so he wasn't going to sneak up on him without being spotted, now that he was watching.

He stood there, waiting. For what? If somebody did jump out from behind one of the bins and head his way, Silk didn't plan to hang around. He didn't have a weapon of any kind and he didn't trust his fighting skills a whole lot, the incident at the school with Buso notwithstanding. So what *was* he doing?

It came to him in that moment:

Whoever was watching him was not behind him.

He was in *front* of him.

He sucked in a quick breath, blew it out. Felt his heart race at the realization. He had no reason to believe it, no evidence. He couldn't hear anybody scritching around up there around the bend, didn't see them or smell anyone, but he was sure someone was there. As sure of that as he'd ever been of anything. His bowels churned and he needed to pee, bad, all of a sudden.

Without another thought, Silk broke into a run, back the way he'd come. He got about fifteen meters, still gaining speed, when somebody behind him yelled:

"Pigfucker!"

Silk was running down the center of the alley. At the sound, he cut sharply to his right, rounded the nearest trash bin, and crouched.

The flat *twang!* of the spring pistol and the whistle of the first needle came almost as a single sound. The next needle hit the plastic bin behind him, made a hollow *thunk!*

He'd been shot at before but it wasn't something he was used to. He tried to run and crouch at the same time and managed neither. He tripped. His martial arts training saved him. Without thinking, he turned the fall into a tuck and a half-assed shoulder roll, came up, and kept going.

The third needle smacked into the bin, the fourth glanced off the wall close enough to his face to spray him with grit from the dirty brick before it ricocheted past.

Whoever it was was apparently trying to run and shoot, and he wasn't any better at that than he'd been at his running crouch. If he shot again, Silk didn't hear it. He reached the end of the alley and cut to the right again, onto the street. A hovervan blew dust and an oily plastcrete stink up in waves a few meters away. A motorized trike cruised along the street toward him on the opposite side of the road.

Silk rounded the truck, startled the driver, who was unloading foam crates onto a hand truck on the walk next to the van. He kept going, nearly ran into a couple coming out of a small diner, but managed to swerve in time.

Half a block away, he slowed. Glanced back over his shoulder.

Nobody following him. Whoever the shooter was, he apparently didn't want witnesses.

He slowed. Walked until he got his breath back.

Who *had* it been? He hadn't gotten a good look at the shooter. A vague impression of somebody in a gray coverall, big, maybe with red hair. He wasn't sure of that last part; it was more a feeling than a memory.

What the hell had that been all about?

He saw a traffic cop cruise through the intersection in a wheeled cart; he considered stopping the woman and reporting the shooting. On Earth, such a thing would be worth a major investigation, plenty of help beating the bushes to find the shooter. Armed assault was uncommon on Earth, though not as uncommon as he'd once thought, he realized after he'd toured the slums of Los Angeles. But that was Earth. Here, you could read about such assaults in the newsfax or see the reports on the 'proj every day. People whipped out guns and cooked each other at the raise of an eyebrow, for real or imagined insults. Good old frontier mentality; shoot first, ask for clarification afterward. *Say, did you* mean *that, pal? Hello? Well. Teach you to fuck with me, won't it . . . ?*

Silk could almost hear the cop's response: *Whassa matter, terry, you don't like our planet, why don't you go home? Don't come whining over every little thing.*

Rugged individualists out here in the *ausvelt*, they liked to think of themselves.

Silk looked around. Still nobody behind him.

What should he do about this? He could com Zia—oh, yeah, that was just what he wanted to do, and what would it accomplish anyway? How's your day going? Me? Oh, not too bad. Went looking for a place to live so I can get some distance from you. And, oh, yeah, somebody in an alley sproinged a couple of needles my way . . .

He pulled his com from his belt and tapped in a search code. He wasn't rich, but he had a few stads in his account. The first thing he was going to do was locate a weapon shop and get something he could shoot back with. Maybe this frontier mentality had rubbed off on him. "Fuck this shit" seemed an appropriate response.

When Zia came out of the fresher, she was naked, ready to give the spy a ride that would loosen his tongue. Easy as falling off a tightrope.

He was on the bed, a big man, hard from the exercise of pushing freight, and he was also naked. Supine and erect at the same time.

Zia moved to the bed, sat on the edge, reached out to encircle his engorged penis with her fingers. He was about average, a hair bigger, nothing to com home about. She moved her hand up and down a couple of strokes.

He gave a little moan. This wouldn't take long. She'd
known that from the first minute she'd picked him up
in the local pub.

She smiled at him, still holding his cock. "What can
I do for you, big man?"

Before he could speak, she noticed something out of
place in the room. She kept her focus on him, but gave
her surroundings a peripheral sweep. It was a hotel room,
basic, not much to see. A bed with a big naked man upon
it; on the sides, a pair of small, drawered nightstands. A
circular table in the corner, a hanging lamp over it; a
cast chair next to that; closets, dressers, a fresher, that
was pretty much it. So, what was wrong?

"Turn around," he said. "I want to come in from
behind."

It nagged at her as she complied, released her grip on
him and went to her hands and knees, facing the foot of
the bed. He rolled up and swung around behind her,
balanced on his knees. Reached under her belly with
one hand and spread her lips.

"You're wet," he said.

She should be, having sprayed herself with vag-lub
in the fresher so he would think just that. "For you,"
she said.

As he positioned himself behind her, the wrongness
about the room weighed on her. There was a mirror on
the wall, but the angle wasn't such that she could see
herself in it. What was it—?

The drawer in the bedside table. It was open slightly.
That was what was different from when she'd gone into
the fresher.

He found her entrance. Put the tip of himself there
and with a hard thrust, drove himself into her. His thighs
slapped against her buttocks. She grunted. Bastard.

He pulled back and slammed into her again. If he hadn't
been holding onto her waist, he would have shoved her
off the end of the bed.

"Oh, yeah!" he said.

Zia figured he would be good for maybe five or six

strokes, if that. She shoved back against him, moaned as if she were having the best time of her life. She didn't doubt for a second that he would believe it. Men always did.

But she felt his weight shift away from her, even though he didn't withdraw, and his right hand left its grip on her waist.

And all of a moment, the open drawer meant something.

He was reaching for something in the bedside drawer.

She had maybe two seconds to decide. Could be it was a sex toy, something he wanted to use on her while they were fucking. An anal plug or even a vibrator he planned to slip underneath to give her a thrill and add to his own as he rammed her.

Or maybe it was a gun and he planned to blow her head off.

There were old ops and Zia had known a few stupid ops, but there weren't any old, stupid ops. Enough errors in this game, and you retired prematurely. Gave up your stipend and breathing, too.

She put her hands against the bed's frame and shoved backward as hard as she could. He was already leaning away from her and the sudden and unexpected move toppled him. He fell, and his head and upper back slammed into the wall.

"Ow! Shit!"

She pulled free of him and did a ragged round-off, hit the floor, came up into a crouch facing the bed.

He had a long, thin-bladed knife in his right hand. He struggled to regain his balance.

She didn't wait. She jumped, caught his hand, did the half-circle aiki technique and snapped his wrist. He screamed. The knife fell from his quivering fingers. She was ready for it, caught the weapon with one hand, still holding him with the other. As he twisted with the technique, trying to lessen the pain, she brought the knife around and thrust it at him, as hard as he had driven

himself into her only a few moments earlier. The point
hit him under the edge of the rib cage. The thin blade
was very sharp; it slid through the hard muscle and into
his heart. Zia wiggled the knife's handle back and forth,
slashed the pump.

He screamed again.

She pulled the knife out of him and drove it under his
chin. The blade was long enough so it must have almost
reached the inside of his skull. Again, the slashing move.
It had taken two seconds to do the entire technique.

He stiffened under her. Gargled wordlessly. Went
boneless.

Zia pulled the knife free and jumped back from the
bed, held the weapon like a sword in front of her. Warm
blood ran down the handle onto her hand. He didn't
move. Wasn't going to move under his own power ever
again.

Well, *shit*!

She slowed her breathing. Looked at the body. He
could have stabbed her, severed her spine, or maybe cut
her throat. Right as he reached orgasm, too, she would
guess.

God.

Zia went into the fresher, washed her hands and face,
considered herself in the mirror over the sink. Had he
meant to kill her? If so, why? Was he just some kind of
pervert looking for a sick thrill?

Or had he somehow known who she was?

Was it generic?

Or was it personal?

Colburn drove the rental cart out into the country. On
Earth, most of the remaining forests had long since been
made into regulated parks. On the *ausvelts*, you seldom
had to go far to find the woods. Fifteen kilometers and
two side roads out of town and for all practical purposes,
he was in the middle of nowhere.

He found a rocky area and stopped the cart. Got out,
took the big plastic bag full of plastic drink cans he'd

brought, and hiked another half kilometer away from the road. According to the maps, this was a tree farm owned by a local timber company. The main portion of it had been logged twelve or fifteen years back, to judge from the slash and size of the forced-growth replantings, so it wasn't likely he would run into anybody. Like a recently planted field, the crop was not to be harvested any time soon, another ten or fifteen years, and care needed would be minimal.

He rounded a hillock and found a flat spot sufficient for his needs. He removed several of the plastic cans from the bag and set them up on various rocks at different heights and distances. He returned to the flat spot and removed a pair of sonic plugs from the small case he carried. He activated the plugs and inserted them into his ears. The semisilicone lumps would mold themselves to his ear canals and the built-in circuitry would do two things: It would suppress any noise over 80 decibels within a hundredth of a second, and it would amplify normal sounds slightly at the same time.

He waited a few seconds for the soft plugs to set. He heard birds singing in the background, the sigh of a soft breeze in the branches of the young trees. He could hear better than normal, but his ears were also protected against loud noises.

He turned and looked at the colorful plastic cans set about him.

With an ease made from years of practice, he pulled the pistol from where it rode in a holster behind his right hip, hidden under his short jacket. He whipped the little weapon up, caught his right hand in his left, and fired. The suppressors chopped the loud noise off so that it was no more than a *snap!*

The yellow plastic can three meters in front of him shattered. Carbonated sweetened liquid spewed in a brownish spray.

He swung his whole body slightly, shot again.

The blue can to his left at six meters tumbled off its rock, bleeding foam.

Again he triggered the pistol. Then a fourth and fifth time.

Three more cans jumped and flew, bled their contents onto the rocky soil.

He spun in a tight circle, pistol held pointed up by his face. He had three rounds left of the eight the weapon had held. There were those who argued that carrying a weapon with a round chambered and a full magazine was too dangerous, even with the safety engaged, but Colburn reasoned that if he needed a weapon in a hurry, the extra second or so it took to chamber a round might be the death of him, and he always carried cocked-and-locked. He could thumb the safety off during the draw and be ready to fire as soon as a target was acquired.

He was alone here, but he also had a rule about not draining a weapon dry unless it was a matter of life or death. He dropped the magazine, allowed it to fall on the ground, and reloaded the spare magazine into the pistol. Eight rounds again. He holstered the gun, picked up the magazine and went to look at the targets.

He'd hit the first can a couple of centimeters high. The second and third dead-on, the fourth slightly high and left, the fifth low and right. The last two targets had been at about ten and twelve meters.

He nodded to himself. The gun was accurate enough. If he could hit a hand-sized target at twelve meters in a hurry, it was sufficient for his needs.

He set up six more cans. He planned to put at least two cartons of the caseless ammo through the piece to be certain of its reliability. A gun that jammed at the wrong time would get you killed, and before he risked his life on it, he wanted to know it would go bang every time he pulled the trigger. Anything left to chance was just that, chancy, and Colburn hadn't gotten to, and stayed at, the top of his profession for as long as he had by trusting to luck. Luck was for amateurs. There were times when dumb luck beat the best skill, but you couldn't depend on luck to be there when you needed it. Skill always was.

He took a couple of breaths and blew them out.

Snatched the gun from its holster.

Filled the air with metal death.

He came up from his shooting crouch. Five for five.

Time for some long-range work, to see how far away he could trust this little pistol. He had a couple of larger cans.

He could hit them four of five at fifty meters. Two of five at a hundred meters. Good enough. He holstered the little gun, cleaned up the cans and all the shards of plastic from the ones that shattered, and went back to his cart. Nobody would ever know he'd even been here. But now he had faith in his weapon, and that was exactly why he had come.

He drove back to town.

NINE

SILK WAS AMAZED at the weapon shop.

He'd been in sporting supply houses on Earth, of course. He'd bought his crossbow in a specialty shop in San Francisco, and the store had been full of stringed weaponry. It had set him back two months' pay, his bow, an Olympic-class piece of equipment from a display with half a dozen similar items. But this—well, he had never seen guns on open display, and there were so many of them. Hundreds of rifles, shotguns, pistols, as well as compound bows, spearguns, the place was a fucking arsenal of killing machines. Moreover, it had been merely the closest of a dozen addresses of such dealers. A town of a quarter of a million people with twelve weapon shops. That surely said something about the folks who lived here. One of the things it said was, he'd better arm himself if he wanted to stay alive.

Silk wandered past a customer talking to a salesman who stood behind a counter. The handguns were inside locked display cases, visible through clear plastic counters, but many of the other weapons were in racks on the wall, some of them right out in the open where anybody could pick them up. Somebody who had such a collection out within reach of ordinary cits on Earth would be liable for locktime.

It was overwhelming, too much to take in all at once. He was comfortable with a shoulder weapon like a cross-

bow or rifle, but those wouldn't do him much good. It
would be fine to have a compressed-gas shotgun ready
to use and stashed under his bed if somebody broke in,
but he could hardly walk around on the street lugging
such a thing. No, he needed something smaller, more
portable, something he could stick in a jacket pocket or
his belt or somewhere—

"Help you with something?"

Silk looked at the young woman who stood there. She
had short, dyed red hair and large breasts under her thin
shirt; otherwise she was thin and kind of leggy in the
tight black pants she wore. He guessed she was maybe
twenty-eight T.S.

"Uh, yeah. I'm interested in a gun."

"Do tell." She waved at the walls. Grinned.

"Something small. A handgun."

"Purpose?"

"Self-protection?"

"Going to carry it?"

"I don't know. Can I?"

"Sure. Unless you have a felony record. Fill out a form
and thumb it, drop it at the local police kiosk. Cost you
twenty-five stads a year."

"Really?"

"You from offworld?"

"Yeah."

She shrugged. "Come on, I'll show you what we've
got. You do much shooting?"

"Rifles and crossbows."

"Same principle."

He followed her to a counter. She moved behind
it, opened the case with her thumbprint on the lock,
removed a tray with three pistols on it. "These are
the three basic types we stock." She picked up one
of the guns, a black carbonfiber or plastic thing
about twenty centimeters long, did something to the
mechanism.

"This is a caseless semiauto. Fires heavy alloy bullets
driven by a molded explosive. Depending on how good

you are, you can thump a man hard enough to kill him out to five hundred meters. That's in theory. A hundred meters is the limit of the practical range, given the sights and all. At five hundred meters, you'd have to point the gun at the sky to allow for the bullet drop. The basic model runs two hundred stads and they go up to as much as you want to pay. This is a 10mm, big enough for humans."

She put the gun back onto the tray, picked up another one. The second handgun had a fat barrel about as long as Silk's forefinger and a thick, squarish body and handle. It was blue steel or some kind of plating that looked like it.

"This is a 12mm shotpistol. Runs one-eighty. Holds five rounds of compressed gas cartridges, fires #4 buckshot. The barrel is smooth on the inside, and it's good for maybe twenty-five meters in this configuration. You can get a rifled barrel that shoots solid slugs for fifty stads extra. No real point in that, might as well get the caseless if you want to shoot solids. At close range, ten meters or so, this one throws a hard spray, bismuth pellets. You don't get much penetration, but the pattern is wide enough so you don't have to be a good shot to hit somebody. You can be a third of a meter off and still put a few pellets into the target. A center hit will make a fist-sized hole in a person at combat distance. It kicks some."

Silk's mouth felt dry. When he'd bought his crossbow, the talk had been about scoring rings and contests for points. The idea that you might shoot a *person* with the thing was not in the cards; it would have been considered criminal to suggest it. Here, the saleswoman knew exactly what you wanted the weapon for; there wasn't any chatter about targets other than soft ones.

She picked up the third weapon, also of black material, plastic or spuncarb or some light metal alloy. "This is an 8mm spring pistol. Fires smart-electrochip or chem needles. It uses spring-powered cartridges, that's where the name comes from. It's only good out to about fifty meters. The basic configuration here runs a hundred and fifty stads. You can choose from half a dozen kinds of ammo ranging from stunners to killers. The standard stunner dart uses a high-voltage electric charge that will put a big man on the ground for ten minutes. The killer darts are lethal within a second; they short out the central nervous system. We sell a lot of these to people who want to stay alive but who don't necessarily want to kill anybody to do it."

Silk took the pistol. Didn't weigh much. He pointed it at the wall behind her and sighted along the top.

"Squeeze the grip, you get a red dot sight."

He did so, saw a pinpoint of red flare. It was similar to his crossbow sighting system, as well as the rented rifle he'd shot the deer with, though not as complex.

She said, "They all come standard with mechanical thumb safeties, nineteen-eleven pattern. For fifty extra, you can get a magnetic ringer. For a hundred, a two-finger printer."

Silk looked at her.

She said, "A reader in the handle that won't let the gun fire unless the magnetic ring is in position or there is a two-fingerprint match. Somebody gets the gun away from you, it's a paperweight, it won't shoot."

"Unless they have a magnetic ring," he said.

"Or matching fingerprints."

"Which do you use?"

She smiled, a lazy, catlike expression. "Neither. I use the mechanical. Nobody is going to get my gun away from me."

Given that she wore a thin, tailed shirt hanging over her tight pants, Silk didn't see where she could hide a weapon, unless it was in her boot or between her tits. He mentioned the general thought without being specific.

She gave him the cat smile again and suddenly she held a brushed mat-blue pistol in her right hand, pointed at the ceiling.

"Jesus!"

"Small-of-the-back holster, see?" She turned around and lifted the shirttail, showed him a thin black pouch mounted on her belt. She put the pistol back into the holster and Silk saw that the barrel ran parallel to her waist, the handle pointed up and nestled into her low back, directly over her spine. When she dropped the shirt, he could see a slight bulge but he never would have thought it a gun.

Until now.

"So. What'll it be?"

Silk looked at the three weapons. He didn't want any of them. But the alley and the man shooting at him in it loomed in his memory. The fact that there were a dozen gun stores in such a small town. "What do you suggest?"

She regarded him with interest. "You're a terry, aren't you?"

What, did he have a fucking flashing sign over his head?

"Yeah."

"Get the spring pistol. With the fingerprint safety."

That was how he'd been leaning. "Okay."

"Good enough. We've got a basement range, and you get an hour free time and a carton of practice needles with the gun. We fill out the computer purchase form and I'll zing your carry permit to the cops, you want."

Silk nodded. "Okay."

"I'll need your credit tab."

Silk nodded again, gave it to her.

"And I need you to press your ring and middle fingers, here. Gun hand first, then weak hand."

"Why both?"

"In case you break your gun hand or maybe lose a finger, you got weak-hand backup."

Jesus. How often did *that* happen?

He put his right hand on the plate where she indicated. There was a flash of light from the device. She did his other hand.

"Be a couple of minutes for the circuitry to burn in. When that's done, I'll pop the chip into the pistol's control and you're ready to go."

"Thanks."

"I work on commission," she said. She smiled, and this time it seemed to be one of genuine good humor. He returned it.

"I've never been with a terry before," she said.

He raised an eyebrow. And wouldn't be with this one anytime soon, either, he thought. But it was nice to have the interest for a change. "Got a com number?" he asked her. He didn't have to call, and he could return the interest without it costing him anything. He knew how to play this game, at least.

She gave him her number.

He wondered what Zia would think when he told her he had bought a gun. Even though it was a common tool of her trade, he somehow didn't think she'd be pleased.

Zia thought about it for a while before she decided what she was going to do with the body. She lay on the bed, away from the blood, propped on one elbow, staring at the corpse. She felt the letdown that usually followed a big adrenaline rush; it was as if she had done a hard workout, she could hardly move. And there was a hint of nausea, a threat of sudden illness in the background. She maintained, but killing somebody who was trying to kill you did that, almost every time. The rush had its price.

She considered waiting until dark, bagging the corpse, and hauling it to a landfill or an industrial disposal unit where it could become useful fertilizer. Normally that thought wouldn't have crossed her mind. There was a section in Nessie whose job was to take care of such matters. You made a scrambled com to a biopath and gave them an address and it was handled. The body would disappear, and the best forensic team on the planet could not tell there'd been a killing at the site. It was a necessary part of the biz.

But as she lay staring at the dead man, Zia had a few reservations. First, if that had actually been his intent, why had he tried to kill her? If he was some kind of sicko who got his spasm from knifing his sexual partners, why wasn't that in her briefing? If Nessie had been watching him close enough to know he was a spy, they damned well ought to know he was a slicer. If he wasn't a sexual psychotic, then the only other reason she could come up with for the knife was that he knew who—and what— she was. And if that was so, how the hell had he found out? They had met for the first time in the pub near the port, had a few drinks, and gone to the room for sport. He couldn't have known who she was unless he recognized her on sight—or had known she was coming.

Neither of those was a pleasant thought.

She supposed he could have seen her somewhere while she was working. Or that whoever had sent him had briefed him well enough so he spotted her. It was possible, but she didn't believe it. More likely was somebody had tipped him, told him she was coming to pump him, and he decided to delete the problem while he was pumping *her*.

That brought up the next question: Who? And why?

She shook her head. It didn't make sense.

She sat up and slid off the bed. She'd have to call the wipe team. Otherwise there'd be too much explaining to do. As it stood, all she had to do was tell the truth. They could slap the electropophy gear on her or use verstat chem and what they'd learn would match what she said. Of course she didn't really want them messing around in her head; there were other things she would prefer Nessie not know. If they went in, she'd have to have a legal eye with her, to make sure they stuck to the subject at hand. Expensive.

Of course, it was more likely they'd believe her without any verification. Why would she lie? A low-level spy pulls a blade, you do what you have to do. They might bitch about her killing him instead of just crippling him so he'd be around to supply some answers. She could understand that. If she hadn't been caught by surprise, she would have handled it differently. That was the problem with defenses against killing attacks. The philosophy was, if they wanted to hurt you, you used sufficient force to negate the threat. A slow punch got a parry or block and a counterstrike. A gun or a knife called for sterner measures. And when you knew it well enough for it to become almost a reflex, well, you didn't stop to think about the long term. As far as Zia was concerned, a man who tried to open you with a sharp blade gave up his right to breathe the local air. Unless he was a surgeon and had your best interests at heart, which she didn't think the dead spy could claim.

She rummaged through her clothes, found her com. Made the call.

"Omega Systems."

Somebody had a warped sense of humor. "I have a package for you." She rattled off the hotel's address and room number.

"Thank you for using Omega," the biopath said. "Have a nice day."

Jesus.

Well. At least she didn't have to worry now about making her next appointment for the Treatment. This job was over. She could go home.

The basement of the weapon shop was well-lighted, and the range itself was a row of dividers along a bench set at the near end of the lanes. The lanes were about twenty-five meters long and ended in a line of targets in front of an angled, thick metal bullet trap.

Silk put the pair of sound suppressors they gave him into his ears and went to his assigned lane, where he put the pistol and the carton of practice ammo on the bench. There was a stack of thin plastic targets shaped roughly like a human head and torso leaning against the divider. He picked one up, attached it to the pulley, and pushed the button on the setting motor. The target moved out to the end of the lane and stopped under a bank of shielded lamps. Three or four other shooters were on the line, firing various weapons.

He examined the gun again, making sure he knew how it worked. Loaded a magazine with the practice needles, which, contrary to the name, looked less like needles and more like sharpened cylinders a little smaller around than a dopestik. Eight mm, the saleswoman had told him.

Once the magazine was in place, he gripped the pistol in his right hand, cupped his left hand around them, and pointed it downrange. The tiny red dot lit, and he centered it on the target. Flicked the manual safety down, and squeezed the trigger.

The gun made a metallic *twang!* he could barely hear through the plugs. There was a little recoil, not much. The trigger was a little stiff, harder than the pull of his crossbow and the rifle he'd used on the deer. He put the manual safety back on, turned the weapon slightly, still pointed downrange, and used a demistad coin to adjust the trigger so it would break at a kilo and a half. That should be enough for a crisp let-off without being so light it might go *twang!* accidentally when he didn't want it to.

He brought the pistol up again, *snicked* the safety down, put the dot on the center of the target, and fired again.

He took his time. After the magazine was empty, a flashing yellow diode lit on the receiver to tell him he needed to reload. He put the gun down and retrieved the target.

Somebody a couple of lanes over fired a big weapon, sounded like a cannon even through the suppressors.

When the target got close, he could see the holes in it, tiny circles a little smaller than the tip of his little finger. Six of them in a group he could cover with his palms.

"Not bad," came a female voice from behind him. The saleswoman. "But you need to think about combat situations."

She hit the motor control and moved the target out about ten meters. As Silk watched, she snatched her pistol from its holster, whipped it around and out, and fired three times. The suppressors killed the noise, but the force of the explosions splashed concussively at him, making him flinch.

He turned to look at the target. He could see the holes from here; they were bigger and cleaner than those of the spring pistol. Two centered in the chest, the third hole was in the head.

"Mozambique double-tap," she said, grinning. "Two in the heart, one in the head. Full wadcutters."

"Want to make sure he's *real* dead, huh?"

"No. It's in case he's wearing body armor. You can hang a spidersilk vest or a titanium shockplate under street clothes easy enough. Both will stop most hand-gun rounds. If he's unarmored, the double-tap to the chest will do him. If he's wearing, those thump him hard enough so he'll feel 'em until the third shot. Most of your shooting is going to take place inside ten meters and it'll all be over within a couple of seconds. That's not a target pistol you bought; you need to practice with it like you'll be using it. Specificity."

He nodded at her. "Thanks."

"No problem. Let's talk about it over supper, hey?"

Zia was out of town and he was on his own. Looking at the gun, all of a sudden he felt lonely. Besides, it was only supper.

"Sure. Why not?"

TEN

THE GUN SALESWOMAN'S name was Hildy, and when she invited him to her cube for a drink after dinner, Silk went. He felt a small stab of guilt, but not deep or hard enough to keep him from following her. He and Zia weren't contracted; she'd made it plain enough she planned to continue the job she'd been doing when they'd met. And if that sometimes included fucking people to get it done right, well, that was how it was. It didn't matter, she said, it wasn't like it was with the two of them. It was just part of the job. It wasn't like she *enjoyed* that part of it.

Silk liked to think of himself as a civilized man. He believed that even being contracted with somebody didn't make them your property any more than it made you theirs. He'd been in a couple of open relationships and they'd been okay; that hadn't ever been the cause of the break-ups. Not in and of itself. But. Something about Zia being with another man—or woman—bothered him. And in one of his deepest and most secret mental rooms, he thought maybe Zia enjoyed that part of her work more than she allowed. Maybe more than she did with him.

In Hildy's cube, the young woman actually did offer him a drink. "Wine or ale?"

"Ale," he said.

She went into the small kitchen and returned with a glass.

He didn't see how she'd done it, but when she came back, she was naked, nothing between her and Silk but the amber liquid in the glass. Not subtle but certainly effective. Silk felt himself respond to her nudity and her obvious willingness to share it with him.

By the time he got out of his clothes he was at full erectile salute.

Apparently they weren't big on oral sex here on E2. When he went down on her, at first she tried to push his head away. That stopped as soon as he touched her, and she orgasmed under his lips in around fifteen seconds, adding a deep and fulfilled moan for sound effects.

Man with the magic tongue, he thought, smiling into her mons. He even chuckled. Well. If you couldn't laugh and have a good time, why bother?

He climbed up on her and she spread wide for him. He slid in easily and began his own triphammer ride. She bucked under him and it wasn't long before he also came, a shuddery, hard spasm.

Afterward, when they were lying side by side and still partially entangled, Silk felt a sense of despair.

Not that the sex wasn't good—it almost always was for him—but the passion had drained with his semen, and he realized he felt nothing for his partner. Moments before there had been lust and curiosity, both his and hers. Now that those were sated, they had nothing to talk about except maybe guns. Not a subject he thought of as particularly appropriate for postcoital communication. The sex had been urgent and hot and good. But it wasn't enough for him. Not any more.

Jesus. What am I doing here? With this stranger?

Colburn watched the woman as she walked toward the complex in which her cube was located. She moved well, an athletic stride that bespoke good balance and centering. Without being obvious, she checked her surroundings, looked for possible danger. She was armed; she had the look of somebody who could produce a lethal weapon in a heartbeat and use it without hesitation. If he

were set on assassination, he would probably do it from a
hundred meters or more away, in the dark just as he was
now, using a rifle. Through the small spookeye scope, the
green-on-green image of her flared as she walked under
the complex's lights. A bullet in the head, one shot, that
would be the way of it. This was not a woman to come
at face on where she could see you coming. Ninja didn't
square off with samurai; the idea was to do the job and
get away in one piece.

Fortunately, this was all moot. He didn't plan to kill
the spy. She was quite attractive, actually, though a bit
younger than he liked his partners. Still, they could certainly talk shop.

Colburn grinned and put the scope down as the woman
reached the entrance. She thumbed the admit plate and
the security door slid open to admit her. Any thief with
half a brain could get past that; he suspected the security
in her cube might be a little tougher.

Well. He didn't have to do that, either. Not yet, anyway.

He started the cart's electric motor. A few of the local
insects, some kind of silvery moth, glittered in the cart's
lamps as he rolled away. He'd seen what he came to see,
that was enough for now.

Zia cycled the alarm system off and tossed her bag
onto the couch.

"Silk? You around?"

Apparently not. She knew he never left the security
system armed when he was inside. She thought that was
silly.

She went into the fresher, took a hot shower, allowed
the air jets to dry her hair and body. Slipped into a robe,
went into the kitchen and dug a self-heating meal pack
from the cabinet and triggered it. Lasagna, and not bad
for prepack.

She finished eating. Had a stem of wine. She had
already dictated a report and commed it to the log computer at Nessie Central. Mintok would have digested it

when she saw him in the morning. It would be interesting to see his reaction to the caper.

She started another stem of wine. Heard the thumb lock click and the front door roll open. There was a pause, then Silk's voice.

"Who's there? I've got a gun."

"In the kitchen, Silk."

"Zia?" He came into the room.

He *did* have a gun.

"Where did you get *that*?"

The gun was pointed at the floor. He looked at it, then back at her. "I bought it today."

"Why?"

"Somebody shot at me this morning."

She stood, tense. "Who? Why?"

He waved his hands. "I don't know. What are you doing here? I thought you were going to be gone a few more days."

"The job got finished sooner than I expected." Boy. That was the truth.

She smelled it on him then. Sex. A woman's musk.

Good God. Silk had been with another woman.

"Did you miss me?" she said.

He flushed.

"Apparently you missed something," she continued. "But it doesn't look like you suffered any. Anybody I know?"

He shook his head, didn't try to deny it. "No. Nobody I know, either."

"A professional?"

"No. Just somebody I met. It didn't mean anything."

It meant something to her, but she would be damned if she would let him see that. She smiled.

The silence stretched. Too long. If he had said he was sorry or had offered some excuse, it would have made her feel better. At least he didn't lie about it. But it bothered her. Gone a couple of days and he was already out fucking around.

Oh? And what were you doing in Touchdown, sister?

Caring for the needy? Polishing your halo?

That was different. That was work! I didn't enjoy it.

Right. And you just forgot to tell Silk all about it before you left.

I—

Besides, look at him. He doesn't look as if he enjoyed it much, either. Let it go, maybe they cancelled each other out, what you did, what he did.

"Somebody shot at you, you said?"

"Yeah. In an alley in the Pearl District." He put the gun onto the table, stared at it. It was a spring pistol, she saw.

"I bought the gun to protect myself."

"What were you doing in the Pearl?"

He sighed. Rubbed his lip with his thumb. Wouldn't meet her eyes.

"I was looking for a place to rent," he said.

Her heart hit a reef and went down, the pressure of the depths crushing it to a hard knot. "A place to rent."

He rubbed at his forehead. "I didn't mean to bring it up like this."

"Oh. How did you mean to bring it up? When you moved your stuff out?"

"Listen, Zia—"

"This is great, Silk. I come home from a lousy fubar assignment to find you've been dorking another woman and packing your bags to move out. Thank you. Thank you so fucking much." She felt the tears gathering— Jesus Christ! She hadn't cried so much in her entire life as she had since meeting him—and she turned away so he wouldn't see it.

"Zia, I'm sorry. It's not you. It's me. I love you. I want to be with you—"

"Great way of showing it!"

"Look, I just want to be able to stand on my own feet without having to have you prop me up."

She turned back to face him, to hell with the tears. "Prop you up? I don't prop you up!"

"Yes, you do. This is your world. I'm an unwelcome

stranger here. How many times have you stepped between me and people who wanted to thump me because I'm a scum-sucking terry? Except for the basic dole, everything I own you bought for me."

"I wanted to buy it for you. I love you, you stupid fucking jerk!"

"I know. But I don't love me much these days. I feel weak, I feel useless, I feel valueless."

"That's stupid!"

"I know. You're right. But it's how I feel. I have to lean on you to keep from falling down, and I don't like the feeling."

"But I love you! I *want* to help you!"

"And I want to help you. But I can't. I'm just a—a weight you drag around."

"That's not true."

"It's true enough."

"You saved my ass on Earth. If you hadn't been there, I would have been dead a couple of times."

"Yes. But that was Earth. That's light-years away and in the past. In the six months since we've been here, the street has one-wayed. Until I got a job, I had to depend on you for everything."

"But I don't mind," she said. And she didn't. She wanted to do for him. Wanted to have him around. Wanted to take care of him in a way she'd never felt for anybody else she'd been with. And at that moment, she would have cut out her tongue with a wooden spoon before she admitted she had gotten him the job.

"I know. And I love you for that, too. But I can't just take all the time. I want to give, too."

"You do, you do give—"

"No, I don't. On Earth, I was somebody. Not much of somebody when you get right down to it, but I had a place, I had a certain amount of respect, I had a life of my own. Here, I'm an extension of you, that worthless terry sex toy Zia brought home like a stray dog."

"You're wrong."

"Really? Nobody ever said that?"

"Not to my face."

He grinned, but it was bitter. Shook his head. "On some things, we aren't ever going to be equal. You'll always be able to kick my ass in a fair fight, and you'll always be more at home with guns and daggers and sneaking around than I will. Probably you'll make more money. But I have to at least feel as if I can run with you, Zia. Maybe I'll never win a race, but I have to be able to keep up enough so I don't lose sight of you."

"I would wait for you," she said. "Always."

Now he started crying. Silently, tears streaming. "I know you would. Then wait for me now. Wait until I can find out who I am and what I'm doing here. Until I can look in a mirror and know there's somebody behind the blank face."

She went to him then, hugged him, but whatever comfort it gave him, she knew it was not enough. He was going to leave her. To go out into the world on his own, and the thought of it broke her heart.

Life was not fair.

ELEVEN

IF MINTOK WASN'T pissed off, he gave a pretty good imitation of it.

Zia slouched in the chair across from his desk because she knew the posture would irritate him more. Irritated men sometimes gave things away they didn't mean to reveal.

"So you killed him. It never occurred to you to keep him alive so we could peel him and find out exactly what it was all about."

"It occurred to me. About the time he stopped breathing. The man was behind me with a knife in his hand and I was maybe five seconds away from being butchered. I used appropriate force to protect myself."

Mintok ground his teeth together. "I don't like it. I don't like it a fucking bit. You haven't been the same since you got back from Earth with your diddle-boy. The Rélanj I knew would never have let some demistad spy get behind her with a knife in the first place. If that's how it really happened."

Zia started to give him a nasty reply but she held it. Truth was, she had thought the same thing. Maybe she *had* lost her edge. Maybe she was better off behind a desk, having conversations with a computer, instead of out in the field with the bad guys. Maybe being in love did make you blind and stupid.

As if to mirror her thought, Mintok said, "You don't go

out to play until we get this sorted out. Consider yourself
on vacation for the next few weeks. Until we crunch this
dead guy and find out what happened and why."

"I'll submit to a truth test regarding the sequence of
events in the room," she said.

"Not necessary at this point. I'll stipulate that it went
down the way you claim. Maybe the guy was a pervert
and our beegee missed it. Could be as simple as that."

"And if he wasn't?"

He looked at her. "Could mean you fucked up and
gave yourself away. Spooked him, burned it."

"Yeah. But I know better, and that only leaves one
other possibility. Somebody in the shop gave me up."

"We'll look into that, too," Mintok said.

Zia nodded, but didn't speak. She planned to do a little
looking into that on her own.

Silk didn't have all that much to pack. Except for his
new trike, everything he owned could be stacked neatly
in a small trunk without crowding. The trike, a low-slung
multigear recumbent, sat parked and locked outside in the
lot, waiting for him. The new cube was only a couple of
klicks away, on the edge of the Pearl, a twenty-minute
walk, five minutes on the trike. The point wasn't how
far away it was, the point was that it was separated from
Zia's cube.

She had commed him from her office to tell him she
was on the way. He sat on the couch, fighting the urge
to strap the trunk onto the trike and leave before she got
home. He didn't want to leave, now that it had come
down to it. He could see it was causing her pain, and
he hated that. It hurt him, too, but even so, he couldn't
stay.

A good spindoc was supposed to be able to turn the
sharp horns of a dilemma into a warm gel massage pad
on one side or an attractive and willing sexual partner
on the other. But this wasn't something he could spin
into a glossy imitation of the truth. This hurt. Him. Her.
Them. And yet—what else could he do? If he stayed

here, eventually, he would resent Zia, and he didn't want that. Better he should be elsewhere and working from a position of strength. Or relative strength, anyway.

She wasn't happy about it and she had to know he wasn't happy about it, either. But there was nothing else to be done.

Silk leaned back on the couch and stared at his trunk. A cheap plastic affair cast to resemble a steamer trunk from the preflight days on Earth. They didn't like terrans here, but they liked the popular historical culture enough to copy it with great frequency. On E2 you could buy art-deco pocket chronometers, Victorian-era lace shawls or Sung-dynasty sculptures. E2 had no culture of its own, so it borrowed from the motherworld while hating itself and Earth for so doing. How they could hate Earth so much when most of the older people here were from Earth or one of the other *ausvelts* amazed him. Anybody older than sixty or so couldn't have been born on this world.

He looked at the trunk again. It had been shaped and colored to ape a leather and steel-riveted box that would have looked at home crossing the North Atlantic on the *Titanic*.

Silk hoped his trunk wasn't going to suffer the same fate as those on that ship had suffered.

Maybe this was a mistake. Maybe he should unpack, put his stuff away, cancel the deposit on the cube. Tell Zia he was a blockheaded fool and beg her to forgive him. No doubt that would make her feel a lot better. If that didn't help his insecurity, well, maybe nothing would anyhow.

He heard the door open, saw her come in. She looked at him, then the trunk by his feet.

"So. You're going."

He fought the sigh, lost. "Zia . . ."

"I just got put on vacation," she said, her voice tight. "They think I fucked up my assignment in Touchdown. So I get a few weeks off to play with myself until they decide what happened."

"I'm sorry."

"I believe you. Just like I believed you when you said you loved me and wanted to be with me."

"I did. I still do."

"Then why are you leaving?"

"I have to."

"Yes. We all do what we have to do. Go. Give me a call sometime."

"Zia, dammit, this doesn't mean—"

"I don't want to talk to you right now, Silk. Go. Get out of here and leave me alone."

Her tone was cold. It was eternity. It was Deep Space, far from any star's light. Silk couldn't stand against it. He picked up his trunk and left without another word.

He heard her sob as the door closed behind him.

The sound was the twin to his own.

Well, now, Colburn thought. What have we here?

He watched as Silk walked to a raked trike parked in the cycle lot and bungeed a small trunk onto the carry rack. He unlocked the trike, backed it out of the lot, then mounted it and pedaled away.

Trouble in paradise? Was he going on a trip, or had he moved out?

Colburn started the cart's motor and rolled out onto the street from where he had been parked behind a small stand of bushes. The morning sun cast hard shadows everywhere. Going to be a warm one, today, maybe up near body heat. Already clouds formed in the distance, building toward afternoon thunderstorms.

He hadn't been keeping very good track of Silk lately. Colburn had concentrated his energies on Rélanj. She was a better target for several good reasons, he rationalized. The man was interesting, but the woman more so. She would be privy to more information, being an agent of the local government. Plus, she was more attractive to him, given that they would be spending some . . . quality time together. Not that he had anything against male lovers, but he preferred a more massive type than Silk when he wanted to walk that side of the street, somebody much more *yang*. Silk was a little too average to call him that. Since the game could get to a genital stage eventually, he might as well indulge himself.

But he followed Silk at a safe distance because he wanted to know what the situation between him and Zia was. A rift would be good; it would certainly aid maneuvers. He only needed one of them, and Zia was his choice, but if something should happen to her, Silk was the other option and he needed to keep it open.

Silk drove to a complex about twenty blocks away, dismounted the trike, and carried his trunk to one of the units. Colburn parked the cart and ambled along after the man, who had no idea he was being followed, not unless he was a very good actor.

Silk thumbed the printlock at one of the cubes and went from the hallway in to the unit. The door slid shut behind him.

Colburn pulled his com from where it was crowed on his belt and tapped in the cube's street and door code. After a moment the small flatscreen built into the com lit, the LCD scrolled the current renter's name: Venture Silk.

Well, well. Trouble in paradise, indeed.

The second installment of the Treatment was not too different from the first. There was the insertion of the tube into her neck and the flow of whatever it was into her. The bitter cum-flavored drink afterward. There was in addition, however, an implant of a tiny capsule under the skin of her chest, between her breasts. The capsule was shiny, black, about the size of her little fingernail, but a little thicker.

As the doctor performed the procedure, she explained.

"This'll stay in place until the third session," Marad said. "It's designed to deliver a precisely metered dose of chem over the next seven days. It should not cause you any discomfort, and you will notice that it will shrink each day until it is about the size of a pinhead. We'll remove the cartridge remains next time."

"I practice martial arts. Will it damage the thing if it gets punched?"

"No. It's a simple bioreactive solid, there's nothing to break or short out. It might shift a little, but that is of no concern as long as it stays subcue—under the skin."

Behind her, Karl said, "Hormone levels are down a little."

"Let me see."

Marad walked over and examined the scan. She looked back at Zia. "Any changes in your life recently to account for a downturn in your estrogen level?"

Zia's grin was bitter. "My boyfriend moved out a few days ago."

Marad nodded. "That would account for it." She waited a second, then said, "Sorry."

"Way it goes. No big deal."

Zia slid off the table.

"Allow a couple of hours for next visit," Marad said. "There are a few new procedures added to this routine."

"Fine. Next week."

"Goodbye."

Outside, the traffic was lunchtime thick, the air hot and muggy. Going to rain again, Zia saw, just as it had nearly every day since Silk had left. She tried not to do it, but things tended to slot into one of two categories these days: Before Silk left. After Silk left. It had only been three days. He had called her every day. She'd seen him in *kolo* class. They'd had lunch twice, dinner once, and he'd stayed over last night. The lovemaking had been frantic, she'd had to work to keep it from feeling desperate on her part, and she was pretty sure he'd felt the same way. She'd almost broken down and asked him to come back. He'd invited her to visit his cube, but she hadn't accepted the offer yet. Something in her resisted it, she couldn't say what. Truth was, they'd probably spent more time together in the last three days than they had in any typical three days in the last three months. She'd been glad to see him, he'd been glad to see her. It was obvious.

But it was different. It felt different. He didn't seem happy to be gone, on the one hand, but on the other hand, he did. She couldn't put her finger on what it was exactly, but it was there, like an unseen cat turd somewhere in your home, it was there. Sooner or later you'd find it, the smell would lead you to it no matter how well it was hidden.

She chuckled as she walked along the crowded street, people going about their business. Comparing love to a cat turd, now there was probably a first.

Despite the hot daylight working to pierce her protective sunblock, she felt a cool, ghostly touch on her neck, a faint stirring of the fine blonde hairs there. It was an atavistic sensation, an unreasonable feeling; it made her want to spin around in a crouch, to snarl and show her teeth and claws, ready to fight or run.

She kept walking, gave no sign of the feeling that swept her, but knew it for what it was: danger, here, close by.

Zia strolled to a stop in front of a shop window, a display of the latest state-of-the-art flexoprene footwear, touted as being totally comfortable and protective at the same time. She pretended to look at the slippers and hiking shoes but allowed her eyes to long focus, using the reflections in the clear plate plastic to show her the street and the walk across it. As she bent to ostensibly look at the display, she flicked peripheral gazes left and right.

There were scores of people going to and from lunch, men, women, even a few children, moving back and forth on the walk, crossing the street. It was a human stream flowing easily in the summer sunshine. There were a few tough-looking folks in the crowd, there usually were, outbackers and badlanders in town for whatever business, but nobody upon whom she could bestow the mantle of quick danger she felt. Nobody who triggered the gut-twisting or the cold fingers on her spine. She didn't see them, he, she, whoever it was, but she knew it to the pit of her soul. She was being followed.

She left the window display, strolled off along the walk,

kept her pace that of the main flow of other walkers. She smiled at passersby, some she knew, some she didn't, and continued to look for the tail. Probably Mintok's doing; that was the first and most likely possibility. Whoever it was, he was good if she couldn't make him, and that argued for Mintok. This wasn't some student practicing his technique on a sister in the biz, something most young ops had tried along the way. Nor was it a stalker looking for a strong-arm robbery or maybe a rape to pass the time, not unless he was a professional op with enough experience to track the best and get away with it. No, this was somebody who knew who she was and who had to be damned good to play surveillance games without being tagged. She'd been watched by experts, and as far as she could tell, she'd almost always known about it on some level. She'd learned to trust her instincts, they were almost never wrong.

Somebody was dogging her.

Well. If she could find out who, it wouldn't take long to convince him—or her—to tell her why. She was pretty sure of that, too.

TWELVE

TWO WEEKS AFTER he'd moved out of Zia's cube, Silk had established a fairly standard daily routine. He'd get up around 0800, shower and dress, go out and have a light breakfast. His shift began at 1000, but he didn't have to actually be in the building if he was accessible by com.

On prime- and threedays, he went to the shooting range—a different one from where he'd bought the gun—and practiced with the spring pistol. It wasn't the same as his crossbow, but it was a similar enough discipline that he took to it comfortably. He'd spend an hour or so putting needles into the target, and after four sessions, he was already a lot more confident. Afterward, he would call and ask Zia to lunch. She met him most days, though it was still awkward at times.

In the afternoons, he went to his office to see if there was any real work to be done. There seldom was. Those events that the company had to have spun generally were the kinds of things a lamebrained primary-school student with ten minutes of training could take care of without any problems. It paid his rent and then some, though. For the first time in his career, he was actually able to save a little money.

He usually ate dinner early, so it would be digested by the time *kolo* class began at 1900. He attended those sessions primeday through sixday, took sevenday off.

Taníto allowed you one day of rest a week. After class, he would shower, and sometimes meet Zia for dinner when he hadn't eaten earlier. Five times in two weeks he had stayed all night with her at her cube. She had yet to visit him at his place. On those nights when she wasn't interested in seeing him, he went home and read or watched the entcom until he fell asleep.

It was a fairly spartan life. He was thinking about finding a pool and adding swimming to his regime. He'd gotten stronger and now had enough endurance to survive the *kolo* classes without falling into utter exhaustion. And he liked to swim.

Oddly enough, on those times when he did go out, to a pub or a public art exhibit or show, he was no longer bothered by anybody because he was a terran. Maybe it was because he carried a pistol tucked into a clever inside-the-waistband holster under his loose shirts, and that somehow came across. Or maybe it was because the martial arts practice had toughened him, given him a more balanced stance. He didn't go out of his way to get in anybody's face, but neither did he walk around with his shoulders hunched and his head down. He'd heard the *ausvelt* worlds believed an armed society was a polite society, and that seemed to be true for the most part. A couple of time he saw offworlders, and there was something about them that gave that away, even when they wore local clothes and seemed to know what they were about. Maybe that was why he'd been bothered at first. Maybe his terran-ness showed and they knew what wimps terrans were supposed to be. Not this terran, not anymore.

It was fourday and Zia couldn't meet him for lunch, so Silk decided to try the new bento he'd heard about, a place within a few minutes' walk of his cube. He dressed, tucked his pistol into its holster, and looked at himself in the mirror. Passable. The little gun hadn't become a part of him or anything, but it was comfortable enough where it rode over his right buttock, just above his wallet. The rangemaster where he practiced had suggested that if he was going to carry, that was the best place. That way, he'd said, if somebody asks for your folding stads, you can come up with hardware instead.

Silk was pretty sure that if somebody pointed a gun at him and demanded his wallet, he was going to come up with just that. The gun would stay where it was unless it was the only way to keep from getting killed. Zia had taught him that: Don't pull it unless you mean to use it—and you know how to use it. But even with only a few hours of practice, he could draw the pistol, line it up and shoot in a little over a second. The rangemaster seemed to think he was pretty good. For a terry.

The food at the bento was passable. It consisted of rice and bits of cooked fowl and vegetables mixed together with a hot sauce over it. It came packed in a paper box so you could take it with you and eat in a nice shady spot outside, if that was what you wanted. Silk sat at a table inside and used chopsticks to eat, something he'd grown up doing, and found it interesting that about half of the patrons in the little place preferred forks. It was good enough so he'd eat here again.

He was on the way to his office after lunch when he spotted somebody following him in the trike's rearview mirror.

He was already on a secondary street, one limited to human-powered or motor-driven vehicles of three horse-power or less. The man tailing him drove a fuel-cell bike, and was in a string of bikes and trikes and a couple of pedal-quads about twenty meters behind Silk's tricycle.

He couldn't have said exactly what it was that drew his attention. Maybe it was the red hair. Maybe some subliminal memory kicked in, something that he didn't know he knew. But Silk was suddenly sure that the big man on the fuel-cell bike was the same man who'd been in that alley a few weeks past, waiting to shoot him.

Let's not get paranoid, here, Silk.

No? Paranoia is an unfounded fear, pal. When somebody opens up on you with a gun, that's about as much foundation as you get.

So what are you going to do?

That was a good question. What *was* he going to do?

Well. The first thing was to find out if the guy really was following him. The bike had an ID plate on the front, under the nose lamp, and Silk pedaled his trike and guided it with one hand while he carefully tapped the numbers on the bike into his com. The query came back in a few seconds. The bike was registered to Nakahashi Enterprises.

No help there, though he filed the information away.

Silk took the first cross-street, made a slow and deliberate right turn, and cranked the trike up a couple of gears and blew past an old man on a little IC scooter that sounded like an angry sewing machine. He passed a woman on a long-handled electric skateboard and pulled in front of her, then watched his mirror.

Red rounded the corner on his bike and fell into the line of traffic.

At the next intersection, Silk moved to the inside lane and made a left, got to a cross-street almost immediately and made another right. He wasn't hurrying, and he wasn't trying to lose his pursuer, if indeed that's what the guy was. If the guy stayed with him, then he figured that would stretch coincidence a bit much.

But after pedaling along for another two blocks with no sign of Red behind him, Silk breathed a little easier. It must have been his imagination.

Then he looked up and saw Red fifty meters ahead of him, going in the same direction he was.

He wasn't sure at first, because this driver had on a lightweight helmet, whereas Red had been bareheaded. But when he checked the bike's numbers to make sure it was the same one, they matched. So did Red's coverall, a dark blue one-piece.

Pretty clever, Red. To put a hat on and get in front of me that way. If I wasn't paying attention, it would have fooled me. Almost did anyhow.

Silk downshifted a gear and slowed a little, got into the curb lane. He needed to think about this.

That he was being followed—led at the moment—
was obvious. Why? Who did the guy represent? Was
it somebody from Zia's organization, keeping tabs on
him? Maybe they'd been watching him ever since he'd
arrived and he'd never noticed before.

But if that were so, why had they shot at him in that
alley? If they'd didn't want him here, they could have
stuck him on a ship to anywhere easier than snapping
their fingers.

Was it somebody from Earth? Come to get rid of him,
since they couldn't extradite him legally? He wouldn't
put it past them, not given the experiences he and Zia
had slogged through to escape. Although Zia was pretty
much convinced after they got back that the guy trying to
kill or capture them there at the end had been some kind
of rogue agent out for his own ends, Silk wasn't sure.
Earth was packed with liars—he'd been one himself—
and some of the best worked for the government in one
form or another.

He was technically a traitor. He'd seen enough entcoms
to believe it possible that Earth might have secret agents
on the *ausvelt* worlds to take care of traitors who escaped
to the freedom of another planet. He hadn't really worried
about it before, because he hadn't really *done* anything
except help Zia escape. That in itself hadn't damaged
Earth's security, the crime was more *malum prohibitum*
than it was *malum in se*. He was a little fish, a minnow;
why should they bother with him now? Zia had concurred
in that belief, but it might be possible.

And if it *wasn't* one of those two, his government
or hers, then who the hell could it be? Some kind of
anti-terran fanatic? A sociopath who had fixated on him
because of something innocuous?

It was a problem, all right.

On Earth, under similar conditions, Silk would have
headed for the nearest police station and reported it. The
cops would have asked Red a few questions and if they
didn't like his answers, they would have detained him
until they found out what they wanted to know. Here,

he didn't know who to trust. Zia, yeah. The rest of the populace was a blank. He might put a little faith in Taníto and Bûso; other than that, he didn't know anybody particularly well. He'd been intimate with Hildy, the gun saleswoman, but they'd satisfied their mutual lust and curiosity and that had been the end of that.

So of the possibilities he could think up, none of them seemed very likely.

Still leaves the basic question, Silk. What are you going to do?

Well. Maybe he should have a talk with Red. Maybe if he asked politely, Red would be forthcoming enough to solve this little mystery.

He smiled. The very idea of bracing somebody tailing him and asking him hard questions, maybe using force, would have seemed so alien to him a year past he would not have believed it possible. He'd come a long way, both in light-years and in his own development.

He considered finding a secluded spot but decided against it. Now that he knew Red was following him, he'd be more alert. If he spooked the man, they might replace him with somebody he wouldn't spot. Better the devil he knew than the one he didn't. For now.

"That's it," the medic said. "You're done."

Zia sat up on the table, rubbed at the cold spot on her neck, looked at Marad. "Let me guess. My line is, 'I don't feel any different.' "

Marad laughed. "Yes, that seems to be the standard response at the end of the fourth session. Technically speaking, the systems are not yet complete—there are some oral medications you need to take for the next few weeks, and the interactive hormones and bacteria colonies haven't, ah, consummated their relationships fully yet. But when it all works properly, in about two months, that won't really make much difference in how you feel, either. It's more of what you *don't* feel. You'll notice that you don't get sick very often, no allergies, no colds or flu, not much likelihood of pimples or minor infections. Your immune system is going to work like a gym full of weightlifters. You'll probably be able to party a little longer before you get tired, and you'll sleep better when you do, wake up feeling better. Offhand, that's about it. You won't get cancer, you won't get gray hair, you won't develop arthritis, you won't go through menopause. If you stay out in the sun too long without block, you'll burn and eventually wrinkle, too, but not as much as before the Treatment. If you cut yourself, it will heal faster. If you sprain an ankle or break a bone, it will also heal faster and with much less scarring.

"If somebody shoots you in the head or your cart plows into a bus at speed, you'll die just like everybody else. You aren't invulnerable, just a more efficient human."

"And I suppose the follow-up line would be . . . ?"

"How long will you have?" Marad shook her head. "We don't know. Based on computer projections, our best guess is a minimum of three hundred years. There are some questions about long-term exposure to cosmic rays and free radical scavenger systems, high-end Hayflick Limits. We won't know until we get there. Some of the big brains believe that the system might be open-ended. That if you take care not to get flattened by a bad driver or don't slip in the shower and break your neck, you might go on for thousands of years. Law of averages says you'll encounter a fatal accident sooner or later, but if you are very careful, maybe it's later."

Zia took a deep breath. Let it out. Thousands of years.

"So I take my pills and that's it?"

"More or less. We'll want to see you every six months for checkups. There is one major restriction: You can't travel offworld. I'm sure you understand why."

Zia nodded.

"Of course, fifty or a hundred years from now, the relationships among the planets could be vastly different. Maybe by then this technology will be something you can pick up at the corner drugstore, and the need for secrecy will be over."

Zia slid off the table, stretched her neck a little. Found that despite the implied impoliteness, she had to ask.

"Dr. Marad, you haven't taken the Treatment. Why?"

"I don't want it. I qualified, given the nature of my job, but I'm a member of the Cyclic Church. I put my faith elsewhere, M. Rélanj. Whatever my allotted span, I have no desire to stretch it."

"I see."

"Probably not," Marad said. She grinned. "But that's okay. Each of us should be allowed to travel her own path."

Without thinking, Zia said, "Amen." It surprised her more than it did Marad, who lifted an eyebrow. Odd that it would come up now. Maybe it was because this was a real miracle and it jogged something in her memory.

When she'd been a girl, she'd gone to church with her mother. She'd stopped when her uncle began giving her lessons in how to please a man sexually. God didn't answer her prayers to make him stop; as far as she knew, her mother's brother was still out in the bush flying delivery hops. And probably still training young women, hardly more than girls, in matters concerning coitus, fellatio, and sodomy. Were he not her mother's brother, were her mother not still alive, he would be dead by now. Or . . . disarmed.

"You're a Believer," Marad said. Not a question.

"Long since lapsed, doctor. My faith went elsewhere."

"Sorry."

"Don't be. I'm happy. Thank you for your work here."

"You are welcome. It's a small town. We'll probably see each other again outside of the checkups. Maybe even in church." She smiled.

"Maybe." But Zia wouldn't bet on that.

Colburn watched as Rélanj emerged from the un-marked medical facility and strode away from the building, talking long, athletic strides. He'd seen her work out at the martial arts class, and he could understand the bounce in her walk. She was very good and also in excellent physical condition.

The medical complex and what it did was a poorly kept secret. His mole inside New Earth Security had laid it out for him, but it didn't take a genius to figure out they were hiding something most important in the complex. An hour inside the building, and he could probably gather enough information about the process to save himself a lot of trouble—but the chances of that were minimal. The security was very tight, and he wasn't going to sneak or bluff his way inside with the old repairman gag. As it was, he couldn't park near the entrance or circle around the block too long without being noticed, so he'd taken to spending time in the small pub across the street to wait for Rélanj when she went for her medical treatments. Or Treatment, as the spy inside Nessie told him. Oh, given enough time, he could eventually come up with a plan that would work, enough time and enough money, but he had more of the latter than the former and they were of equal importance. There were always chinks in the best armor, weak links in a chain, and he could exploit them if he did so carefully. A guard with a fondness for things expensive or a secret to hide could be influenced. A technician with a family could be threatened. There was always a soft spot that would yield to pressure; the trick was taking the time to find it before you risked applying the pressure. People were the keys to doors with unpickable locks. Unfortunately, he didn't have months to spend here, only a few more weeks at the outside, and one couldn't hurry such things and expect to maintain one's own security.

So, snatching somebody who carried the magic in her was a better plan. If you couldn't bring the process, bring somebody who had been processed. One could learn how to build a machine by carefully taking it apart.

The truth was, he could have selected any of the patients who flowed in and out of the top-secret Treatment process, isolated one from the small pack and spirited him or her away, doubtless a lot easier than kidnapping

a trained undercover operative who could break bricks
with her hands and who carried a pistol under her shirt.
Silverman had given him carte blanche; he wouldn't care
what the container looked like, as long as it held what he
wanted.

Ah, but Silverman was a bottom-line man, and he
wasn't interested in testing himself in the field any more.
He'd paid his risky dues and was done with that.

Not so Colburn. Anybody could shoot a fish in a barrel; only an expert hunted Great Whites in their own
territory with nothing but a deep breath and a speargun.
For Colburn, it wasn't just about doing the job, but doing
it with *style*. With elán. Any thug could pull a trigger or
clonk somebody over the head and drag them off. An
artist must be subtle. Colburn was, after all, the best of
the best.

And it was time to make his next move.

THIRTEEN _____

AS THEY LAY side by side in her bed, his heart still pounding from their frantic lovemaking, his small secret popped into his mind. Silk considered it, but decided not to say anything to Zia about being followed. He figured he would handle it himself. One of the reasons he moved out was to take charge of his own business.

"You okay?" he asked.

Nestled next to Silk, feeling his warmth, Zia didn't mention that she was being tailed. It wasn't his concern, and while she wanted to share herself with him, this was her business. It was just a little secret. No big deal.

"I'm fine," she said.

FOURTEEN _____

ZIA GENERALLY PRACTICED her pistolcraft at the indoor range under the Justice Center. She tried to manage at least one session a week, usually on fiveday. As a Nessie op, she didn't have to pay for time or ammunition; each police agency had a contract with the range. The range was open to the public but most of the shooters were local, national or planetary peace officers or government agents who went about armed under the provisions of their various charters. All needed a place to practice shooting because all had to pass tests with their weapons. The parole officers had to qualify once every sixteen months. Local cops had to demonstrate their skills once a year, tax collectors every six months. Nessie ops had to shoot passing scores four times a year.

She'd offered to help Silk with his shooting, would have been happy to go and practice with him, but he wasn't enthusiastic. Probably worried she'd make him look bad.

Well, hell. It wasn't her fault she was a razor and he was a butter knife.

Well, okay, actually it was. But she didn't see how he could *blame* her for that. He'd known what she was when he'd agreed to come with her to E2.

Like he had a lot of choice by that point.

Shut up. I don't need this from you.

Me? But you are *me, sweetie.*

The rangemaster saw her coming and put a box of

ammo, some targets, and a pair of throwaway earplugs on the counter. Smiled at her and pushed the button that unlocked the electronic lock on the range entrance door. Said, "Lane nine."

She nodded, put her plugs in, and went through the soundproof door. As she walked to her assigned lane, she saw there were eight or ten shooters on the line. Some she recognized as other fiveday-morning shooters, some were strangers. She stepped over the blinking amber caution strip and put the ammo on her lane's bench, quickly set a pair of targets on the conveyor and ran them out to ten meters. She took a deep breath, drew her weapon as fast as she could, stepped into a modified Weaver stance and started shooting. She fired twice at the first target, shifted the red dot up to the head, shot again, shifted to the right, capped off two-and-one at that target.

She reeled the targets back and examined them. Each of the thin plastic sheets had two holes in the chest where a man's heart would be and a third punched-out circle in the forehead.

She marked the holes with a yellow paintpen tied to the bench and sent the targets back out, to fifteen meters this time. She reloaded the magazine, inserted it into the pistol, reholstered the gun.

In the lane next to her, a matching target floated out and stopped next to hers. Before Zia could draw, she heard the guy in the lane next to her open up. He fired six rounds, fast enough so it sounded almost like a full-auto. She couldn't see him for the high divider, but it sounded as if he were wasting a lot of ammunition. That kind of speed didn't make for much accuracy.

She paused a second and watched the next lane's target float back toward the firing line. When it was three meters out, she saw the holes. She only counted four, but the one in the middle was big and ragged enough to encompass three bullets, easy. The entire group would fit inside a circle she could make with her thumb and forefinger.

That was good shooting at fifteen meters with a service handgun at slow speed. Real good shooting done rapid-fire.

Zia pulled her own piece and tried to copy the group. She fired six times, a bit slower, aiming at the head. When she reeled the target back, she found she'd hit it five of six, but her group was not nearly as tight as the shooter's next to her. They were all in the head, but it would take her whole hand to cover them all.

She frowned. She was pretty good, better than most of the cops and ops who shot here on fivedays, but the guy next to her—and it was a guy, she remembered seeing him when she walked in—was better. Unless this particular group was a fluke, a lucky happenstance.

As Zia put the rest of the box of ammo through her weapon, she kept a peripheral eye on the target next to hers. Wherever she put hers, the guy would line his up beside it. Five meters, fifteen, twenty, seven. And as far as she could tell, he outshot her every time.

It pissed her off. For all practical purposes, it didn't make any difference; she was getting "A" hits, all kill-zone taps. Shoot a guy in the heart, and a centimeter or two probably wouldn't make much difference. Plus the guy could be using a better weapon, longer barrel, cleaner sights and trigger, like that. Still . . .

She sent a fresh target out to the limit of the range, forty meters. Took a series of deep breaths and went through the quick meditation mind-clearing exercise Taníto taught. Forget everything, concentrate on the here and now. She shook her arms to relax them, defocused her eyes for a few seconds, and drew her pistol. The little 6mm became an extension of her hand, as much as her fingers were. Grip, sight picture, breathing, trigger control, it was all locked into automatic, non-thought-involved, a thing of feel. In that mode, it was either right or it was wrong, and it felt right. She put the red dot in the center of the target and pressed the trigger with crisp strokes, emptying the entire magazine in about three seconds.

As soon as the gun ran dry, the shooter next to her cranked up. He fired at the same pace, same number of rounds.

Zia reeled her target back, saw his target also start to return.

As the two targets neared the line, she knew she had beaten him this time. Her group was about seven centimeters, very good at that distance. Better than good. His was maybe nine centimeters, and there was a flyer that opened it up even more.

She grinned. About damned time.

She pulled the pistol apart and cleaned it, using the bench's solvent and push rods, reassembled the weapon, reloaded it with her carry ammo. She holstered the gun, collected the empty ammo box and the used targets, and clicked off the stall's lights.

As she left, the shooter next to her also moved out of his stall.

"Good shooting," he said. He nodded and smiled at her.

Zia looked at the man. He was lightly tanned, had thick hair cut moderately short that was once brown but mostly gray now, and looked to be in his late thirties or early forties at first glance. Fairly muscular, a little above average height. He wore blue synlin pants and a snug and matching T-shirt over spun dotic boots in a darker blue. Zia looked at his hands and the smile lines next to his eyes and upped her estimate a few years. Mid-forties, T.S. The little signs gave it away, but if he wanted to claim to be younger, most people would believe him; he moved well and was fit. He had an accent she couldn't place, so he wasn't a local boy.

"Thanks. You shot better."

"Not that last round."

"Last time doesn't matter, it's the first time that's important."

He smiled again. "True enough. I'm Croft Colburn."

"Zia Rélanj."

They nodded at each other.

"Well," he said. "I have to go. Work calls. See you around."

He left and she puzzled over his accent for a moment. Nein Gepack? New Australia? Maybe even Earth?

When she reached the rangemaster's desk and gave him the used targets and ammo box, she was curious enough to ask.

"Milos, that guy who left just ahead of me, who's he work for?"

"Dunno," the rangemaster said. "He's nonaffiliated, he paid street rates. A civilian."

"Hmm. Would you punch up his stats for me?"

"This business?"

"Personal. Did he log in his carry permit?"

"Nope, didn't need to. He shot a rental gun."

"A rental? He did that well with a rental? What kind?"

"Same as yours. Six mm Risthawk."

"Jesus. Let me see the stats."

Milos shrugged. Said, "Computer, display stats on last checkout."

The holoproj appeared. "Reverse image."

The image turned itself inside out so Zia could read it.

She blinked. The name at the top of the sheet was "Clete Claibourne."

She frowned. That wasn't the name he'd given her. He'd called himself "Croft Colburn."

Hello?

She glanced at the rest of the stat. "You run a hard copy for me?"

"Is this guy trouble, Zia?"

"No reason to think so. But maybe it's business after all."

"No problem. Computer, print a copy of this image."

It only took a few seconds until the laser finished the sheet and Milos handed it to her.

"Keep me posted if it's something I oughta know?"

"I will. Thanks, Milos."

She left, looking at the sheet. Why would the guy

give her a phony name? Was he maybe contracted and looking for a playmate he didn't want his spouse to find out about? If so, why hadn't he pitched her? Other than complimenting her on her shooting, he didn't try a line. Smiled and left. Didn't seem interested in her that way.

Was it something else?

Given the way things had been going lately, maybe it was a good idea if she found out.

Colburn smiled as he wheeled the cart out of the parking lot under the Justice Center. She'd stopped to check him out, just as he figured she would. She was a good shooter, better than most, and he'd outdone her all but once. He grinned wider. And that last round had been a deliberate loss on his part; at least the flyer had been. It had to pique her curiosity, the dead-shot stranger next to her. It surely would have piqued his, had their positions been reversed. She'd want to know something about him. And when she found out he'd used a rented gun and a different name, well, how could any agent worth a bent demistad let that go by? She'd have to check him out.

Exactly as he had intended. He had dangled the bait, and she had nibbled it. A little more work and she would be hooked solidly. Then it would only be a matter of time until she was his.

When Silk saw Hildy sitting at a table in the front of the bento eating lunch, he was tempted to walk past without speaking. He had avoided going back to her store just so he wouldn't run into her again. He didn't think she was bothered by it, she hadn't given any indication she'd wanted any more than a quick fuck to see what it was like to do it with a terry, so no loss on either side.

But she looked up and saw him as he approached and broke into a big smile. "Silk! Great to see you."

Well, at least she remembered his name.

"Hi, Hildy."

"You gonna eat here?"

He had been, but he didn't want the entanglement. "No, I just had lunch."

She gave him a catlike smile. "I have something you can eat for dessert, if you're interested."

Silk's heart sped up. She'd been good in bed, but they didn't have anything else in common. On Earth in his younger days, he'd played the wham-bam with others who'd liked the game. Meet a stranger for lunch, go into the fresher together, fuck each other silly, smile, go back and finish your meal. It had been fun, but it was a kid's game. Pleasant friction, cheap thrills, something to release a little tension. Nobody got hurt, but it was very limited. This wasn't exactly the same, but it was similar enough.

Hildy wasn't Zia, and maybe that was worth something. He didn't feel inferior to her. Oh, maybe she could shoot better than he could, but he didn't know that for sure. Zia reserved the right to screw other people if it was part of her job—why couldn't he have something on the side?

It was tempting for a moment. But the truth was, he didn't really want her, not when he would be in Zia's bed tonight. His days of marathon fucking were long past. There had been a time when pleasing three or four women in a single day had been a challenge. He supposed he might still be up for it physically, but psychically? No. Cost too much.

He said, "I'd like that but I've got to get back to work. Another time?"

"You got my number," she said. She didn't seem too disturbed that he wasn't hot to leap on her right there.

"That I do. See you."

He strolled off down the walk. Only if he ran into her by accident again would he be likely to see her. There was a time when he wouldn't have even considered refusing. Today, however, temptation had arisen and he had turned away from it. He grinned to himself and felt virtuous.

FIFTEEN _____

COLBURN WHISTLED A bit of Pachelbel's *Canon in D* as he let himself into his cube. He gave the vox alarm his code and thus disarmed it, thumbprinted the lock, and stepped into the building. The coolness of the conditioned air inside was welcome after the hot and muggy afternoon. He'd spent a couple hours at the pharmaceutical company, driven through the slow traffic in a cart whose cooler had been malfunctioning, and was now sweaty and just a little irritable. He intended to grab his exercise clothes and to spend an hour or two at the local gym working the tension out.

The sight of Zia Rélanj seated on his couch startled him enough so that he almost went for his gun. He moved his hand a couple of centimeters, then stopped. Smiled at her. "Good afternoon."

If she had wanted him dead, he would already *be* dead.

He hadn't seen her working him, hadn't sensed her inside, and he'd known that sooner or later she would tail or approach him. That she was here was delightful—and a serious mistake on his part. For her to be on his couch, her hands empty, was a complete surprise and it meant two things: First, she was better than he'd figured. Second, it meant there was a very good chance he wouldn't be taking her back to Earth. That remained to be seen.

"Good afternoon," she replied. "Do sit down. Like a drink?"

His smile grew. Oh, that was a nice touch. To assume command of his very premises. "A soft drink, perhaps."

She waved at the bar. "Help yourself. You know where things are."

Colburn walked toward the bar, smiling, striving to maintain as cool a demeanor as he could manage. He remembered the old joke about the definition of a sophisticate, a definition he'd heard applied to himself by others: a man who has never done *any*thing for the first time. But this was a new one. He'd never been caught with his metaphorical pants down before. It was an interesting feeling.

He opened the cold drink compartment under the bar and removed two bottles of seltzer water. "One for you?"

"Okay."

He broke the plastic seals and twisted the caps from the bottles, then went to where she sat and put one of them down in front of her. She had to be nervous, but there was no sign of it as she leaned back against the cushion and watched him settle into the chair across from her. The distance was just shy of four meters, too far to cover in a single leap. If either of them tried, the other would have time to pull a weapon—

He mentally chuckled to himself. Old habits, the calculation of such vectors. Neither of them would be bounding at each other, not like that, not now. And the last thing he wanted to do was shoot her. He raised his bottle and inclined his head in a silent toast. More of a salute, actually. Saw her get it and match the move.

Excellent.

He took a sip from his drink, as did she from hers. The ritual finished, he put his bottle on the small table next to his chair, watched her carefully set her bottle on the couch's side table.

That she was here meant she knew what he was, so they could skip the first level of cover stories. But how much more did she know?

"You're very good," he said. Might as well acknowledge the obvious.

"Thank you. And you are better than you pretend to be."

Colburn could not stop the grin. Excellent!

"How so?"

"The set-up and little name game at the range. A man smart enough to get my attention with the gunplay wouldn't be clumsy enough to give it away with a phony name, M. Colburn."

"And why not Claibourne?"

"That's the name you've got on record." She smiled.

He inclined his head again in agreement.

"Anything else, M. Rélanj?"

He saw her assimilate his use of her name and nod slightly. "Well. I know *what* you are and *who* you are. Why you're here is more of a guess but not really very hard to figure out. The Forever Drug."

He was impressed. He said so.

She shrugged. "We don't really have a lot worth stealing out here in the space woods, now do we? Not so much that Earth would send one of its best to get it. We know somebody figured it out, after my recent adventures there. We *ausvelters* aren't as sophisticated as you terrans, but we aren't completely stupid."

Again, he had to nod in salute. She really was quite incredible. She knew he was a spy, knew where he was from and what he had come to fetch. But more importantly, she knew he wasn't going to be surprised by her revelation of what was supposed to be a top secret. That she wasn't giving anything away by admitting it.

It was a wonderful dance, the best he'd had in years. So delightful to deal with a professional. Logic dictated his next step.

"And why aren't I face down in an alley, then, Zia? If I may be so informal? Or dogged down in a cell with the brainpickers digging into my synapses?"

She said, "Would our strainers get anything from you under drugs or torture?"

He smiled. "Not really. I have an embedded block. The first probe to get past my name, rank, and ID number would trigger it." He touched his closed fists together then spread his fingers quickly in the silent USL gesture for an explosion.

She nodded. "You're ahead of us there. As for the alley, M. Colburn—"

"My first name is Croft. Please."

"We both know how the game is played. You could have a backup or a replacement standing by, maybe one even you don't know about. We have a saying here; 'It's easier to follow the wolf in the snow than the one in the den.' "

"True enough," he said, "but there's more, isn't there? If you were really interested in bagging me, you would have done so."

"I still could."

"I don't see a gun, but I assume you have one. Do you think you are good enough to take me? After our game at the range?"

"Yes. At this distance, speed is more important than pinpoint accuracy. I'm younger and faster."

Oh, he liked her. She was brash, confident, bright. Younger than he would have liked, and maybe a little rough around the edges, but those weren't major problems.

"Let's get back to that another time," he said. "The real reason you haven't taken me out or, more importantly, given me over to the powers-that-be is that you want something."

It was her turn to nod acknowledgment of his clever reasoning, and she didn't disappoint him.

"And that would be . . . ?" he prompted.

"Silk. I want him left alone."

Another smile lit his face. He was beginning to feel like a grinning idiot. It had been a long time since he had felt so delighted in an adversary. Was it that she was really that good? It had been a while since he had played out in the field; maybe he was projecting his desires onto her?

No. He had been searching for an equal for what

seemed forever. Never found one, and even this beautiful young woman wasn't that, but she was as close as any had ever come. With training and a little work, she could get closer still. She already could at least respect and appreciate him. And he appreciated her for that ability. And with her comment about her lover, she had given him the lever he needed to pry her loose and launch her into the orbit he desired. Plus it meant she wasn't so far gone into the cynicism that eventually claimed most secret operatives that she couldn't be salvaged. She could still care. She was attractive, she was adept, and she held within her the secret to longevity. In that moment, Colburn decided. He wouldn't be taking her back to Earth for Silverman's medics to dissect.

And in fact, he wouldn't be going back to Earth at all.

Silk pedaled his trike along one of the secondary streets, glancing over at his mirror now and then to make sure Red was still behind him. It was hot, sweat darkened the polyprop shirt and pants he wore, but the heat was the least of his worries. He'd had enough of being tailed without knowing why.

He'd checked out the place where the scooter was registered, but it had been a dead end, some kind of holding company that was nothing more than an E-mail box. That could mean a lot of things, most of them not good. So it was time to take things into his own hands and find out what the fuck was going on.

Earth had been a relatively peaceful society compared to E2. He'd heard that some of the other *ausvelts* were even more violent, hardly a pleasant thought for a civilized man.

But was he a civilized man? He had killed two other humans on Earth. True, it had been slay them or die himself, but the idea of it would have once made him sick. Now? Now he could shrug it off as if it had been no more than a bad dream. Supposedly, killing somebody left deep emotional scars, wounds that might take years to heal, if they ever did. But the truth for him was, what he felt when he thought about it was not grief, but outrage. He had been minding his own fucking business, and people he didn't even *know* tried to kill him. That was not *right*. It burned down to his deepest being that somebody would try to take from him the most precious thing he had. They had stolen Mac's life, killed her almost in passing, as if her death had been no more important than swatting a mosquito. They had tried to kill Zia. Those things burned in him, too. A man who would come out of nowhere and threaten you and your loved ones that way deserved whatever he got. It was maybe simplistic, but Silk had no problems with it. Anybody who said you shouldn't defend yourself in such a situation was full of crap. Period.

Maybe Red back there wasn't a threat. Maybe when he'd been shooting at Silk back in that alley he'd only mean to scare him. If so, it had certainly worked. His reaction to the threat had been to buy a gun and learn how to use it. That wasn't right, either. A man minding his own business ought to be left alone. I won't bother you, you don't bother me—another simple philosophy, but he could live comfortably with that one, too. But there Red was, dogging him. It was time Silk found out why.

He had checked his route carefully, over a period of days, the final time on foot and alone. He'd slipped out of his cube via a back door and left his trike—which could be bugged, he knew—to reconnoiter the location he wanted. When he found the right place, he finished his plan. Like his most current philosophical thinking, it was simple.

Ahead, Silk saw the turn coming up. He slowed his trike, downshifted and braked, and swung a tight curve into the alley. This particular artery was bounded by light industrial or storage buildings and shaped much like a letter T. The crossbar of the T stopped on the left end against the back of a plastic recycling plant, on the right end at the normally closed back exits of several small businesses.

Silk reached the intersection and turned right. He picked up his speed a little. The second-to-last door on the left was a corrugated roll-up big enough to admit a truck unloading freight. The door, and a smaller one twenty meters ahead of it, both belonged to a public storage company in which Silk had rented a locker. That bought him the access code to the freight door; the smaller exit could be opened from the inside.

Silk pedaled to the freight door, hopped off his trike, and quickly tapped the code into the ancient keypad lock. The corrugated door moaned once and squeaked as it rolled up. Before the door reached its apex, Silk had the trike inside.

There was a human attendant, but his kiosk was in the front of the building, through a web of halls and not within sight of the back. Here was only a simple stationary robot reader to check IDs. The robot scanned Silk's rental tag and opened the inner door.

Silk rolled the trike into the hall, then left it and hurried down a side corridor.

He reached the smaller exit door and carefully slid it open a hair, just enough so he could see somebody pass it.

This was the tricky part. If Red wanted to know where he had gone, he would have to come into the alley. His timing would be tight. If he followed too closely, he had to figure Silk might see him. If he waited too long, he could lose his quarry. If he went to the left, he would see there was no place for Silk to go. When he arrived at the end of the right turn, there were several possibilities. In order to eliminate them, he'd have to see which doors were accessible. He could stay on the scooter or he could be on foot.

Silk glanced around. The storage building might be doing business, but none of it was taking place by the rear exit, one of the reasons he'd chosen this alley and this time of day.

His hands sweated and he wiped them on his pants, themselves damp enough so it didn't help much. His

breathing came faster than normal, and he forced himself
to inhale and exhale slower. Couldn't do much about his
heart's rapid thumping, or the dryness in his mouth, or
the clammy goosebumps stirring the hair on his neck.
Until what happened to Mac, he hadn't had much
experience with this sensation, but he'd had more than
his share since and he knew it better than he wanted to:
fear. Gut-churning, watery-boweled, sphincter-tightening
fear. One part of his brain kept insisting that this was
incredibly stupid, that he ought to fetch his trike and
leave via the building's front entrance, to pedal home
as fast as he could and hide under the bed until all of
this went away.

Another part of his brain said, *Fuck that. They want
to play games, I'll show them fucking games—*

The shadow passed over the hairline crack so quickly
he almost missed it, but he took a deep breath and eased
the door a little wider open in its track in time to see the
man walk by.

Red.

Silk blew out the breath. Took another one, deeper,
and drew his pistol. He checked to make sure the print-
safety diode was green, then slid the door wide. The
track grated a little and stuck before the door was fully
open, but he had plenty of room to step through and into
the alley.

Red, alerted maybe by the sound the door made, started
to turn. His hands were empty.

"Don't fucking move!" Silk said.

Red froze for a second, and Silk thought he had things
under control.

Then Red dived to the side like a gymnast, rolled, and
came up in a twisting move to face Silk. When he did,
he had a gun in his hand.

Shit—!

SIXTEEN

WHEN ZIA LEFT Colburn's, it was all she could do to keep
her legs from trembling. She had played her hand pretty
well, she thought, but this guy Colburn was mesmerizing.
He had that ultra-competent feel, the presence of a man
who knew what he was about and how to accomplish it.
He reminded her of one of her first Nessie instructors, a
gray-haired man of about fifty who'd spent thirty years
in the field. The instructor had been cruising through a
final tour at the ops academy to cash out his retirement
and he'd taken a few hits along the way and was slowed
some, but he was always at least two jumps ahead of the
sharpest students in the class. If you showed up thirty
minutes early, he was there waiting. If you got there an
hour ahead of schedule, he was there. He was like the
wild dogs outside her mother's town when she'd been a
girl. They'd let you feed them, sometimes even get close
enough to touch them, but a sudden move and they were
fifteen meters away, teeth bared, ready to run—or bite.
That old instructor and this Colburn felt the same way
to her. Dangerous. Unpredictable.

When he'd first walked in, she was sure she'd surprised him; yet, aside from a tiny start, there was no
sign of it. It was as if he expected her.

Which, she supposed, he might have, given that little
clue he dropped at the range. If the name he'd given her
had matched the one he'd left at the desk, that would

probably have been the end of it for Zia. Had he figured the discrepancy would put her on his trail?

Had he done it deliberately?

She thought she'd been very careful not to let him spot her, but maybe he'd known she was there.

What kind of game was he really playing?

She didn't doubt he'd come for the Forever Drug; he'd confirmed that with his offer.

But there was something else . . .

She reached her cart, slid in, bounced a little on the hot seat. The solar-powered vents kept the air in the cart relatively cool, but the seat was in direct sunlight, breaking the first rule of summer surveillance: Always park in the shade.

She engaged the electrics and rolled off, punched the cooler up to high. To help evaporate the sweat that drenched her clothes, the sweat that had begun even while inside Colburn's comfortably cooled cube. She wasn't a sparrow to his snake, she had teeth of her own, but she wasn't sure she could have taken him in a one-on-one. Because he was maybe twenty years older didn't mean he was that much slower. It wouldn't matter if she beat him to the draw and fired first if he managed to get off a shot or two of his own. In this game, there was no second-place winner and a tie was just as bad.

Now what?

She was pretty sure he'd been the unseen watcher following her. It would have to be somebody good, and he was that. While she didn't trust him for a second, there was the problem of Silk to consider.

She knew about the spy business. Knew that sooner or later the terrans were going to figure out a way to get the Treatment; it was only a matter of how long. If she nailed Colburn, she would slow it down a few months, but maybe they'd take a run at Silk next time.

Of course, failing to report Colburn was treason. Then again, cross the line and the punishment was the same for so-so treason as it was for really bad treason: They could only kill you so dead.

When push came to shove, what was more important? A secret that would out sooner or later, or the life of the man she loved?

And would she feel that way if she hadn't already completed her own Treatment?

When Red dived and rolled up, Silk was surprised. He'd thought he was prepared, and he was, in a kind of theoretical way, but not for the reality of it.

Once, he'd rebuilt an antique electric stove in his cube on Earth. Put in new burners, put it all back together, and then grabbed the control knob to test it. He wasn't sure if he'd wired the new switches in right, so there was a possibility of a short circuit. He knew that, had read the manuals and halfway expected it, but when he twisted the control and a shower of hot sparks blew out of the stove all over him and the kitchen, he'd jumped a meter away anyhow.

Red fired the first round from his weapon, and Silk felt just like he had the day his stove had spat fire at him. Prepared for it, but surprised anyway. That whole thought went through his mind in speeded-up time, between the sound of the first shot and the second.

The second needle *twanged!* from Red's weapon.

Silk dropped into a deep crouch, heard the projectile zip past his left ear only a few centimeters away—

Silk fired. It all happened so fast he didn't think about aiming. He pointed his pistol at Red and pulled the trigger.

Red jerked, sprawled backward on the alley's dirty plastcrete floor, his arms flew wide. His gun clattered and skidded into the wall, bounced and came to a stop three meters away.

He stared at the downed man for a time. He was aware of a yellow light flashing on his pistol, and for a moment he couldn't think what it meant. Then reality retracked itself and he blinked at the pulsing diode. Empty. The gun was empty. He'd shot all of his ammunition. He couldn't remember doing that, not at all.

He looked around. If the sounds of the guns attracted any attention, he couldn't see it. Nobody came running, nobody yelled for the police, nobody stuck a curious nose out into the alley. They were alone.

Silk moved to where Red lay. He kept the empty gun pointed at Red, as if it would do any good, and squatted next to the fallen man. He was breathing. The missiles weren't supposed to penetrate very deep—they only needed to get through clothes and under the skin—and he saw the circular butts of the needle cylinders stuck in the man's chest, outlined in meniscal rims of welled blood. At least four of them. He wondered where the other shots went. Probably into the wall as Red fell down.

The bullets weren't supposed to be fatal one at a time, but four doses might be dangerous. Now what? His chance to question Red was gone; the man might be unconscious for a few minutes or a few hours, there was no way to know. He didn't want to hang around here in the alley with what looked like a corpse—what might *become* a corpse. He could drag Red into his locker in the building and wait for him to recover, he supposed, but that didn't have a whole lot of appeal, either. He hadn't figured on this. Red was supposed to put his hands up and do what he was told, to come up with some answers—only it hadn't happened like Silk envisioned. What good was a threat if nobody paid any attention to it?

Shit.

What was he going to do?

As much as he didn't want to call her, Zia was his best bet. She'd know how to handle this.

He stood, put his pistol into its holster. Hell, he hadn't even thought to bring any extra ammunition; he hadn't planned on shooting any of his bullets, much less all of them. He did go and fetch Red's gun, one similar to his own, except it had a mechanical safety and was shaped a little differently.

Then he pulled his com.

•   •   •

"You did what?"

"It's a long story. I'll explain it later. What should I do now?"

Zia shook her head. She was still in her cart, halfway home, when Silk called. He'd shot somebody, somebody he said had been following him for days. Must be one of Colburn's people who got careless and let himself be spotted. He'd have to be pretty sloppy for Silk to pick up on him.

"Go into the building and shut the door. Go to your locker. What's the number?"

He gave it to her.

"I'll meet you there in . . . ten minutes."

She broke the link and shook her head. Poor Silk. He seemed to draw trouble like a magnet drew iron filings. First all the stuff that had happened to him on Earth, of which she was no small part, and now here, light-years away. Some cosmic joker enjoying himself, no doubt.

She got as close as she could on primary roads, then parked the cart and rented a small motorized bike. As she fed coins into the rental comp, she did a quick scan to make sure she wasn't being followed herself.

It took another five minutes to get to the storage company. She parked the bike, went into the front entrance, told the guard she was meeting somebody, and gave him Silk's locker number. He scanned a file and nodded. "Yeah, he came in through the back."

She wound her way through the maze of halls and found Silk's locker. He stood outside it. Or rather, leaned on the wall next to the door.

"Hey," he said. "I'm sorry about this."

"Not your fault."

He glanced down at the floor. "Yeah, well, it is, actually. I knew the guy was behind me. I . . . led him here. Snuck up behind him and tried to ask him some questions. At least that was the plan. He pulled a gun and I had to shoot him."

"Jesus, why didn't you call me when you first noticed him?"

He shook his head.

"Silk?"

"I wanted to take care of it on my own."

"Dammit, you aren't an op! You're a PR man! Just because you've taken a few fighting classes and got yourself a gun doesn't mean you're qualified to be playing cloak-and-dagger games!"

He sighed. "So I noticed. I'm sorry. What do we do now?"

"Let's go see this guy."

He led her to the back of the building and into the alley.

Red was gone.

Silk looked around frantically for a few seconds. She followed him up the alley, but the man's vehicle—a fuel-cell scooter, according to Silk—wasn't around either.

"He must have waked up and taken off," Silk said.

"You hit him four times, you said?"

"At least."

"And you were using standard bioelectric darts?"

"Yeah."

"Then he should have been out for thirty or forty minutes at the very least. He didn't get up on his own unless he's got the metabolism of a fruit fly."

"Then where is he?"

She shook her head. "Maybe he had backup. And if he did, you are lucky they didn't take you out."

Silk looked distressed. Good. She wanted him distressed. He could get himself killed doing stuff like this. Deal or no deal with Colburn, an op who found himself looking down Silk's gun barrel might shoot and worry about the consequences later. She was pissed off at him. At the same time, he hadn't done so bad. He'd trapped a pro and, when the guns came out, outshot the guy. She had been with field ops who wouldn't have done as well. Plus, he'd spotted his tail, and she hadn't seen hers, not until Colburn gave it away on purpose. Silk had done okay.

Not that she would tell him that.

"Okay. You remember anything about the guy?"

He gave her a description of a red-haired man. Didn't sound like anybody she'd seen around. He said he had the scooter's registration number and the owner's name and address but that he'd checked it and it had been a dead end.

"Maybe I can find out something else about them. Who owned the scooter?"

"Somebody called Nakahashi Enterprises."

Zia's heart leaped under a sudden prod of adrenaline. She didn't let it show on her face as she nodded at him, but it surprised her.

Nakahashi Enterprises was one of Nessie's front corporations.

He stored his trike in the locker and went with Zia on her rental scooter to where she'd left her cart.

"I think maybe we ought to stick together for now," she said. "There's something going on."

"No shit. My place or yours?"

"It doesn't matter."

"You mean you would come to my cube and stay if I asked?"

"I'd rather my place, but, yeah, if that's what you want."

That she was willing to come to his cave made it okay to go to hers. "Well. Your place is bigger and the security is better, too. Let's go there."

They did, and Zia drove with one eye on the mirror the whole way. If they were being tailed, Silk couldn't spot it.

He felt drained, tired, worn out. He wanted to go and take a long nap somewhere. The letdown after the excitement, he knew. It had happened to him before, back on Earth. He was exhausted, but there was something else going on, too. During the heat of the moment, when he and Red were exchanging fire there in the alley, Silk had felt something in the fluttery bowels and tight scrotum other than just fear. Excitement. And he realized something else as he sat here next to Zia, watching her drive and looking around for more danger:

On some basic level, he had enjoyed the sensation.

SEVENTEEN

IN ZIA'S CUBE they lit the alarm and locked the doors. She swept the place with a bug sniffer, waved it around like a priest giving a benediction. When she was satisfied they weren't being watched or overheard, she started to lay it out for Silk.

When she did the part about the terran spy, he interrupted, said, "Ratshit! We cancel this guy's ticket. We don't give him squat."

"Let me finish," she said. "It's not that simple."

She told him about her adventure in Beagle and the man she killed there. Told him that the scooter Red had been riding was registered to a New Earth Security front corp. Told him that she had finished her Treatment.

Silk shook his head. "What does it all mean?"

"I don't know. At the very least, Nessie has got a finger in this pie somewhere. They've got somebody watching you, and that doesn't make any sense; it's too expensive to have a permanent tail working anything other than an active case. There are other terrans who've defected or emigrated or whatever and you can tape it, they aren't being shadowed full-time, even some of the the ones we *know* are spies. Why would they be working you? And why wouldn't I know about it?"

"Maybe they think you're not objective."

"Maybe they'd be right. But why would somebody try to stick a knife in me? No, there's something gone bad in this barrel of fruit and we need to know what it is. Before it rots on us."

Silk nodded. "How?"

"We start running things down. The guy who tried to do me in the hotel room in Touchdown. The guy following you. They had to leave trails of some kind. I can reach out to some people who owe me. I can do some direct investigation; I'm on 'vacation,' I've got the time."

"Makes sense. What do you want me to do?"

"You? Go back to work. This is my area of expertise, not yours. You don't have any official standing and this isn't your thing. No offense intended, but you'd only muddy the waters."

"I see."

"Jesus, Silk, don't do that! I'm trying to take care of you!"

"By making sure my nose is wiped and my ID is tagged to my jacket seal."

"These people are dangerous. I don't want anything to happen to you. Besides, you're on conditional-citizen probation. If you get into any kind of trouble, they can deny your application and deport you."

He didn't want to hear that. "I'm the guy Red pulled a gun on. It was me he was following. I have a right to know why."

"And the minute I find out, I'll tell you."

It was the wrong thing to say, and she knew it immediately from his face. She tried to soften it. "Silk, I love you. Do you believe that?"

"Yes. I believe it. What does it have to do with anything?"

"If I were a mechanic and your trike threw a sprocket, you wouldn't mind if I fixed it, would you?"

"If I couldn't fix it myself, no. But I would give it my best shot before I gave up."

"You are determined to make this difficult, aren't you?"

"No. I'm determined to take care of my own life. I don't plan to walk behind you forever. I realize I'm not up to speed with you, but I'm not going to get that way by ducking into a hole every time I hear a loud noise."

"Silk—"

"And if we're going to be something other than a parasite and a host, I can't let you spend your time having to shove me out of harm's way, Zia."

"Christ on jet skates! We're not talking about your manhood here!"

"Yes, yes we are. We're talking about exactly that."

She shook her head. "Listen. The smart thing here would be for you to go about your normal business until I can clear all this up. You know that. I know you know it."

"Maybe. The smart thing would have been for me to call the police the minute I saw you in my front yard in Hana. What I got for listening to you then was a one-way ticket offplanet, plus a charge of planetary treason good for total revision if I ever put myself inside Earth's territorial limits again. But you know what? It was worth it, because I also got you. I came out way ahead."

She shook her head again, but smiled. "You're an idiot, you know that?"

"I do believe you are right. But I'm here and this is my life now. A man's gotta do what a man's—"

She grabbed him and they fell to the floor laughing. "Don't say it! Don't!"

Silk returned her laughter. It was the best he'd felt in months.

Colburn made a call to the mole. His voice and the spy's voice were both scrambled and electronically altered when they spoke. If somebody managed to break into the opchan pipe and somehow decode the computerized scramble, he and the spy would probably sound like entcom monsters; certainly the spy did to Colburn. The voice was deep, fuzzed, echoey, and a listener couldn't say whether the speaker was male, female, young, old, nothing. They spoke Standard, and the speech patterns they used were idiomatically clean.

"Anything new?"

"Nothing," the spy said. "I've kept watch, and he's doing what he usually does."

"Good. Keep me updated."

"Of course."

He cancelled the connection. No names, no places, nothing in their conversation that could be traced, even if somebody was good enough to tap into it. He hung the com onto his belt's cro-patch and went to work out.

In the gym, Colburn went through his routine with machinelike precision. Thirty minutes of heart-lung-circulatory exercise, running this time on the treadmill. He alternated that each session, sometimes in the magnetoflex field with the wrist, ankle *and* waist strapmags. Sometimes he worked the rower or the flybike; sometimes he swam. It depended on what equipment was available.

After the warmup, he did Kajukenbo forms for another thirty minutes, *kata* and attack-and-defense sets. Not as good as working with sparring partners, but enough to keep his flexibility and speed from fading too much.

Finally, he did resistance exercises. This E2 gym was not as advanced as some on Earth, but it was well supplied with piston and magnetic field machines, plus a decent selection of freeweight barbells and dumbbells.

The kiloage Colburn used for most of his exercises was low to moderate; he had long since given up heavy weights. He wasn't interested in building more muscle and strength per se, but in endurance and explosive power. He tended to do several sets of high reps for each body part. His muscles were dense, thick, but not overly large, and he stretched between sets to hold off the pump as long as he could. Weightlifting was for general conditioning; he did enough specific combat work to keep his edge.

He was nearly through his third set of bench presses, using a barbell instead of the air or magnets, to get the collateral work. Unlike the machines, a barbell had to be balanced and held steady, and the smaller muscle groups in the shoulders and arms had to work to keep it that way. He had a hundred kilos on the bar. Once, he could press nearly twice that, but the wear and tear on his tendons and joints were not worth the gain in muscularity. There was a point of diminishing returns. He had seen weightlifters pop connective tissue under massive bars, watched torn pectorals curl up like leaves in a fire. There were lifters who used clutch straps or hook gloves to hoist monster kiloages because their hands weren't strong enough to hold onto the bar, and Colburn did not see the point. If all of the muscles necessary to move a weight weren't sufficient to do so without artificial aids, then maybe you ought to consider the logic of trying. Except for competitive weightlifters, nobody needed to *be* that strong. Certainly he did not.

Nine. Ten. Eleven . . . Twelve!

He finished the set, racked the bar, sat up, and wiped his face with a towel.

There was another man waiting to use the station. Colburn nodded and slid off the cloned-leather bench, mopped up his sweat as a courtesy to the next lifter. The man nodded and smiled his thanks.

This kind of exercise bored many people, and he could understand why. It wasn't intrinsically interesting, picking things up and putting them down. Serious lifters developed a concentration that allowed them to focus on the body part being worked, to put themselves into the exercise in such a way that it took as much mental energy as physical. Colburn had long ago learned the trick of talking to and listening to his body. He was never bored while working out.

Nor did he allow himself to become bored while doing his job, though his sense of ennui was sometimes stultifying. It was mostly the lack of challenge, save that he provided for himself, that did it. The failures of the opposition to provide players of equal caliber. He sometimes felt like a grandmaster playing chess with the mentally retarded—he could make *his* game interesting but not theirs. And sometimes he had to work harder than seemed worth the effort. Not that there hadn't been times when he was at risk, especially earlier in his career. But the last few years had been, well, uninspiring. He found himself pitted against competent agents now and then, but usually they were so rule-bound or politically conscious they offered no real threat. The game wasn't nearly as much fun when you knew you would win.

He moved to the curl station. Put fifty kilos on the cambered bar, grabbed the weight, and stood. Took a deep breath and began his first set. Stopped thinking and concentrated on movement.

After the tenth rep, he put the bar down and took several deep breaths. Knowing you would win was one of the perils of being the best at what you did.

He was pretty sure he could outthink and outmove Zia Rélanj, but he found to his delight he wasn't positive. Seeing her in his cube had been a surprise, and he hadn't been surprised on a caper in a long time. She was physically attractive enough, but it was her ability as an op, her mind, that really called to him. A man needed an equal, or one who was nearly so, to talk to. Of the players he'd seen, Zia was right up there. There had been a couple of others along the way who might have made the cut: Twenty years ago, Orinda, the New Australian counterespionage agent; she had been sharp. But she'd been betrayed by a fellow agent and been killed. The traitor was later pushed into a metal recycler by a person or persons unknown. And there'd been Anna Maria, on Earth, who had been a SWAT chief for SuePack's elite Crowd Control Unit; she could have kept up with him. A big, strong, smart woman, except she had a thing for living on the edge and taking risks that caught up with her in the Singapore Riots. She survived, but as a vegetable until the mysterious grid failure that cut not only the main power but somehow also bollixed the backup generators at the hospital in which she lay drooling.

He had been fond of them both.

But he'd been at the top of the game for a long time, and here was a bright and adept young woman who not only might be able to run with him, but who held within her a secret valuable enough to buy anything either of them would ever want. Earth wasn't the only market for such a product—any of the *ausvelts* would love to get their hands on it. So what if in a hundred or two hundred years Zia and he went their separate ways? With that kind of time in one's personal bank, one could spend it seriously or frivolously, a choice he'd never felt leave to do before.

He would have her, and he would have her priceless secret. She had already given him the lever. It now only remained for him to insert the tip of the bar and carefully pry her loose and into his grasp.

Into his loving grasp.

EIGHTEEN _____

ZIA TOOK THE maglev rather than a shuttle. First, because she wanted a little time to think. Second, she wanted to see if anybody was riding her tail. She booked passage to Drain, a small town about a hundred kilometers short of Touchdown. She intended to leave the train there, rent a cart or maybe a small flitter, and take a slow ride across the Black Plains. This was a forty-klick stretch of old lava, a remnant of a long-dormant volcano. Except for a few scraggly plants that managed a stunted growth in the acidic rock, the plain looked much like the surface of a dead and airless moon. Anybody who followed her from the maglev or who might be hanging around the station waiting for her would have a hell of a time keeping visual or radar contact without her spotting them. They would have to back off or get burned, and by taking that route, she would put anybody with half a brain on notice: I know you're there, suckers—try to stay with me and I'll nail you.

The procedure for investigating somebody's background was an old one and easy enough, and even though she hadn't put in many hours doing that kind of work in a while, she didn't think it would be hard. Once she got to Touchdown without unwanted company. Of course, there could be somebody there waiting for her, somebody who anticipated what she was doing, but she'd deal with that if and when she ran into it.

She moved all the way back to an empty row of three seats in the rear of the last car. So far, she was alone. Good. She hurried to the rear exit and put a stikstop on the door's lock. The stop was a cheap, clever little device designed for travelers worried about being attacked in their rooms by nightstalkers. It was a small, fat, semi-circular chunk of dark gray rubbery material. To work it, you pressed it into place against the lock, then squeezed a pair of buttons simultaneously, one on either side. This released a penetrant, a liquid so volatile it would flow easily through a keyhole, a card slot or even the cracks in a standard keypad. Most locks, even electronic ones, had some kind of mechanical component—a bolt, pins, tumblers, magnets—and the penetrant in the stikstop, once it set, would essentially jam the mechanism so it wouldn't operate. It had something to do with the coef-ficient of friction. Once set, the door would not respond to normal keying methods. In the event of a fire or other emergency, you had only to double-squeeze the buttons to release a second chemical that neutralized and washed away the locking penetrant within a couple of seconds. Stikstops sold well to people who traveled a lot and who had reason—or thought they had reason—to fear unwanted company. They were only good for one time each, but they sold in convenient little six-packs and were inexpensive insurance.

Of course, for every safety device, there was a counter. If somebody knew your door was stikstopped, they could attach a similar device of their own to the other side of the lock and inject the neutralizer. It hadn't taken the makers of the things long to figure that out, and so as a bonus, each unit had built into it a backup. If somebody else's neutralizer released your stikstop, it would fall to the floor. When it hit, an impact switch triggered a loud buzzer. At the very least, you would have some warn-ing that your door had been unlocked and was about to open.

With the back door to the train protected, Zia felt a little better. Anybody who might be following her would have to come at her from the front, and she would be on guard for that. She loosened her pistol in its holster and sat angled so she could reach it without shifting. The trip to Drain would take three hours, and there'd be a couple of other stops along the way. This wasn't an express but a local train, and she'd picked it because it was apt to be empty of anybody but small-towners.

The bar car was three cars ahead of this one. Those who wanted to smoke or drink or eat while the train flew along over the magnetic rail bed usually clustered closer to the bar car. Plus this was a midweek, midmorning run, so it ought not to be crowded.

It wasn't crowded. As the maglev thrummed away from the station, Zia found that she was almost alone in the car. Save for a young and apparently horny couple near the front who were all over each other, the seats stood empty. They could be agents, of course, the couple, and she would keep them plotted, but even if they were watching her, they'd established a cover that wouldn't let them wander back to where she was—the fresher was in the front of the car and up a level.

Twenty minutes out of the station, the rumble of the repellors and the rocking motion of the maglev lulled her into a doze. She'd always been able to sleep on trains, ever since she was a kid. The first time she'd ridden alone, she'd been nine, sent to spend a summer with her grandmother in Neese. The old woman—she must have been all of fifty that summer—was a widow who lived with two small dogs, a cat, and three large tropical birds she had trained to recite poetry, plus her father. Her place was a sprawling U-shaped ranch-style house on the banks of a sluggish, dirty brown river on the edge of the Eeberville Swamp. Her grandmother, who made a small living teaching piano and complicated card games to other women her age, had installed Zia's great-grandfather in a guest room. The old man was eighty but still in good shape, originally from Earth, one of the First Wave to settle E2. He drank whiskey, snorted kikdust and smoked illegal tobacco cigarettes and looked like a prune left out in the sun too long. He was lonely, and he and Zia took to each other immediately. She spent much of those hot summer days on the river bank, shooting at frogs and snakes with an antique small-caliber air pistol her great-grandfather gave her. The old man also taught her how to fish, using nothing more than a thin bamboo pole strung with a weighted, hooked line run through a cork from one of his liquor bottles. He dug up greeworms for bait, showed her how to lace them onto the barbed hook. They caught bottom-feeding whiskerfish, carp, sunfish, and even alligator gar now and then. Mostly they threw them back; once in a while her grandfather would produce a blackened iron skillet from somewhere, fill it with oil, then cook some of the fish, coating and frying it to a crisp brown. She'd never tasted any fish so good, not before, not since.

"Secret's in the coating," he'd said. "Cornmeal and crushed potato chips. 'Course you gotta get the oil temperature just right. You know it's ready when you can drop a bit of meal in and it bubbles just like this."

Fascinated, Zia watched the oil hiss and foam as her great-grandfather sprinkled a bit of the yellow powder into the pan. When he cooked, her grandmother stayed out of the kitchen, so it was just the two of them. "And the seasoning, 'course, you need some coarse ground pepper . . ."

It had been a wonderful summer. She hadn't thought about that time in years. She and her great-grandfather in the shade of a spin oak tree fishing, her grandmother in her house teaching one or another of the neighbors how to play the piano, halting chords of classical music chasing flies and bloodgnats in the sunny afternoons. When it rained, as it did frequently, the old man would sit with Zia in the den or kitchen and tell her stories about his youth. Sixty years earlier he'd worked in the new petroleum industry in Southland, first as a roughneck in the oil fields, later as a drilling foreman. The times had been exciting, colorful, dangerous. Twice he'd gone to jail for fighting, once he'd killed a bandit trying to

steal the company's credit computer, shot him dead in
the doorway with the old smoothbore he'd kept in the
portable field office . . .

She'd already been working for Nessie when the old
man finally died. Drunk, he fell out of his small boat
and drowned. He was ninety-three—

Zia came out of the dreamy memory with a sudden
start. Something was buzzing . . .

The stikstop alarm—

She reached for her pistol as the car's back door slid
open.

Silk had no intention of sitting idle and scratching his
butt while Zia went out to slay dragons to keep him safe
from harm. He'd never been a man of action—it hadn't
been necessary in his life on Earth—but it was necessary
now. Besides, he found he could understand why Zia did
it. There was a certain pleasure to it, being able to take a
risk and survive, to triumph and keep going.

He sat in his office and thought about the best way
to go about it. True, he didn't know enough to poke into
smoky pubs and get information out of greasy informants
like the spies in the entcoms did. He didn't have any
kind of underground network of colorful characters who
would tell him what he wanted to know. He grinned. But
there was more than one way to cook an egg. He was a
spider, he knew how to spin a nothing story into a cotton-
candy fluff, or to carve a steel plate down to a needle, and
those skills could serve him here. One of the first rules of
a spindoc was that if you didn't know it, look it up—it
was only if you couldn't find it that you faked it.

The public record system on New Earth was not nearly
so extensive as that of the motherworld, but it was there,
and since you couldn't bend information if you couldn't
locate it, a good spindoc knew how to do research. The
problem usually wasn't in coming up with enough information to bolster your story, but in winnowing it. The
amount of minutia about virtually any subject was mind-
boggling, you could get lost in it, and a spider learned

fast how to walk the web or he'd fall out of a job.

He had hunted and found men for stories with less to go on than he had on the guy who'd been following him. It might take a while but he could do it.

Silk leaned forward in his chair and spoke to his biopath. "I want an identity search," he said. "Scan all license bureaus, local and planetary, military records, police and planetary agents and include offworld travel visas for the two-year period immediate prior to this date. Parameters: Subject is male, Caucasian, between the ages of thirty T.S. and forty T.S. Height, between 177 and 185 centimeters; weight, between 75 and 85 kilograms, his hair is red, eyes are blue, complexion fair. Flag any possible matches with connections to Nakahashi Enterprises."

The biopath said, "Searching."

Silk leaned back. On Earth, an order like this might well be impossible to execute. Even the sharpest system would have to slog through so many records that the search could take weeks, and the number of possible matches might number in the hundreds of thousands, maybe even millions. With six and a half billion people onplanet, it made for a lot of sifting. But here on E2, there were fewer people on the entire world than in any medium-sized town on Earth. How many of them could there be like Red, even given the rather wide descriptive latitude he'd used for parameters? If he was in the system officially anywhere, Silk's biopath should be able to find him, unless he was hiding. His hair color could be faked and his eyes altered with droptacs. Then again, if he drew a blank, well, that might tell him something, too.

"Search completed," the biopath said.

Silk blinked at the holoproj, which was blank. That was quick.

"How many possibilities?"

"Four."

Four? Was that all? Jesus. "Put their holographs on-screen."

The air lit with a swirl of colors as the pix appeared in the air.

One, two, three—

There he was.

"Discard images one, two and four," he said. "Give me the third image and stats only."

The image shifted, increased in size a little. Under it, several graphs of data appeared.

Well, well. That had been a real tough problem, hadn't it?

Silk looked at the man's face. Yes, it was the guy he'd shot all right, no doubt about it, unless he had a twin. He glanced down at the name under the holograph. M. Ampul Reilly Bec, whose listed occupation on his vehicle operator's license was that of Nonaffiliated Inquiry Agent.

Inquiry Agent? Some kind of private investigator? One with ties to New Earth Security, at least to the extent he had been riding one of their scooters?

Now that was interesting. Who would pay money to have somebody follow Silk? And why?

Colburn watched Zia board the maglev train. He had determined her destination easily enough and he made no attempt to follow her as the train floated out of the station. She'd bought a one-way ticket to a small town a few hours away and whatever was there, he didn't see it as any kind of threat to his plans. Maybe she was going to visit a friend, maybe she had some kind of work to do there, it didn't matter. She would be back here soon enough, of that he was fairly certain. Her paramour, M. Silk, was parked in his office even as the train departed and wherever the terran was, Zia would eventually wind up.

She did seem to care greatly for him, maybe even love him, and while that was Colburn's lever, too, it was a bit worrisome. People in love did strange things, unpredictable things, and that could be dangerous were you not prepared for it.

He turned away from the platform and walked across the hardcast faux-marble floors of the station. When this place had been built, it had apparently been in vogue to copy ancient train stations from the days of coal or diesel engines and rickety metal and wood rails. Except for the cleanliness of it and a few anachronisms here and there, this station could have been right at home in the late nineteenth or perhaps early twentieth century on Earth. A big analog clock was mounted over the exit to the platform; baggage claim and ticketing areas were bordered by large wooden counters; the waiting benches were padded and sculpted of hardfoam and therefore comfortable enough, but also colored and shaped to resemble dark wood. The floor was of alternating black and white squares, like a giant chessboard. Given that the place was nearly empty of passengers now, Colburn's boots echoed as he walked. So quaint. A wonder they didn't put fake smokestacks and driving wheels on the trains themselves.

He emerged from the station and went to his cart. For some reason, the train station brought up an old memory, from the time when he was fifteen.

It was almost 1800 hours, and the November night was already dark and cold. The watcher in the shadow of the burned-out Intel factory had marked his target when the sun was still high then spent the next few hours hiding out until the last of the Day Patrol finished its rounds. He sat with his back to a fairly solid wall, a stolen fire blanket draped over himself, the shiny inside keeping most of his heat from escaping. There were a few rats or other small animals prowling around the old building but no other humans in this particular section. Probably that was because the roof was gone and the sky was building toward a rain that would start in the next hour or two.

He went by the ruenom Spidercat and he was a thief. Not a great thief, but he hadn't gotten caught and he got by. He could afford a stall most nights, and he knew the streets of the Beaverton-Aloha-Hillsboro Sprawl as well as anybody. The main corridor was the old Sunset Highway and it ran all the way from Portland to the coast. The Bah Sprawl had once been a string of separate cities but had long since joined into one big and rapidly decaying bedroom community. Most people with money had left for Seaside or Astoria or moved to the Valley, and those who were left were either too poor to have much worth stealing or rich enough to protect what they had. The Spidercat was fifteen and smart enough to stay away from the wired estates, where an invisible light trigger could crank an alarm that would sic the cools on you before you could run a hundred meters. Or a genedog who might run you down and chew your throat out even if you darted him.

But there was a thin line of middle-classers, those who had a few items worth snagging but not enough stads to afford the best protection. They were the prey of the Spidercat. A decent computer, an okay voxbox, even some hard curry or a credit tab you could fence if you hurried, those were enough to buy a stall, an hour now and then with one of the cleaner stall whores, food and chem. It was an exciting life and better than trying to work at a straight job. Not that the Spidercat could get one of those, what with Chillserve ready to ship any runaway it caught home on the first lockbus out of town.

The first few drops of light rain pattered down. He'd checked the climesat 'cast earlier and it was supposed to be a mild rain, not much of a front moving through, probably over by morning. It was enough to absorb enough city glow to make it a little darker than usual, though, and that was what was important.

The Spidercat shucked the fire .blanket and moved out.

He kept to the darkest shadows as much as he could, and hurried the two blocks to the transformer box that carried the power for the street where his target was. There was a meshed-lamp over the box and he didn't have anything but his knife, so he couldn't put out the light by smashing through the protective covering. But if he hurried, he could be done before anybody spotted him. He'd paid the Keyman fifty for a one-time slider that would let him open the box. He had a plastic vial of chort, a liquid metal that should do the trick. The lamp fed off the transformer like the rest of the street did.

The Spidercat looked around, saw that the street was shut tight. He ran the slider through the reader slot. There came a metallic *click!* and the box's door reeled to the side. The unit looked solid, but there was a prepunched slug still in place on the top of the hard plastic. He used the butt of his knife to pound the metal circle enough to make a gap. Quickly, he poured the silvery chort into the hole. He turned and ran.

Five seconds later the transformer shorted out in a nice shower of blue flame and yellow sparks. It made a noise like a small bomb going off inside a metal barrel, *whump!* The security lamp blinked out. And all the lights on the street and in the houses also went out.

He could count on ten minutes before a repair truck from PGE arrived, twenty if he was lucky. There were a few houses that had backup generators, but his target didn't. The cools would be notified that it was a power-down, so they wouldn't be busting their asses to scramble scooters to check out the fifteen or twenty cheapshit burglar alarms that kicked on when the power was cut. Nor would they be checking his target out, because while it had an alarm, the system was a KMA midrange, which had a battery backup so it would not ring unless it was breached.

The Spidercat ran. A couple of houses came on-line with exterior lights but he avoided the rainy cones the lamps threw.

He made it to his target and circled around to the back. Hopped the wooden fence—no dog—and moved to the sliding plexplast door. It was locked, she wasn't that stupid, but the lock was a joke and it took all of five seconds to stick the knife into the gap and break the latch. He slid the door open, set his wristchrono's timer, plugged the timer's receiver into his right ear and darted inside.

He had thirty seconds before the internal alarm went off. The system would com the KMA computer and report an intrusion. The monitor would wait one minute to give the homeowner a chance to reset the system, in case it had been accidentally triggered. If it was reset with the proper code, the monitor would log the event and make a courtesy call in another few minutes. If nobody recoded the alarm, then the computer would call immediately. Anybody who answered had to have the bypass code word or the computer would call the police. If nobody answered, then the system would call the police. Either of those could take another thirty seconds to a minute. Once the cools were alerted, they would send somebody to check, and that could take anywhere from five minutes to half an hour, depending on how busy they were. So the Spidercat could figure on a minimum of seven minutes before a patrol came by and rattled doors to see what the trouble was. The timer on his wrist was set to beep at three minutes. That would give him plenty of time to grab what he could and get away, even at the minimum. By the time the cools showed up, he'd be back at the Intel ruin, where he'd stash the loot. He'd catch the bus back into Beaverton with clean hands, carrying nothing but his knife, which was good ceramic and would easily pass the bus scanners. He'd return for the stuff tomorrow night, pack it into a bag, and haul it to Fat Louie to fence. A piece of cake.

The woman who lived here was at work, she was a nurse on the swing shift at St. Vincent's. The Spidercat wasn't greedy, it wasn't like he was gonna back a truck up and rip her clean, he was just going to take a couple things. She had a good job, she could replace stuff.

He hadn't been inside the house but he knew where he was going to look. First the bedroom, a fast run through her dressers or chests, then the medicine cabinet in the fresher—a nurse might have some quality chem—finally the living room. A minute each, the timer would chime once every sixty seconds, and he'd know it was time to move on.

The audible alarm kicked on. The hee-haw horn blared, filling the house with noise. He'd learned to ignore it.

He grinned and hurried to the bedroom. No sweat—

Somebody jumped out of the fresher and grabbed him.

The Spidercat screamed and twisted away. He felt the hands locked around his chest loosen and he kicked and drove his knee up like a piston, hitting flesh and bone. A man's voice cursed.

The Spidercat shoved with both hands, broke the grip, heard the man slam into the hall wall.

Panicked, the Spidercat pulled his knife. It was a short, fat, one-piece drop-point ceramic, the black blade half as wide as his hand, as long as his middle finger. He turned to run but the dark figure lurched in front of him.

Got between him and escape.

Blocked his way.

He lost all sense of time, and that was probably as much a part of it as anything. The alarm blared. He dropped the earplug somehow in the struggle, and he wouldn't be able to hear the timer's beep without the plug. How long had he been in here? It seemed like hours. The cools would be here any second, they'd get him. They'd stick him in lock and the cell monsters would have him bent over and plugged in two minutes, he knew what happened to juvies in lock, he'd heard the stories.

"Move!" he yelled.

But the attacker loomed over him. "I'm gonna kill you, you little prickhead!"

The Spidercat lost it. He punched the attacker, once, twice, three times, drove the ceramic blade into him, felt the tip slice flesh, grate on bone—

"Fuck!" the man screamed. "Fuck!"

But he fell back. Hit the wall and left enough of a gap for the Spidercat to run past, bloody knife clutched in his fist. He sprinted for the door, ran into the yard, somehow cleared the fence without realizing it, ran down the dark street in a daze, seeing nothing but a tunnel of safety directly in front of himself.

He was at the end of the block when he heard his chrono beep softly. Twice.

It had only been two minutes since he'd slipped the sliding door's lock and gone into the house.

He wiped the blood from his knife, sheathed it under his jacket. Caught a bus heading out toward Hillsboro, rode to the end of the Bah Sprawl before catching a second bus toward Aloha. He got off at the transit mall and caught a third bus to Beaverton. Jesus!

Jesus.

In the faxsheet the next morning there was no mention of a killing in the neighborhood. But the evening edition carried a short piece, couple centimeters, about an elderly man killed by a housebreaker in the central Bah Sprawl. From the name, the Spidercat figured the man must have been the nurse's father, maybe an uncle.

He hadn't known anybody lived with her. Bad luck. For him and for the old man.

And when a week, then a month passed and nobody came for him, he realized he'd gotten away with it. He never spoke to anyone about the killing, not as the Spidercat, nor later when he'd put the ruenom and those days far behind him. Never told anybody he'd done it.

Never told anybody that when it was done and he was away, he had *enjoyed* it . . .

Colburn shook his head, as if that would clear the old recording his mind had brought up. It was not something he allowed himself to feel very often, that rush of pleasure he got when he faced another and danced to the death. It was a dangerous energy, one he didn't want to become ensnared in, even if it was one he couldn't ignore. He hadn't killed anybody in several years and he thought he was past having to do so, but it was always *there,* just like some addictive drug, waiting. Just like a substance addict who knew he might not take that next drink or toke or pop, but that the Siren would always call to him even if he pretended he couldn't hear her, Colburn knew:

Once a killer, always a killer.

NINETEEN _____

THE STIKSTOP ALARM gave Zia a second or so of warning, and she didn't hesitate to draw—anybody who knew enough to pop the jam on the train car's rear door was dangerous on the face of it.

The shooter was a woman and she screwed up, she should have fired through the opening as soon as she had a gap; instead she waited for the door to open enough for her to jump inside. She was tall, heavyset, well built. She wore track worker's grays, loose-fitting coveralls, but that didn't fool Zia for a heartbeat. Aside from the trick with the door, the gun in the woman's hand was pretty much a giveaway—

Zia had the advantage. By the time the door was wide enough for the shooter to slip through, Zia had her pistol lined up. She was fully focused on the threat. The shooter's gun was pointed up and she tried to bring it down, but she was too slow.

Zia fired twice, centered on the woman's chest.

The force of the bullets wouldn't have been enough to do it, but the sudden panicked contraction of the shooter's legs was—she flew backward through the still-open door as if launched by rockets and—

—So did Zia.

—*Oh, shit she got me, fuck I'm falling—! The spidersilk chest plate stopped the slugs but she tried to get away from them and, oh, fuck, she was falling off the train, going*

152

*right over the safety rail and it was happening so fast
and where was Bally? Oh, Mama, help me, I'm going
to die—! And she hit the ground and bounced and hit
again and it all went black—*

Zia came back to herself and found she was standing in
the open doorway staring out at the track bed behind her,
at the body of the woman she'd shot rapidly dwindling
in the distance. The train was moving at maybe three
hundred kilometers an hour and even though they were
on a straight stretch, the body shrank and disappeared in
a few seconds.

The stikstop buzzer was still going and Zia kicked it
out, watched it hit the track and tumble off to the side.
Five seconds passed.

"Wh-what happened?"

She turned, keeping the pistol hidden behind her hip.
The young couple stood three meters away.

"We thought we heard shots," the man said.

The couple looked at each other. Zia realized they
hadn't seen anything. Smoothly, she holstered her pistol
and covered it with her jacket, turning the move into a
hand wipe on her pants. They couldn't see her do it.
"Shots? I don't think so. The door, ah, malfunctioned.
Blasted open on its own. I think the noise was a circuit
or a hydraulic piston or something blowing out."

"That's freaky," the woman said.

"I think I can close it." She turned around and hid the
control button with her body, tapped it. The door slid
shut. The sound of the rushing wind cut off.

"Should we, you know, tell somebody?"

Zia said, "Nah, the onboard computer will have logged
it. They'll probably send somebody back to look at it at
the next stop. Just stay away from it, we'll be okay."
She strived to project a calm she did not feel.

The couple turned and went back to their seats. Zia
watched them, then took a seat across the aisle from
where she'd been earlier. Maybe they bought it, maybe
not, but as long as they didn't do anything, it didn't
matter.

Must be tired, she thought. Nothing like that had ever happened to her before, Christ, it was almost as if she had been inside the shooter's head there at the end. Like the young woman said, it was freaky.

And it was one more brick she didn't need to add to the overload she was already carrying. Twice recently somebody had tried to cancel her vital signs and it was beginning to piss her off.

She was positive the shooter had a partner. During that . . . dislocation, she'd become aware of it. It must have been that the shooter had yelled, called for help, only somehow Zia logged the cry as some kind of mental thing. That must be what it was. One thing for sure, she'd better be on the watch for the shooter's backup in case he made a run at her. Bally.

Silk had an address on Red, and he didn't waste any time getting there to check it out. Red, aka Ampul Reilly Bec, had some answers and he was going to give them up, damn straight, end of sentence, put a period right *there*. Being chased and threatened by people to whom he'd never done anything was not right, and Silk was rapidly getting to the place where the next person who crossed him was going to be real sorry they did.

It was a crappy neighborhood, one that had obviously been thrown together and pushed up cheaply, with no intention of it lasting very long. The inquiry agent had a small office in a building made of cast plastic slabs that had been flocked with what now looked like old, greasy snow. The coating had worn off in big patches under the sun and rain and the building was piebald, like a street dog with mange. The entrance had a robotic control but it was broken and partially stripped and the cracked glass door was propped open by a wedge of wood jammed under it.

Apparently Red's business wasn't all that hot.

Silk walked into the building. No reception area, no watchcams, no security of any kind he could see. No people. He found a directory and noted that Bec Inquiries was located on the third of five levels. He went to the lift, a tired and wheezy unit that smelled strongly of urine, and ordered the lift to the third level. The car jerked and moved upward, accompanied by a metal-on-metal grinding like a huge bearing going bad. Maybe he would use the stairs coming down.

The hallway on the third level was dim, half the glowstrips in the ceiling burned out, the windows at the ends of the hall caked with grime. Real nice place.

Silk moved to the door of Bec's office. He pushed the control button but the slider motor didn't work. He stuck his fingertips in the slot and pushed it aside manually. When it was halfway open, he drew his pistol. Better safe than sorry. If Bec could afford a human secretary or a biotech, he probably wouldn't be in this dump, so Silk didn't worry too much about scaring anybody. Let Red explain it. Probably a lot of his clients came armed in this neighborhood.

There was a reception table but it was empty. Beyond that, an inner door led to what Silk figured was Bec's office. He moved to it. Took a couple of deep breaths and a better grip on his gun, then shoved the thin plastic panel roughly to the side.

Ampul Reilly "Red" Bec was there, sure enough. And he was the guy who'd been tailing Silk. He sprawled in a chair behind a cheap plastic desk.

And to judge from the amount of blood on him and the gaping wound across his throat, he was as dead as he could get.

Shit.

Silk knew he should leave. Wipe his prints from the doors and get out of the building before anybody saw him. All he needed was to be detained for killing some seedy private snoop; that would do wonders for his probationary status on this world, wouldn't it?

The little voice of self-preservation bleated in his head: *Out, get the hell out and go home, lock your door and take a long nap!*

Fuck that. Red—Bec—was dead. He didn't do it, and if they caught him and it came right down to it, they could strain his brain and find that out.

He went back to the outer door, dragged it closed—using the barrel of his gun so as not to leave any more prints or cells—and tapped the lock into place. That ought to slow anybody who might want to sneak in behind him, at least long enough to warn him they were coming.

Back in Bec's office, he looked around. There wasn't much to see. The computer on the desk was old, not even a holoproj but a battered flatscreen. The screen's hinges were broke and the screen was propped up by what looked like half a brick. The desk had three drawers on one side. He was careful to avoid touching the body as he opened the top drawer. Bec's gun and holster were in the top drawer, along with a variety of what Silk figured were burglar tools: odd-shaped plastic and metal shims, thin stretch gloves, a couple of strange-looking electronic keycards. The same drawer had a small reader with a videocam built into it, a belt com unit, and a personal carrycomp.

Well, the gloves would be useful. Silk put them on and felt better about rummaging through the dead man's effects.

The second drawer had a box full of pornoproj recordings, mostly straight heterosexual titles, a couple of what looked to be mild S&M bondage. There was a plastic flask of something that smelled like gin, and a roll of plastic cuff tape.

The third drawer held a lockbox, unlatched. Inside were stacks of platinum hundred-stad coins, at least fifty of the shiny coins.

Silk stared at the gleaming disks. Whatever the reason Bec had been killed, robbery wasn't the motive. With five thousand in hard curry sitting there for anybody to lift, either somebody was in such a big hurry they didn't look, or they did and didn't care. Interesting.

The computer's voxax might work but Silk didn't want to leave a record of his voice, so he dragged the keyboard to one side and used it to start the unit. The screen lit and the system software opened, but all of Bec's files were encrypted and he couldn't get into them. Same for the little carrycomp.

There was a printer in the corner on a table but the hard copy bin was empty.

He looked around. Well. So much for his own investigative abilities. Bec was dead, and if there was a clue to who had done it or why, he couldn't find it. Maybe it was best he leave now.

He kept the gloves on and took the portable comp—Zia might be able to figure out a way to break into the encrypted files. After he thought about it for a second, he took the com, too. He left the platinum coins, even though he was tempted to pocket them. Not worth the risk, the coins; they could be tagged somehow, and maybe there was a way to identify particular lots. Too bad, especially since he was pretty certain Bec had earned that money by tailing him and Silk could have used it himself.

He found a roll of paper towelettes under the reception table and used one to wipe the doors where he'd touched them. He shoved the towelette into his jacket pocket with the little hand comp, the gloves, and the com and hurried toward the stairs. He didn't see anybody as he exited the building, and he hoped nobody had seen him.

Whatever the hell was going on, it wasn't getting any clearer.

Feeling spent, Colburn checked into a room at one of the bigger hotels. He contacted the bell captain and arranged for "female company." He specified somebody athletic and young. Unlike in a long-term arrangement, this would be a partner he didn't need to talk to afterward. They would finish their transaction and they would go their separate ways. All he wanted was a warm and willing receptacle, someone to drain his tension competently.

It was twenty minutes before the woman arrived. She was short, muscular, and attractive, probably in her mid-twenties though she looked younger, long dark hair, light milk chocolate skin.

"An hour," he said. "Round the system."

"Two hundred," she said. "That's for plain, no toys, no pain."

"Plain is fine." He handed her his credit tab, watched her punch the number into her reader. She turned it around so he could see she wasn't cheating him. He nodded as she handed the card back. She hung her bag over a chair back, kicked off her shoes, and started to undress as she walked toward the bedroom. She moved well enough, and her body was clean and fit. She laid on the bed, face down, naked, spread her legs. "Pick a target," she said. "I'm Maya, by the way."

"Clete," he said, staying in character. He stripped, not in any hurry, and was ready by the time he got to the bed.

"How about we start here?" he said, touching her mouth with his forefinger.

"You're in charge, Clete." She scooted around as he stretched out onto his back.

He smiled as her lips touched him. Yes. He was in charge.

TWENTY

THE MAGLEV REACHED the station in Drain without any further incidents. After the shooting, the couple in the front of Zia's car went back to their previous activities. The thin blanket under which they groped each other was enough to hide their bodies but not the little groans and quickening moans as they climbed toward their releases. Zia, alert for the shooter's backup, couldn't help but hear them.

She smiled and looked elsewhere. Ah, to be young and in love, so full of dammed-up passion you couldn't wait to let it flow. That's how it had been with her and Silk, not so long ago. Yes, they still fell on each other like starving wolves on fresh meat, but there had been a bubble of hesitancy injected into their vessels of mindless desire. After the near-death experiences they'd had on Earth, this was the part where they were supposed to live happily ever after—only it hadn't quite worked out that way.

Zia listened to the young woman under the blanket give herself to the hands of her lover as she reached orgasm and cried out softly.

Did that myth at the heart of all the fairy tales her mother had told her, that part about happily ever after, ever really work out that way? How many children around the galaxy had been given that pretty picture, had swallowed it entire, only to grow up and find that reality was not so simple, not so beautiful, not so easy? The story didn't end when the brave princess killed the wicked queen and rescued the prince. That, she was learning, was the easy part. The hard part came when the guns were cleaned and reholstered, the bodies of the villains cremated, and the day-to-day business of life reared its ugly cobra's head and grinned down at you. When your prince had doubts you couldn't answer for him, when *you* had doubts he could only shrug at, that, *that* was the hard part. That was the part the stories hadn't addressed.

The maglev slowed as it approached the little town. Zia had commed ahead and had a rental cart waiting, not that she intended to use it. Anybody who might be set up to work her would have a long wait before she picked up that particular vehicle.

The couple composed themselves as the train pulled into the station. The late afternoon looked hot past the cooled air rising from the vents beneath the polarized window. Before the maglev stopped completely, Zia walked to the back exit and let herself out. She jumped to the track and covered the ground with long strides, looping around the station toward the parking area in the front. Anybody waiting for her inside the terminal would make fit company for somebody watching the pre-rented cart. If they were that dull, they deserved each other. She grinned again, feeling confident and adept. Maybe she'd stumbled a little since Earth, but she was resharpening herself pretty quick. She didn't know what was going on, exactly, but that was mere ignorance. What you didn't know, you could learn. Being stupid was a lot harder to get past. She would find out what she needed to know, and when she did, she would take care of business.

One thing for sure: As long as she was careful, she had plenty of time.

She started to grin again, but stopped. As she trekked across the parking area, she had a sudden realization, something she hadn't even considered until just that moment: If the shooter on the train had gotten her, instead of the other way around, she would have lost a whole hell of a lot more. Before, if she got tagged and the game was over, she might give up seventy or eighty more years, given the current life expectancy on E2. Now? Now she would forfeit hundreds, maybe even thousands of years. All that potential, gone in a heartbeat.

It was a sobering thought. When you didn't have any more to lose than the next guy, it was no big deal. Everybody dies. You take a number and wait your turn. You could get flattened by a hoverbus, go down in a ferry accident, splash across the landscape in a suborbital accident and die a lot younger than the average, too. But when you might give up a dozen or even a score of lifetimes, suddenly the game was not quite the same. A gambler who wouldn't hesitate to bet a month's pay on the flip of a card might not be so willing to risk the whole ranch. When the stakes got large, a smart player got careful. It might not make any difference to the thief trying to take her life, but Zia realized for her, it now *would* be a big deal. If you had five hundred years to play with, there were a lot of things you could do. But if you got killed before you were thirty, well, that would be a real loss, wouldn't it?

Silk happened to notice he was half a block away from the gun shop where he'd bought his pistol; it was just ahead on the left. At that moment, he was suddenly taken with the urge to see a familiar face, one that wasn't threatening. Maybe he would just pull his trike into that conveniently empty slot right over there and pop in to say hello to Hildy. He didn't have to do anything else, it wasn't a life commitment or anything; besides, he needed some more practice ammunition anyway, didn't he?

He angled the trike toward the empty space, pedaled in, parked. He locked the trike's steering, climbed off, and walked to the gun store.

Despite his new familiarity with this kind of hardware, his recent shooting practice, the place still impressed him when he went inside. All those guns . . .

A young man with hair swept fifteen centimeters straight up, cut flat across the top, and dyed a dark blue walked up to him and flashed a grin full of capped teeth. The caps alternated in color: candy apple red with metalflake blue.

Silk wanted to shake his head. Kids and their fashions.

"Help you?"

"Uh, yeah, I need some ammunition for a spring pistol."

"Caliber?"

"Eight mm. Standard stunners. A couple of cartons."

"Easy breezy." He started to turn and go get the ammo.

"Say, uh, is Hildy around?"

The blue-haired kid stopped. "Hildy?"

"Yeah, she works here. She sold me my gun. Red hair, kind of thin and leggy, fairly well endowed up top?"

The kid flashed his purple smile. "I wish. Nobody like that here on days. Maybe she's on swing or graveyard."

Silk nodded. She could have transferred to another work shift. It had been a few weeks. "No big deal," he said.

The kid collected the ammunition and took Silk's card, ran it through the scanner, and gave it back. He made conversation as the store's computer worked the transaction. "So, what kind of eight you carrying?"

Silk was embarrassed; he couldn't remember the brand name. He started to reach for it, stopped. It was considered polite, the rangemaster where he practiced told him, to warn somebody when you were about to pull your piece—unless you planned on shooting him or maybe scaring him into shooting you. He said, "Okay to show you?"

The kid nodded. "Sure."

Silk drew his pistol slowly and held it up.

"Hey, a Harrison Model 10. Nice weapon. They only came out with that a couple of months ago."

"Yeah, Hildy said it was new."

The kid shook his head. "You sure you got the right store? I've been here for a year and a half and nobody named 'Hildy' has worked days here since I logged in."

Silk blinked. "I'm pretty sure I bought it here."

"Lemme see the serial number."

Silk handed him the gun, and the kid tapped the number into a keypad. The holoproj lit up. The kid looked at it and nodded. "What I thought. No record of it in our files. You musta got mixed up. There's a shop over on 20th, not far from here. Maybe that's where you got it."

Silk knew an exit segue when he heard one. He smiled. "Yeah, maybe you're right. I'm new in town, I haven't learned my way around real good yet. I must have gotten confused."

The kid gave him the colorful porcelain again. "You a terry? It true that Earth women walk around naked on the beaches and if you want to fuck one all you have to do is ask?"

"Not quite," Silk said.

Outside, he walked to his trike. Unless the kid with the hot-rod teeth was crazy or on chem—and those were possibilities—Hildy wasn't exactly what she claimed to be.

He was beginning to wonder if anybody on this damned planet was what they said they were.

Even this backrocket planet had some culture, though most of it was imported, and Colburn discovered that a local chamber orchestra was performing a baroque concert that evening. He bought an admit and went to see what the *ausvelters* thought would pass for music.

The performance was heavy with J. S. Bach pieces, one of the Brandenberg Concertos, the Toccata and Fugue, the No. 5 Trio Sonata, plus a few odds and ends by Christian Bach and a couple of lesser known German composers of the period.

It wasn't terrible. True, the synthesetic keyboard didn't have the full timbre of a cathedral pipe organ—nor did the tuned acoustics of the chamber quite get the traditional high-ceilinged echo effect right. Still and all, he'd heard worse on Earth and he was a Bach fan, all those tight and methodical variations on a theme that were so precise, almost compulsively so. Amazing what variety a genius could wring from contrapuntal and fugal constructions. Bach wrote to the glory of his God, and surely that particular deity must have been mathematically inclined, did he like the man's music. Colburn thought that the hairy thunderer God must have appreciated Bach well enough, since he hadn't struck the old boy down with the death bolt until he was in his mid-sixties, a decent age for the times, and since he'd allowed him to father some twenty children, half of whom survived to adulthood. The composer had been potent in the bedroom and obviously well practiced with that organ, too.

After the concert Colburn found a restaurant that served passable TexMexThai. He ate chili and satay and drank an excellent local beer. One of the first things most *ausvelt* worlds did well was learn how to brew good ales and beer. That was a plus.

He ordered a second draft of the dark honey-colored beer and considered the logistics of his new and self-imposed challenge. Money was not a problem; until he made the break, he could draw on The Scat's accounts pretty much as heavily as he wished. There were limits, of course, but given the prize they sought, those were a lot higher than he'd ever been able to play with before.

The waiter returned with the second beer. The container was real glass, heavy, and there was a centimeter of foam on the top. He took the beer, sipped at it. Ah.

So, he could siphon off a few hundred thousand stads from Terran Security's petty cash, no problem. They wouldn't miss it, and it would pad his own funds nicely. They always watched your money when you worked for them, The Scat did, especially if you went offworld, but that wasn't a real problem, either. The first thing a good op did was learn how to protect himself, and unless Terran Security was willing to shut down the entire electronic banking system on Earth, he could transfer his money no matter how hard they froze his personal account.

Those escape doors had been in place for a long time, shifted often enough so they wouldn't be noticed even if somebody had been looking for them. And it was a lot cheaper to live on any of the *ausvelt* worlds than it was on Earth.

ID wasn't a problem, though he would want to see a good surgeon to have his face and ears done. The drugs that distorted the retinal patterns weren't fun, but he wouldn't have to keep taking them once he relocated and got settled. He had enough of a supply to last for years.

The Scat wouldn't just roll over and let him go, of course; they'd keep looking for him at least as long as Silverman was there. Silverman would take it personally and he was bright enough to be dangerous. That would be something he'd have to watch, but time would, after all, be on Colburn's side, wouldn't it?

He grinned into the beer. He could stay hidden for twenty or thirty or fifty years, until Silverman retired and a younger man or woman took over. They wouldn't be personally offended, and there would surely be other more important items on their calendars than finding a rogue agent half a century gone. The secret would be a long time out by then, and life would have moved on.

The immediate problem was to secure a ship, one large enough to make the stellar leap but small enough to go relatively unnoticed when it did so. A courier, maybe, or a corporate parcel delivery vessel, something along those lines. He didn't have a network on E2 to speak of, and he didn't want to risk The Scat finding out, so he'd have to step cautiously in that direction. True, he could spin a story that would satisfy them if he needed it, but why give them any clues at all? Better he should just disappear and leave them scratching their asses.

"Another beer, sir?"

Colburn smiled at the waiter. "I believe I will have one."

The waiter returned the smile and went to fetch the beer. Three beers would be too many—he never allowed himself to get drunk or stoned while working—but he could take a couple of sips and leave the rest. It really was good beer. At least he wouldn't have to give that up.

What had worked once for Silk might work again. It was late, well into the night, and he was alone in his office with the biopath. He gave the system the parameters and leaned back.

A minute later the holoproj of Hildy smiled at him.

The name on her vehicle operator's ID wasn't Hildy, it was Korin Piki. And her occupation wasn't listed as gunseller but as private inquiry agent.

Why didn't that surprise him?

Silk shook his head. For such a small town, there seemed to be an awful lot of these professional snoopers within his reach.

There was a home address for Hildy or Korin or whoever the hell she really was. The street and cube number were not anywhere close to the cube where she had taken him and they had screwed each other's brains out—certainly his brain, at least.

It was the middle of the night and not a normal hour to go calling, but as Silk shut down the 'proj, he figured it was probably as good a time as any to catch her unawares. Somebody sooner or later was going to tell him what the hell was going on. He was long overdue.

He pulled the magazine from his pistol and checked it, put it back, and headed for his trike.

TWENTY-ONE _____

CUNT!

The voice in the night sounded as if the speaker were right behind her, and it was not speaking a term of endearment. Zia tensed, took a long, quick step to get out of punching or kicking range, and turned, ready to fight. It was dark, but the street lighting was bright enough for her to see her surroundings clearly.

There was nobody there.

She blinked, startled. Slowly turned, scanning for the speaker.

The second of the town's two vehicle rental stations lay ahead of her, a squatty, mashed, glazed green brick with a wall of glass facing the street. Part of the glass was fogged with condensation where the night's tropical heat lapped at the cooled building. There were two people inside the lighted structure, behind a counter, but the clerks and their counter were across the street and behind a wall, even if it was glass. She could see them but not hear them.

Carts and vans went past on the street, but at that particular moment, nothing on wheels or fans was anywhere near her, nor had any vehicles passed close enough for her to have heard a conversational voice.

There was a man looking into a shop window to her right, but he was fifty meters away, and unless he yelled she wouldn't be able to hear him. And the voice had not been a yell; she was pretty sure of that.

But unless she was losing her mind, she had heard the remark and she was sure it was directed at her—

Stupid twat, I see you looking at me. You're gonna be fucking sorry you killed Laurel. Soon as we get to a place where nobody'll see it, I'm gonna delete your ass, I don't give a shit about my goddamned orders. You don't fuck with Bally's partners and walk away.

Zia turned back toward the rental station, shaken. It was just like the woman who'd fallen from the train. She was inside somebody else's head. Reading his thoughts. It couldn't be. It was impossible.

Maybe something had broken in her own brain and she'd tumbled over a mental precipice into psychosis. Lost her connection to reality. Gone insane.

Or maybe not. She didn't *feel* crazy.

Of course, maybe nobody ever did feel crazy, even those who were raving, but if anything, she felt sharper than usual, fast on her feet physically and mentally. If she'd slipped a gear and gone mad, there wasn't much to be done about it, save to get herself to the medics and hope they could fix it. Maybe this was some side effect of the Treatment; maybe it had cooked her brain.

But—put that possibility aside for a moment. What if she wasn't crazy? What if there was another answer? Once was an aberration. Twice might be a pattern.

What if she *was* able to reach inside somebody's head and read their mind?

If that was the case, if it wasn't some hallucination, then the man looking at the sports display was Bally, the same Bally the shooter on the train had thought about as Zia put her down. If so, then what should she do?

Stall for time.

She continued across the street as if nothing had happened. How could she check it? If she had a chance to put the guy under her gun without having to delete him, then she could find out who he was and why he was following her. If his name happened to be Bally, that would go a long way to convincing her she wasn't bugfuck crazy.

She entered the rental station and smiled at the clerks. If the man behind her had any further thoughts about her, she couldn't hear them. Nor could she pick up anything from the two clerks. What did that mean?

"May we help you, M.—ah . . . ?"

"Rélanj," she finished. It didn't matter who knew she was here. "I need to rent a flitter. Something small and fast. I'll need it for a day or two and I'll drop it back here when I'm done." A small lie, but if somebody following her lost contact, better they should return and wait here than poke around looking where they might find her. That had been her original idea.

"Let me see what we have available," the woman said.

But she was running on autopilot in renting the cart. As she stood there waiting for the clerk to finish, Zia knew her plan to go to Touchdown to find history on the man who'd tried to kill her was no longer necessary. Now she had something better.

Now she had Bally.

Silk found the cube complex easily enough. The front entrance had a keycard lock that controlled what looked like accordion-style metal security doors. The structure was five or six stories tall, could be a couple hundred units in it, depending on how large they were. He sat pondering a way to get inside when he saw a couple park a low-slung cart at the curb and alight, then walk toward the entrance. The woman was tall, heroically built, athletic; the man was short but broad-shouldered. Both were dressed in evening silks. A couple of muscle workers back from a night out, Silk figured. And his pass into the building, if he played it right.

He dismounted from his trike and started across the street, timing his arrival so he would get there a couple of seconds after the tall woman and short man. He pulled the keycard for his office from his wallet as he approached the doors.

"I got it," the man said. He nodded at the keypad.

Silk nodded his gratitude. "Thanks. My card has been screwing up lately anyhow. Must have set it down near a magnet or something." He put the card away.

The tall woman flashed him a bright smile as her escort ran his card through the reader and the doors fan-folded open. Silk walked into the building and stopped by the mail comp and printer. He pretended to punch up his mail as the couple walked past him to the elevators.

When they were gone, he went to the stairs. Hildy—or whatever her name was—had a cube on the third level. Maybe he could work off a little of his nervous energy by walking up instead of taking the lift. His stomach was fluttery, his bowels felt loose, his scrotum had ridged and drawn up so it was a corrugated knot in his groin. This was scary stuff, skulking around, playing with spies and guns and people killing each other. When he'd seen Zia in action, it hadn't looked as if she was worried. She was as cool as a tank of liquid nitrogen, impervious to the heat around her. Did Zia, so calm with Death's breath hot in her face, ever feel as nervous as he did now? Could you ever get used to this feeling?

And yet, there was an attraction to it. He sure felt *alive*. He might not be in a few minutes, but right in this second, he was aware of things around him with an almost supernatural sense of sharpness. As if the air had turned into some potent psychedelic that increased and magnified his attention with every fresh breath he drew. As though his personal bit of the universe had turned to crystal and razorwire and amphetamine rushes. He felt edgy, tricky, and in a way he couldn't explain to himself, *competent*. Zia would probably have laughed at that. He wished she were here now.

The third level was quiet. He padded down the carpeted hallway until he was outside the door marked 315.

Now what? Somehow in his scenario, he hadn't thought about this part. He'd been clever getting into the building, but how was he going to get into the cube itself? The lock looked to be a print/voxax combo; it would be set to respond to the occupant's thumb or voice pattern, maybe programmed with those of frequent visitors, if she had any. Certainly his print and pattern wouldn't be in it.

He could use the annunciator: *Hey, Hildy, I just happened to be in the neighborhood, thought I'd drop in.* Right. Sure.

And how, my terran stud, did you happen to know I lived here, under another name, hmm?

He could stand around out here in the hall and wait until she came out—or more likely, until somebody saw him and called the cools or security and had him hauled off for trespassing. How would he explain that?

He could throw himself against the sliding door until he broke through it. Although from the look of it, it was solid densplast, and what was more likely was that he'd break himself.

Well, shit. How was he going to get in?

He wandered down the hall, looking for inspiration. When he found the laundry room with its bank of ultrasonic clothes washers and cheap heating-filament dryers, the idea came to him.

Somebody had left some clothes in one of the dryers. Too bad for them. He found a trash can and dug a handful of newsfax and hard copy 'zine paper out of it. He piled that inside one of the dryers, then arranged a tent of clothing around it, cotton and acrylics and synsilk that looked as if they would burn well. Silk had long ago given up smoking, even though denatured tobacco and dopestik were still common enough, but he still carried a keycard lighter out of habit. He lit the paper, watched it flare green when the magazine inks caught, then hurried out of the room. The burning paper and cloth should produce a fair amount of smoke and CO_2, enough to trigger the smoke detector over the door. Since the fire was inside a metal dryer designed to withstand a certain amount of heat, Silk didn't think there was much danger of the fire getting out of control before somebody came to put it out. Given that there was an extinguisher mounted on the wall five meters away, some brave soul would probably have the fire doused in a hurry. Meanwhile, if this complex was like the one he lived in, the smoke alarm would set off a siren or hooter or something noisy in every cube— at least on this floor and maybe the entire building. When that happened, it would be prudent to stick one's head out into the hall and see what the problem was.

Silk moved past Hildy's door and ten meters farther down the hall. He stood in the middle, facing the laundry room. After a moment, he saw the first wisps of smoke curl out.

The alarm went off. It was an ear-grating buzz that sounded like the noise Silk imagined a really constipated giant robot might make straining to take a dump: *Annnhhh! Annnnhhh!*

Some of the tenants were light sleepers. Doors opened, people stepped out into the hall, both in front of and behind Silk.

"What the hell is going on?"

"Them damned kids fucking with the alarm again?"

Silk added to the walla: "Looks like maybe one of the dryers shorted out or something."

"Oh, shit, my clothes!" A portly barefoot man in a robe thundered down the hall toward the laundry room. A couple of others also started that way. Silk followed but he took small steps.

The door to Hildy's cube opened and she leaned out to look, her back to him.

Silk moved toward her. He pulled his gun carefully and slid it around his body under the front of his shirt. It didn't seem as if anybody noticed. He angled over so he was next to the wall as he reached Hildy. She wore a nightgown of translucent red silk and another time, it would have interested him in a different way. Now, it just meant he could see she was unarmed.

When he was close enough to touch her, he said, "Good evening, Hildy. How about you invite me in for a nice long chat?"

She jerked and turned to looked at him.

He pulled his shirt aside and showed her the gun.

"Fuck," she said, when she saw who he was.

"Not this time, sweetie."
They went inside.

"Who hired you to follow me?"
"I can't say," she said.
"Oh, you can say, all right. Or maybe I'll shoot you, just for the hell of it."
"That's a stunner," she pointed out.
"Yep, sure is. And while you're unconscious, I can shove you out a window or strangle you or set your cube on fire and you won't ever wake up, if that's what I feel like doing."
"Come on. You would kill me for following you?"
"How did you pull off that business in the gun store?"
She grinned. He was talking and not shooting; Silk could see she thought she could worm her way out of this, could manipulate him. She leaned back on the couch and let her knees gape a little.
Please, he thought. I'm not *that* stupid. And the little voice that wouldn't let him get away with fooling himself said, *Yeah, well, it wasn't too long past that you were. A natural mistake for her to make.*
"Easy," she said. "I followed you into the store. While you were gawking at all the hardware, I flashed my ID at the manager and told him I needed to be a clerk for a few minutes. He went along."
"Why would he do that, if you were a private inquiry agent?"
She hadn't thought about that, he saw. It flustered her. She tried to cover it: "Money, Silk. I downloaded a big chunk into his account. Simple."
"I don't think so. I think maybe he went along because you convinced him you were something else. Maybe some kind of official operative. Let's take a look at your wallet, Hildy. Or Korin, if that's your real name."
"I'll get it," she said too quickly.
"No, I don't think so. I think you'll show me where it is and I'll get it."
She nodded. "It's in my pants pocket, in the bedroom."

"After you. Move funny, and you get to take a short nap and wake up with a nasty headache. Speaking from experience."

"You are a terran spy, aren't you?" she said, as he followed her toward the bedroom.

"What makes you think that?"

"Because you're too good to be what you pretend to be. You deleted Red and you found me; no flack for a timber company could do that."

Silk wanted to smile. A spindoc dealt in information, and that *was* how he'd found her. The part about canceling Red, that wasn't him, but if she wanted to think he was more dangerous than he was, fine. Maybe it would keep her from doing anything stupid.

Once again he was wrong.

She pointed out the pants, where they lay neatly folded on a dresser. He moved to the dresser and dug into the pocket with his left hand, his right holding the gun on her. His attention shifted a hair when the synlon wallet came free. In that instant, she jumped past him and ran.

"Stop!"

Before he could shoot, she was through the door and out of sight.

Silk ran after her. He rounded the doorway and saw her slap the exit control. He pointed the gun and fired at the middle of her back, but she was already dropping and the round thunked into the opening door. He lowered his aim but he was used to shooting with both hands on the pistol, and the wallet got in the way. By the time he got the weapon shifted right, she had scrabbled out into the hall on her hands and knees. A fold of red was his only target, and it vanished fast.

"Shit!"

Well, she wasn't going to get out of range in the hall. The fire was out and the residents had gone back into their rooms. He hoped.

He ran to the exit and half slid into the hall.

Hildy was up and running. He started to target on her—

She screamed and veered to the side, and Silk saw three men past her. He got no more than a glimpse of them but it was enough to tell him they were young, wore plain gray coveralls, and had guns.

Hildy tried to turn around.

The three men started shooting. Silk watched in slow time as the bullets hit her. Five, six, maybe a dozen rounds. Flesh tore, blood erupted, Hildy kept screaming.

A stray shot pocked the wall next to Silk's head.

Maybe they weren't shooting at him. But if he got killed by accident, he would still be dead. He thought about ducking back into the apartment but the reptile in his lower brain hissed and shook its head. *No! Danger! Run!*

He believed that. Only thing was, if he ran, that wouldn't stop them shooting.

He already had his gun up and pointed their way.

Silk opened up, swung the weapon across the hall, pulled the trigger as fast as he could. Spray-and-pray was not the way to do it, but too late to stop.

The first man went down. The second man dropped. The third man dived into an open door and vanished.

Silk didn't know if he'd hit any of them, but his gun was empty and the hall behind him was clear. He turned and ran.

When he was halfway to the stairs, Hildy stopped screaming.

TWENTY-TWO

THERE WAS A wide river that meandered in and around the city of Beagle, and since it was deep enough for pusher boats and barges to ply all the way past Frogtown to the islands beyond, there were also docks. Colburn stood on a pier near the end of one of these heavy wooden structures, near a piling as big around as a large man could encircle with his outstretched arms. He listened to the river slosh past, to civilization noises in the background: carts, airliners, the sad moan of a distant train horn. An acrid tang of wood preservative tainted the damp night air. The jutting pier where he stood should have been sufficiently illuminated to make it as bright as any city street, but somebody had shot out most of the big pole lights. The single one still burning was seventy meters away, and it cast a cone of yellow that swarmed with insects too stupid to know they couldn't see the light that attracted them.

Colburn preferred doing this kind of business during the day, when more people were about and it was easier to blend in. The best place to hide, after all, was in a crowd. Unfortunately, not everybody he dealt with felt the same. Certain individuals felt the night was safer, that it offered dark shadows into which they might scurry if frightened. These were the brothers of the rat, the roach, the owl, men who depended on staying out of sight rather than speed. There was a time before electric lamps shoved the night into corners and held it at bay when such feelings might have been justified. Now, all it took was the flick of a switch to destroy the darkest natural umbra. A copter with a spotlight could turn this pier into a nighttime soccer stadium. In his back pocket he had a blastcell diver's light no bigger than a candy bar that would do a pretty good imitation of a spotlight itself; certainly it would blind anybody within twenty meters were he to shine it into their unprotected faces. A smart watcher wouldn't even have to do that; he could slip on a pair of spookeyes and see in the dark as if it were noon. A man who depended on the night to protect him was a fool.

But. The man he was to meet was a creature of the shadows and since he had what Colburn needed, it was his call. Colburn wasn't afraid of the dark. He was armed and adept and he was more valuable alive than robbed for his pocket money and jewelry—if somebody were stupid enough to try.

He heard the footsteps coming.

"Claibourne?"

"Who else?"

"You have something for me?"

Colburn wanted to laugh. People who weren't ops had a distorted idea of how the game was played. They thought the entcoms they'd seen about code phrases and passwords and spookeyes had some connection to reality. Stupid, but it didn't cost much to stroke the fantasy.

"The food is terrible in the Blue Gull," he said, deadpan.

"Yes, but the liquor is cheap," the man replied.

God. Who thought these things up?

"Can we get to biz?"

"Sure. Bulletin says you're looking for a suborbital ship."

"Not quite. What I'm looking for is something I didn't particularly want Bulletin to know about, if you get my meaning."

"Ah. And what might that be?"

"A starship. One with enough range to get me to New Australia. Big enough to carry a crew and some small cargo, small enough to slip around a system coast guard cutter if the pilot knows what he's doing."

The man, no more than a shadowy figure backlighted by the single lamp, sucked in a quick breath. "You're talkin' a lot more money for that kinda craft than for an airship."

"I kind of figured that. I can get the stads—can you get the ship?"

"How soon would you need it?"

"I needed it yesterday. I'd like it tomorrow. I can wait a week. Ten days at the outside."

None of what he'd said was true, but like everything else in this transaction, misdirection was important. The ship would be stolen and the money the seller wanted would be a lot, though hardly anything near a ship's true value. There wasn't much of a market for boosted starcraft. Each Pull drive was handbuilt, every part in it computer ID'd, and there wasn't any way to hide that. You'd never be able to sell a stolen ship legally without changing the engines. The Claibourne ID would die when he left, so that was no problem. He'd thought about using a different name, but on a planet this small, it was easy to find him if somebody really wanted to do so. The size of the ship wasn't that important, as it had only to haul two passengers. New Australia wasn't his destination, either, but if the ship could get that far, it could also get to York or Fuji or Shinto, and might even stretch enough to reach Mchanga. It was SOP to point anybody who might ask in the wrong direction. Not that this particular thief was going to say anything else once Colburn had the ship in hand. M. Night Crawler here was going to disappear about the time Colburn left this world, as were any others Colburn suspected might give The Scat the slightest clue about where he'd gone. Silk, the boyfriend, would be tricky. He had to keep him alive until after they left normal space, in case Zia didn't trust him.

If he were her, surely he wouldn't trust him. But Silk was doable later.

Nobody could possibly know yet where he was going, since Colburn himself wasn't sure of his destination. He had two strong possibilities in mind, York and Fuji. In both places he had a drop-in ID waiting; all he had to do was slip a current hologram of his new face into the log and *poof!* he would be a new man. A man with established history he could hide behind. Both York and Fuji boasted larger populations than E2; both were places where Terran Security had poor networks. He could access his money from either and there would be no way to trace it—not after the terrible disaster at the Omninet Earth Orbital Transfer Station that would coincidentally take place within seconds after a TOF courier ship left there bearing his account transfer. And the ship, alas, would have a similar hull dispatency right after it downloaded the squirt on whichever world he chose *not* to live on. By the time he routed the transfer through a dozen dummies and then to another planet, the greatest human tracker who ever lived wouldn't be able to stay with it, nor would a dislinked biopath be likely to get past the loop he'd leave behind. He'd had years to set it all up, and it should be bulletproof.

"Cost you a hundred kay."

"I can live with that."

"I'll see what I can do. I'll com you."

The footsteps retreated. He hadn't gotten a good look at the speaker, at least not here. He had excellent surveillance holographs from earlier in the day, however, so he wouldn't have any trouble recognizing the thief when the time came.

Until this caper, the bolt-hole project had been nothing but an intellectual exercise. Colburn hadn't expected he'd ever have to use it, it had been more of a game, one he'd played when he had nothing better to do. Part of his low-profile and evasion plan. Better to have it and not need it than to need it and not have it. A smart man looked as far down the road as he could see, at possible turnoffs, for places where a sudden truck might lumber into traffic to block or even hit him. You couldn't be prepared for everything, but you could avoid a lot of problems by spotting them in time to go around or even back up. You either took care of biz, or it would eventually take care of you.

As a serious student of the old American gunslingers and the retro-Nihonnese samurai, Colburn had discovered that the very best players were those almost nobody had ever heard of. Men who never walked into a building without first knowing all the ways they could leave it in a hurry. Men who were deadly but who never developed major reputations because they were more interested in survival than glory. They didn't have colorful names like "Kid" or "Blackie" or "Korusu." You never saw their pictures in the hardcopy periodicals of the day, and what stories there were about them were vague because the best of the best kept very low profiles indeed.

Colburn grinned to himself as he sauntered along the pier toward the main body of the dock. It had taken years of research to learn about two of the better unknown experts, he'd had to travel to Tombstone and El Paso, to Reigendo and Narita, to speak to the few who had documents and oral stories about the men of mystery. Sure, every scholar who studied the martial arts in Japan knew of the great seventeenth-century fighter Musashi, who won nearly eighty duels, but—who knew of Izumo, born four years after Musashi, who defeated half again that many men in single combat? According to one of Colburn's more reliable sources, Musashi, traveling in the company of a priest and three nuns, had once met Izumo in passing on a country road. Musashi was then thirty, at his physical peak, having already won more than sixty fights with blade and spear. He was a master of the twin sword technique he did much to improve, if not invent. He was thought to be a man utterly without fear, and he was arrogant in his strength. He had once beheaded a man for laughing too loud. But when he came upon Izumo, he bowed low and hurried along his way. When the priest asked who the ronin they had passed was to deserve such a deep bow of respect, Musashi said, "That was the deadliest man in the world. Were I to challenge him, he would strike me down in an instant."

Izumo died at eighty, surrounded by his grandchildren and great-grandchildren.

Billy the Kid and John Wesley Hardin were famous shootists in the American wild west, and their histories well documented, but they were little more than self-centered psychopathic thugs. Almost nothing had been written about Tom Hardwicke, who traveled through Texas and Kansas and Montana during that same period and who, if the reports could be believed, had shot forty-seven armed men without ever sustaining a wound himself, more than the Kid and Hardin and any other two infamous killers of the day put together. Arrested only four times, Hardwicke was never convicted of a crime, and he died in bed in San Francisco in 1933 at the age of eighty-nine. He left a diary covering the years 1870–1885, begun when he was in his mid-twenties, and each of the shootings in which he was involved was detailed. At least a dozen of these were corroborated by other sources, and the details were similar enough so that Colburn believed the remainders were probably true. Colburn's favorite entry was an early one:

"Octbr. the 31st 1872, the evening, at Mrs. Peab'dy's Fancy House, Ellsworth, Kansas.

"Blackfoot Bill Harris, having become overly drunk while playing poker, got into an argument with G. K. McCoy over the ownership of a ceegar laying upon the table nearest the pianoforte. As it was chilly, Bill wore a long coat and he drew from its pocket a small pistol and proceeded to shooting. His first shot missed McCoy and instead hit the gambler Geo. Ashly on the left leg. As I was one of the players seated next to McCoy and thus endanger'd by Bill's action, my only safe recourse was to draw my Navy Colt .36 from my belt in self-defense. I fired one time and the ball took Bill just over the left eye, killing him and thus ending the engagement. All agreed the incident was unfortunate and the policeman Ed Hogue came and saw that it was provoked and informed us that he would tell Marshal Norton and that would be the end of it."

Colburn smiled. He felt a strong kinship with those unsung experts. His boots were quiet on the dock as he walked, since they were built for silence and traction, but he could almost imagine jingling spurs and the *clock-clock* of nailed-on leather heels upon the wood. He was the best of the best in his own time, and only a few people had any idea of who he was, all of them in the biz. Mostly, that was enough, but now and then, he wanted to be with somebody who could really appreciate who and what he was. Like the woman Rélanj. She was the perfect audience. And shortly, she would be his.

Silk didn't even consider trying for his trike. He hit the street and scrabbled across it, dodged between two parked carts, and looped to his left, looking for a place to hide. Even as he ran, though, he realized that wasn't a good idea. If there were more of the men in gray, staying in one place wouldn't be to his advantage. If you were still, they could find you; if you kept moving, they would have to figure out where you went before they started looking. True, you were easier to spot running down the street than hiding under a bush, but if they trapped you inside a search area, it would only be a matter of time before they flushed you out. Zia had told him that.

Fortunately, he'd learned from his first experience with shooting at somebody and emptying his gun. He had two spare magazines in his pocket, and he managed to reload one into the pistol even as he ran. He holstered the weapon so he could pump his arms faster.

Who were these guys?

Obviously they had some kind of official weight, else they'd be worried about the law showing up to stop their party. But why were they after him?

As he dodged and ran, keeping to cover when he could, Silk realized he was not far from Taníto's school. He'd missed a couple of lessons; she'd probably be pissed at him. This time of night, nobody would be around. And he had a key . . .

He headed for the school. Any port in a storm, and it ought to be far enough away from the dead woman's building—surely she must be dead after all the bullets she'd absorbed—that maybe he'd be safe there, for the moment, at least.

If the men in gray were after him, though, why had they blasted Hildy? Surely they could tell the difference between a woman in a red nightgown and Silk?

Maybe they'd been after her and not him.

Well. They were after him now.

He ran.

The school was mostly dark; a couple of small lamps cast a dim glow on the hardwood. Silk let himself in and shut the door behind him. He bent and rested his hands on his thighs, took several deep breaths, trying to slow his heart and get his breathing back to normal.

When he felt a little better, he headed toward the fresher.

He was halfway across the workout floor when the door burst open behind him and three men ran into the building. He half spun. Saw they weren't the same three in the hall. That meant something.

His gun was in its holster, and they had their handguns out and pointed at him.

Oh, shit!

"Don't move a fucking muscle," one of them said. "Twitch and you die."

Silk kept his hands away from his body, his fingers spread wide. He also kept absolutely still.

"What are you doing here?" came a woman's voice.

The three men froze. Looked for the speaker.

Taníto stepped from a shadow. The green tattoo on her bald head gleamed dully in the dim light.

"Who are you?" one of the men asked.

"I am Taníto. This is my school. You have broken my door and are threatening one of my students. Explain yourself."

Silk stared at the woman. Was she crazy? Yeah, she was an expert fighter, but these three were armed with guns and much too far away for the fastest person who ever lived to get to them before they started shooting. She wore workout clothes, and her hands were empty.

"We're, ah, special agents of New Earth Security," one of the men said. "This man is a criminal. We are arresting him."

"I see. Do you have a warrant for his arrest?"

Two of the men looked at each other, then at Taníto. "Hot pursuit," one of them said. "No warrant necessary. He, ah, murdered somebody."

"Is this true, Silk?"

"No, Taníto. I didn't kill anybody. They did."

She looked at the men again. "Do you have official identification?"

One of the men laughed. "Identification? Do you see this gun in my hand? That's the only identification I *need*!" He waved the pistol.

None of the three had a weapon pointed at Taníto; they were still covering Silk.

"Ah, well. I see. In that case, I don't suppose I can argue with you, can I?"

"There's a smart idea," one of them said. "Okay, you, come along—"

He never got to finish. Silk was looking right at Taníto when it happened and even so, he could hardly believe it. One second she was standing there barehanded, the next second she had a gun in her hand, shooting. She fired six or seven times, a spring pistol she shot so fast it made a single, long *tut-tut-tut-tut!*

Silk had once seen a nature edcom of a mongoose attacking a cobra. The little ratlike beast had moved with a blurring speed that looked fast even when rerun in slo-mo. The cobra hadn't had a chance.

Taníto's shots were like that.

By the time he turned around to look, all three men were down.

When he turned back toward his instructor, there was no sign of the gun. Like a magician.

Maybe his mouth fell open.

Taníto said. "A martial artist who can't use modern weapons is a cripple. Spinning kicks and fancy postures are best reserved for the entcom vids." She paused. "Do you know who these men were? And why they were chasing you?"

"No, Taníto. Somebody has been stalking me and Zia. We haven't been able to determine why. I believe they or somebody with them have killed at least two people, private investigators."

"Hmm. It would be wise if you found out who they represent and why they are trying to kill you," she said.

Now there was an obvious statement.

"Best you leave now. I would not have the school involved in such things publicly. I will take care of these three."

"But when they wake up, they will—"

"They aren't going to wake up, Silk. The darts in my pistol are lethal."

"Jesus!" He couldn't help saying it. "Bu-but, Taníto, they might really be some kind of planetary agents!"

"I doubt it. They would have followed procedure and shown me warrants and identification if they had been here officially. I know something of these things. If they were agents, this business was unsanctioned."

Silk looked at the three men. Corpses, now. When he looked back at his instructor, his throat was as dry as sunbleached wood. She'd killed three men, just like that. It must have showed on his face.

She spoke as if she were giving him a lesson in class, and her voice was matter-of-fact: "They drew weapons in my school without permission," she said. "They *threatened* me." She gave him a small and tight grin. "I don't allow that."

Ah. She didn't *allow* that.

Jesus.

TWENTY-THREE

ZIA DROVE THE rented flitter slowly toward the edge of town, looking for the right place. There was a little pub not far ahead, she'd been there a couple of times, it might work . . .

She kept the flitter in ground-mode, and she didn't see Bally behind her but she assumed he was somewhere out there in the dark. He could be running without lights, on a scooter, maybe, or even ahead or parallel to her. Could have maybe tapped the rental place's com and hustled ahead to slap a tracer on the flitter before she got it. That way, he could let her go anywhere she wanted and home in on her from klicks away.

She didn't think this last was likely. If he could have gotten a bug on the flitter, he could have also planted a bomb on it and saved himself a lot of trouble. Of course, maybe he didn't happen to have a bomb with him. Besides, if her flash of whatever it was had been valid, he wanted to kill her in a more personal manner.

And she was beginning to believe that mental zap was real and not some dementia. It had happened again, twice more.

The young woman in greasy mechanic's clothes who had brought the flitter around had smiled when she looked at Zia, but her thoughts had been bleak:

God, what a great-looking woman. I'd really like to be with her. But she wouldn't be interested in me, I'm so ugly and so stupid. I should kill myself.

And when she'd stopped later at a traffic signal as a group of people left a theater and crossed the street in front of her, a thin, slight man of maybe thirty glanced at her flitter as he passed in front of it:

If this stupid split-tail tries to run me down, I'll pull my gun and put seven through the windscreen before she can fucking blink.

Zia hadn't spent much time wondering how telepathy would work, but she would have guessed that it would be more empathic than language-driven, if anybody had asked her. She'd read spec stories for a time when she'd been a kid and in those, the telepaths tended to walk around downloading everybody they passed, like being in a loud party and hearing the buzz of many voices droning all at once. If she wasn't crazy and this was what it was, she was only able to pick up a few people, and those concentrating on her, it seemed. More, they were all upset in some way, and the idea of murder or suicide had figured into all three of the overheard thoughts.

Was it that only a few people could send? Or maybe it required some kind of strong emotional threshold to be crossed for the connection to establish itself? Did somebody have to be angry enough to be contemplating homicide, or despondent to the point of suicide? She hadn't picked up anything from the couple making love on the train, but then again, past a certain point, that didn't involve much thinking per se, did it? Not unless they were ops and faking it. She knew how that worked well enough.

As she approached the pub, Zia tried to concentrate her focus on it, she strived to "hear" mental voices from within.

—and the guy said, 'What do you mean, wrong hole?' Oh, man, that's fucking funny—*!*

Zia grinned as she pulled the flitter to the curb and shut the engine off. She'd heard that joke. So maybe the emotional driver just had to be any strong one, as long as it was strong enough. And it meant the thinker didn't have to be focused on her, unless the joker in the bar could see through walls.

Interesting.

She got out of the flitter and walked toward the pub. She didn't think Bally would follow her into the place, at least not for a while. In his boots, she would set up on the flitter and wait for the subject to return to it. You'd have to allow for the possibility that the subject might be meeting somebody inside and could be leaving with them, so you'd want to make a quick run around the back to see if there was another exit, any carts or flitters parked there. If there were two doors and you were alone, you'd have to let one go and hope you guessed right on the one you picked. You'd need to be where you could see the most likely exit *and* the subject's transportation. Since she'd been here and knew the back door to the pub was for deliveries and emergencies and not patrons, Zia would set up on the front. If Bally looped around back, he'd figure that out and he'd probably do the same. Five minutes from now, Bally ought to be parked on the street, somewhere close enough so he could eyeball or put a scope on the door good enough to recognize her in the dimly lit doorway if she came out and left with somebody else instead of going back to her own transportation. There were small buildings across the road, but none of them had an alley directly in line with the pub's door. Besides, parking in alleys was best avoided; it called attention to you, and even if you had ID to flash at the local police when they came to check you out, you didn't want a patrol cart advertising your presence when your subject came out when they might see it and you.

Zia walked into the pub. She'd draw attention, even though she wore a baggy shirt and nonflattering pants. She was female and alone, and she'd been in enough pubs to know the barstool brigade would hit on anything it thought had a hole big enough for use.

She hadn't gotten ten meters inside the place before the first semi-drunk was in her face. He was big, hairy, dressed in business blues. A junior exec, she figured. Banker, lawyer, like that.

"Heya, baby! Wanna drink?"

She smiled at his artless approach. And she could read his thoughts, too. While muzzy, they were unmistakable:

Pussy! And she wants me, she smiled at me!

Well. It seemed as if lust qualified as a strong emotion. Big surprise. It didn't matter. She had a few minutes to kill, and he was as good as any.

As he guided her toward the bar, one hand on her arm, Zia concentrated on listening to his thoughts. They were more or less in tune with his words, up to a point.

"Heya, I ain't seenya in here before. Whaddaya wanna drink? They make a good red lightning here."

Zia smiled again. She didn't need to be a mind reader to know why he wanted her to try one of those. It usually had forty or fifty cc's of two hundred proof alcohol in it.

Get her swacked, take her to to the Waytel, get a room, fuck her, get home in a couple hours, Carla'll never know.

Zia let him buy her one of the big potent drinks. She sipped at it. Jesus, if she finished this, she might as well let him hit her in the head with a hammer.

"Drink up!"

"I have to go to the little girl's room, sweetie. Be right back."

"Need any help?" He waggled his eyebrows.

Hell, fuck her in the fresher, that'd be okay. She sits on the bidet, blowjob, that'd be all right!

It was all Zia could do to keep from laughing. This telepathy could be fun. She said, "No, I think I can manage. I'll take this with me." She shook her glass lightly, made the cubed ice tinkle.

In the fresher, Zia poured most of the drink into the bidet. Well, she did need to pee, too.

At the bar, Morley—he hadn't told her his name but she could pick up the tender thinking it at him—waited, his stupid grin plastered on like a rictus.

"Let me buy you one of these," she said, waving her nearly empty glass. "Tender, two more like this."

She guessed she could probably drink Morley off his stool, given his head start and all. When she'd been fine-tuned as a spy, they'd tinkered with her metabolism some, done things with insulin and thyroid and her liver, and she burned alcohol a lot faster now anyhow. But since she wasn't going to be drinking, or even here, much longer, Morley would have to suffer alone.

She gave it another ten minutes to be safe, then said, "Hey, what say we leave?"

Morley was ready. "You got it."

Oh, boy, pussy, oh, boy!

"Uh, let's go out the back way, okay? I got a boyfriend and I don't want it to get around I'm going with other guys."

Morley, despite his intake, had the beginning of an erection that was uppermost in his lusty thoughts. She guessed that if she'd asked, he would have offered to tunnel under the wall barehanded to get to a place where he could put that erection into her. He said, "Sure!"

But at the back exit, Zia stopped and put her hand on his chest. "Morley—" she began.

He wasn't quite as drunk as he looked. "I didn' tell you my name, did I?"

"No, you didn't. Carla told me."

"Carla?"

Oh, shit! She knows Carla? Oh, shit! But wait a second, maybe it's okay, maybe she just wants some of what Carla gets. As long as she doesn't find out, it's okay. She got a sudden mental flash of a dark woman holding a knife, a carving or fillet knife. Interesting. Pictures and not just words could come across. She was getting more adept at this.

To Morley she said, "Yep. If she ever finds out you've been playing dork and bush with blondes you pick up in pubs, you'd better sleep with one eye open around her from now on. Know that kitchen knife she likes? The real sharp one?"

He knew; both his face and his thoughts gave it away.

"Well, you can't spike paper without a paper spike, now can you?" Her smile was the sweetest one in her inventory.

Oh, shit—*!*

She left, and he stood there staring open-mouthed after her. *My dick. She would cut off my dick!*

This telepathy stuff could be a *lot* of fun.

Outside, she looked for somebody standing around or sitting alone in a cart or flitter, but didn't see anyone. She moved to the back of the parking area and made a big circle toward the street in front of the pub.

Bally was parked right about where she would be if this were her surveillance. He was thirty meters behind her flitter, his flitter pointed the other way, using his mirrors to watch the door and her vehicle. That made approaching him a little harder.

Zia kept to the shadows and went far enough down the street so when she crossed it, Bally wouldn't be able to see anything more than a distant dot. Then she worked her way back toward him, using the buildings for cover, staying behind the nearest one and working her way toward the street until she was within a three-second dash to his flitter. It would be too much to hope for that he'd left the passenger door unlocked, but as she looked at the flitter, she realized he had lowered the window on that side, probably to allow what little breeze the humid night had to offer to blow through the vehicle. A small nod from a minor god, but she'd take it.

She squatted behind a long rectangular trash bin, pulled her pistol, and waited. Fortunately, there didn't seem to be any other foot traffic on this side of the street at this hour, so nobody was apt to spot her.

Fifteen minutes later the pub's door opened and a couple emerged, arm in arm.

Now!

Zia scooted toward the flitter, staying in a semi-crouch. Bally's attention would be on the couple for a few seconds—

She reached the flitter, put her gun on the sill, aimed at his head. "Good evening, Bally. No sudden moves, okay?"

The word and thought were as one:

"Fuck!"

Zia had no intention of getting into the flitter, nor of allowing Bally to step out. If anybody passed on the street, all they would see would be a woman leaning into a flitter window talking to the guy inside. Maybe a street whore looking for a customer, maybe a contracted woman saying goodnight to her lover, nothing threatening.

"So," she said. "Who sent you?"

He glared at her. His mind ran like a motor:

Stay calm, stay calm! Wait, you'll get your chance. The spare gun clipped under the control panel, only a few centimeters away from your hand on the wheel, she won't expect that, a fast sweep and you'll have her. Stall, make up a story, she starts to shoot, break down, cry, tell her you're a jealous spouse, that's it, tell her she's been looking at your husband, then when she relaxes, get the backup but be careful! She's good, you've got the spidersilk vest but she took Laurel even with her armor—

"Bally? Your vest won't help, I'm lined up on your head. Who sent you?"

Fuck, she knows! Mintok'll be pissed I let her sneak up on me, she must have spotted me on the train or at the rental place. Fuckin' cunt—

Mintok? This guy worked for Mintok? Shit.

"Were you supposed to kill me?"

No, stupid cunt, we were supposed to bring you back alive so Mintok could do whatever it was he wanted to do to you, shove it up your ass, who fucking cares? But you shot Laurel! And you are going to die for that. I'll tell him it was an accident, he won't be too upset. I can manage him.

"Listen," he said. "You've mistaken me for somebody else."

*Fucking Treatment won't help you, bitch, a bullet in
the face will stop your clock. Get ready . . .*

"Don't do it, Bally. You'll never get to the backup
under the panel before I blow your brains out."

*How does she know about the backup? She can't know
about that!*

"I'm sorry about Laurel," she said. "She shot and I
returned fire."

*How does she know Laurel's name? What the hell is
going on here? Did Mintok sell us out?*

"Mintok sold you out," she said. "The game gets complicated sometimes, you know how it is."

*Oh, man! The bastard sold them out! No wonder she
got Laurel, no wonder she spotted me—!*

He moved then, and because he did it without thinking,
all she had was her reaction time. It would have been iffy
even if she hadn't frozen, if her own thoughts hadn't
bloomed like an explosion to betray her.

A thousand years down the tubes. That was the thought
clogging her brain when he lunged at her. He was past
going for a weapon; the primal rage was unconscious. He
hit her with his open hands and knocked her backward. It
was only the years of training that saved her from a bad
fall. She twisted, tucked partially, turned the fall into a
roll. Hit the plastcrete of the walk hard enough to bruise
herself, came up facing the flitter—

He lunged through the window, fell, hit on his hands
then his knees, scrabbled to his feet. Now he went for
the gun on his hip under the tail of his shirt—

A thousand years down the tubes—

Her own learned reflexes kicked in. She still had the
pistol in her hand. She shoved it at him one-handed and
fired three times. Two to the heart, one to the head—

He had his gun clear and coming up when his skull
exploded.

She wasn't aware of the noise the shots made, she'd
blocked them out in tachypsychic reaction, but she knew
others might have heard them. She didn't want to have
to explain this to the city police, especially not when her

own supervisor was who'd sent the man she'd killed.

She hurried around the body and opened the passenger door to Bally's flitter. Slid in and across to the driver's seat. Saw that the flitter's keycard was slotted. She punched the engine up and on-line and pulled away from the curb. She looped around and headed out of town. As soon as she cleared the outbuildings, she engaged the lifters and put the little flitter into the air. She kept the altitude low and turned toward Beagle, shoved the throttle to full. The little flitter jumped as if kicked and streaked through the dark night.

She had to get back to town fast. Mintok could tap big resources, he was up to something deadly, and she needed to get somewhere she could figure it all out—

Silk! Jesus, he could be in trouble, too.

She reached for her com to call him.

TWENTY-FOUR

SILK WALKED THE humid night streets, feeling as he imagined a rabbit being hunted by dogs must feel. He couldn't go home—that would be the first place they would look; neither could he go to Zia's, his office, and now, not Taníto's. What was he going to do?

"Take it easy, don't get into a panic. You're alive, the bad guys are not doing so well, you're walking around free. It could be a lot worse."

A couple of men going the other way passed and stared at him. He kept his hand near the butt of his pistol until he realized they were staring because he'd been talking aloud.

Paranoia went right to the bone, didn't it?

Paranoia? They are *out to get you, fool, it isn't paranoia! It's survival!*

Okay, okay, what do you have to work with? You got the little computer from the dead guy's office; no help because you can't get into his files. You got his com, for whatever good that'll do—wait a second. Maybe that might be useful. You had something in mind when you decided to take it along, didn't you?

Yeah. If Red Bec made calls on that com, they could be in storage. Especially since he met an unexpected death and might not have had time to delete the most recent ones. But it might be a good idea to get off the street and find a cozy spot to play with the com. A temporary den was better than none.

There was an all-night pub a block or so ahead. Silk
went there.

Inside, he ordered a beer and moved to a booth out of
the glow of the stage. There were ten or twelve people
scattered around the inside of the pub, smoking or drinking. People who looked as if they didn't have anywhere
better to go. On the stage under pale blue lights, a naked
woman moved listlessly back and forth. She had a good
body but her dance was by the numbers, no passion, no
joy in it. After a moment, a well-built and well-hung
naked man joined her. The pair went through a halfhearted imitation of stand-up sex. Had to be imitation,
since the guy's interest was obviously more than a little
flaccid. As far as Silk could tell, none of the patrons was
paying the dancers much attention. Tough audience, the
vampire crowd.

He powered up Red's com. It was a standard hand-held
with a belt clip on the back. The tiny flatscreen lit up,
over the com's keypad, the liquid crystal colors dim
but viewable. He hit the recall-last-call key. A number
scrolled across the screen. Okay. Now, who did it belong
to? He tapped keys for the query. This could be just what
he needed.

And the winner is . . . ?

Nakahashi Enterprises.

Well, shit.

It wasn't such a major surprise, but it was a dead end.
Somebody connected with Zia's agency somehow was
causing all this grief. There had to be a way to run him
or her down. Maybe there were other numbers in the
memory . . .

Silk's own com vibrated silently on his belt, an incom-
ing call. Should he answer it? Couldn't they backwalk
a signal and trace it, if they wanted? Maybe it was the
bad guys, thinking he would be stupid enough to set up
a link. Then they'd swoop down on him. They could do
that on Earth; he and Zia had almost gotten caught that
way once when he made a call to his old buddy Xong.
Could be them.

Yeah. And it could be somebody trying to sell him miracle carpet cleaner or an encyclopedia, too; even at this hour, commerce never slept.

Or it could be Zia.

Silk pulled the com from his belt. Took a deep breath. If it were anybody but Zia he could cut the power and get the hell out of the pub, be five blocks away in a minute. They might get a general area during the two-second transmission, but he wasn't too worried. Yeah, they were dangerous but so far not that good, certainly not if a know-nothing like himself could stay away from them. Well. A know-nothing who had been painted with a thick coat of good luck, anyhow. Maybe it would weather a few more storms.

"Hello?"

"Silk?"

He let out his mostly held breath. "Zia. You okay?"

"Yeah, I'm fine. But we've got problems. Anything unusual happening to you?"

He laughed. "Me? No. I figured out who the guy on the scooter following me was and went to ask him a few questions. A private inquiry agent. Only thing was, when I found him, his throat had been cut and he was as dead as a plastic boot. Then I discovered that the woman I slept with that one time was a liar, so I poked around in my computer and guess what? *She* was an inquiry agent, too. So I went to her cube. Only I didn't get a chance to talk to her because a bunch of guys showed up and shot her to death. Then they chased me and I went to Taníto's but they somehow traced me and showed up there. Where they made the unfortunate mistake of drawing weapons in the school and Taníto shot *them*.

"Other than that, nothing unusual, no."

"Been busy, haven't you? Well, I shot somebody who attacked me on the train, developed telepathy, and almost got killed by another shooter when I locked up at a critical moment. I'd say we're having a pretty busy day. Where are you?"

"In a pub. Telepathy?"

"Tell you about it when I get there. Be another hour. I'll call back and get the location when I reach town. Watch yourself. We're in fairly deep trouble."

"Thanks for pointing that out. It never occurred to me."

Forty minutes later the com vibrated again.

"You're early," he said.

"Oh, were you expecting my call?" a man's voice said.

Silk reached for the power button to kill his signal. Before he could thumb it, the caller said, "If you want to keep Zia alive, I think you and I should talk, M. Silk."

"Who is this?"

"She didn't tell you about me? I'm Colburn."

Silk frowned. Colburn? The terran spy? What did he want? Did he have something to do with all this?

"There's a warehouse on Cue Street, at the corner of Loca. Meet me there in fifteen minutes."

Silk considered it. It was only a ten-minute walk from here, if he remembered right. He had his com. One place was as good as another, wasn't it? And if this spy was threatening Zia, maybe this was the right time to take care of this little problem. He could handle it. He'd done pretty good so far on his own, hadn't he? Luck or skill, it didn't matter as long as it worked, did it?

"Okay. Fifteen minutes."

He slid out of the booth. The naked heterosexual couple had been replaced by two busty women, one dark, one light, who pretended to take great pleasure in each other's nude bodies. At least it was easier to fake—a moan could be real but a limp rod was hard to hide.

Silk went to deal with the terran spy.

Colburn had augmented his armory with a dart stun pistol. If Zia's paramour wanted to play, he'd have to put him down without hurting him too bad. The idea was to demonstrate that he could kill Silk at any time but that he would not, if Zia would go along with his

contrived offer. He had to be believable but he also had to
demonstrate that the stick he had was sufficient to justify
his speaking softly. As in a game of *Go*, subtlety had its
place, but there were times when direct and brutal force
could be just as effective and a lot less complicated. The
boyfriend was not a player, he was a civilian. He might
be courageous, but he was dealing with a professional
and in the end, he—and thus Zia—would see the light.
Colburn was sure of it.

Zia flew in the commercial lanes now, so as not to
attract unwanted attention from some traffic cop. She
kept her airspeed just below the maximum allowed; the
windscreen was thick with smashed bugs. This late at
night, most of the traffic, such as it was, consisted of
vans and these were easy enough to whip around.

Mintok wouldn't be so easy to circumvent. There were
ways, of course; she'd have to stay alive long enough
to get to Mintok's supervisor, and Mintok was smart
enough to have begun covering his ass there: *I'm worried
that Zia's lost it,* something like that. *No, no, I'll handle
it, we don't want a public problem, I'll see if I can reason
with her . . .*

It wouldn't be easy, but if she could get to the Assistant
Ops Director, she could convince him that it was Mintok
who had the problem. She had an advantage now, didn't
she? She'd know what the AOD was thinking and she
could counterpunch in just the right place. If the AOD
had any doubts, Zia could exploit them to her advantage.
Why Mintok had done this was something she could
worry about later. Could be it something as simple as
her spurning him for Silk? Was he that screwed up? It
was possible, she supposed; men had killed other men
for less, but God, could Mintok have that big an ego? If
she got a chance to talk to him, she supposed she would
find out.

She wondered if this telepathic business was permanent. It could be really useful. And had it happened to
others who got the Treatment? Because it had to be a side

effect of all that chemical, hormonal, and viral tinkering, didn't it?

What she tried not to think about was the incident with Bally. It kept coming back, naturally. The instant when she'd frozen. For the first time in a long while, she'd truly been afraid of dying. Not just the usual reaction she'd learned how to use to her advantage, to spike her survival hormones and ratchet her operating systems up a couple of notches. No, this had been a deeper fear. She had something to lose now, something she'd never had before.

She might lose forever.

Somehow, she'd have to get past that. If she was going to stay in the biz, she couldn't do it afraid. Once doubt took hold, you were handicapped. She'd seen it happen to other agents, even those she thought were better than she was. They crossed a line, some stray ricochet chinked their intellectual armor, and that I'll-live-forever mindset stopped working. Once you knew you were going to die, really *knew* it, it began to happen. If you were lucky, you got out. Hung up your gun, bought a store or a farm with your retirement account, and settled down to watch the grass grow. Had coffee in the mornings with other retirees and bragged about the old times. If you were unlucky, you stayed on and tried to pretend it hadn't happened. You might fool the people around you, but you couldn't fool yourself, and sooner rather than later, you'd make a mistake. Usually a fatal mistake. Benoit had gone that way, so had Franklin. Stubens had survived his error but as a cripple. It had been a miracle the surgeons had pulled off that much.

The irony of it was, now Zia might well live forever—or long enough so the normal hundred-and-some would seem like dying in childhood. Knowing you were going to live for a long, long time was not the same as the communal denial of death most people bought into. Except that in this business, hesitate at the wrong second, and you could kiss all that extra kilometerage goodbye.

It was not a problem she'd ever thought about before and she didn't like having to think about it now, but there it was.

Okay. First things first. She had to keep herself and Silk intact until she could take out Mintok's troops and bypass him for help. After that, she could sort out all the other stuff. First you drive the wolves off, *then* you clear the forest.

TWENTY-FIVE _____

THE WAREHOUSE WAS a low and broad building, gray permaplex prefab. It had lights over the doors and a few shining through high and small windows from inside. Silk walked to the door and tried it. Unlocked. He opened the door and looked into the place. There were wide rows bounded by stacked plastic crates. A powerlift was parked nearby, and overhead cranes and lines crisscrossed the ceiling. He stepped inside, drew his pistol, and immediately ran straight to his right as fast as he could.

During one of his practice sessions he had heard two other shooters talking about a game they had played. You were given a low-powered laser pistol and a light-reactive vest and put into combat scenarios with other players. In one of the situations, you had to walk through a warehouse with half a dozen opponents who knew you were coming. The idea was to survive the test without getting tagged. You got points for each player you took out, but you lost big points when one of them got you. The two shooters had been laughing because one of the gamesters had opened the warehouse door and sprinted for the other side before his would-be assassins could get set. He hadn't tried to shoot any of them and thus got no points that way, but since he was the only one who survived without taking a hit, he won the game. That struck the two shooters as funny, but it made a lot of sense to Silk. Staying alive seemed preferable to taking three or four others with you when you went down.

He was wearing softsoled boots, his feet didn't make much noise, and he reasoned that anybody waiting for him to enter the building would assume he would move cautiously once he got inside. If they weren't looking right at the door when he came through it, maybe he could get clear and get behind them before they realized what he was up to. It was as good an idea as any. He still had a few minutes before Zia's call was due. Maybe he could have this all wrapped up by then.

He circled to his left and kept to the shadows of the crates as much as he could. He searched carefully for Colburn, gun held out in front of himself, ready to shoot. If he saw the man, he'd needle him, knock him out, and, while the guy was unconscious, tie him up and disarm him. When Colburn woke up, he would do so in a position of weakness, and Silk would have the advantage.

Moving carefully, Silk sought his prey.

Colburn frowned. He had left only one of the entrances unlocked, and he'd been hidden in a side aisle a dozen meters off the main corridor leading from the door. He heard the door open and he took a deep breath, waiting five seconds for Silk to look around, then jumped out into the main corridor to dart the man.

Where the hell was he?

Instead of going up the main corridor, he must have gone to the left or right. No matter. He would be creeping along, and Colburn could just pop out behind him and pot him that way.

He reached the intersection. Peeped out quickly and looked to the right. Not that way. Crossed the main corridor and moved to that corner, peered around it.

Not there, either.

Damn! This didn't make any sense. Silk shouldn't have gotten more than a few meters from the door—

"Don't move!" came the voice from behind him.

• • •

He came out behind the spy, who was looking around the corner near the door, his back to Silk. Gotcha! Silk lined his glowing dot sight up on the middle of the man's back and ordered him to hold still.

The man dropped and twisted.

Silk fired but he was high. He shifted his aim down at the spy, who was prone and rolling on the floor. He couldn't get lined up, the guy was moving so fast—

Silk heard the *twang* of the spy's gun and felt a jolt. Things went gray—

Silk awoke to find himself lying on a couch. A hotel room somewhere. What the hell had happened—?

Colburn sat in a chair two meters away, watching him.

Oh. Yeah. The warehouse. The spy. But he had screwed up. So much for his luck.

Silk sat up slowly. His head ached, and his entire body was sore. His mouth was gummy, and he felt parched. He rubbed at his eyes.

"Sorry about that," Colburn said. "I sympathize—I know the sensation. There is a tumbler of cold water on the table to your right."

Silk nodded. "Thanks." His com was gone, his gun, and he felt like shit.

He drank a little of the water.

"For an amateur, you're not bad," Colburn said. "You should have shot me in the back, though."

Silk managed a wry smile. "That would have been sporting, wouldn't it?"

Colburn shook his head sadly. "If I hadn't already known you were a terran American, that comment would have given it away."

Silk drank more of the water.

"You grew up watching entcom vids, didn't you? Saw a lot of westerns? And easterns? Cowboys and samurai?"

Silk blinked at him. The questions were rhetorical, for Colburn went on: "High noon kind of thing, right? The villain and the hero on the dusty street facing each other, hands held stiff over their low-slung holsters, ready to draw. The bad guy goes first, naturally, and that gives the hero leave to snatch his ivory-handled Colt six-shooter so fast it's a blur. Blam, blam—the bad guy's shot goes wide, and the good guy cancels the bad guy's license to breathe with a hip-shot to the heart from thirty meters."

"I've seen the vids," Silk said.

Colburn smiled. "And bought into the mythos, too." He came out of his chair in a smooth movement and walked toward the window to his right. He had turned his back, but the pistol snugged over his right hip would be in his hand a lot quicker than Silk could get to him— he didn't doubt that after their last encounter. He had no desire to repeat that scenario and add fifteen minutes of downtime and a fresher headache to his current misery.

Colburn said, "I understand your feeling. I once believed in all that entcom crap myself. Since then, I've become something of an authority on those days. The Japanese samurai and the American wild west. It never was like the entcoms showed it, you know."

He turned around and looked at Silk. "Those show-downs on the frontier main street were nothing but romantic, fictionalized versions of the earlier eighteenth-century duels of Europe and the eastern U.S. They never happened in the American west. Most of the gunfights of the day were in saloons or brothels or back alleys. Men carried their weapons in canvas-lined coat pockets or stuck into their belts or occasionally in holsters made of clingy, soft leather. It was the work of several seconds to get their guns out and on-line. Until the 1870s, the most common handguns used large charges of black powder, and after a shot or two, the air would be so thick with choking, smelly smoke you very likely couldn't see your target any longer. The sights on the guns were crude and not particularly well adjusted. Most shootings took place at very short range, and most were fueled by a loss of temper or chem, or both. The drugs of choice in those days were alcohol or patent medicines, which contained everything from cocaine to strychnine."

Silk was a captive audience. He wondered where Colburn was going with this.

"Here's a typical incident," Colburn continued. "It is the evening of 27 September 1869. The place is Hays City, Kansas, United States. A bunch of already drunk cowboys enter into a saloon and begin drinking large amounts of beer. During the evening, they drift in and out, mostly to the vacant lot next door where they can drink and urinate freely. Eventually the bartender starts to run out of glasses, as the drinkers return for more beer but without the containers. The tender asks the cowboys to bring the empties back, but they laugh and refuse. So the tender sends for the town policeman, who arrives and obligingly fetches a half dozen or so of the glasses and returns them to the bar. One of the cowboys, a local bad man known as Sam Strawhim, takes umbrage at the policeman's interference. He tells the policeman that he will, by God, throw the glasses into the lot if he so wishes. He further says he shall shoot anybody who tries to interfere with his fun. The policeman, one James Butler 'Wild Bill' Hickok, advises Strawhim that if he attempts such a thing, he himself will have to be carried out when he leaves. Strawhim grins and picks up one of the beer glasses. Whereupon Wild Bill draws his revolver and shoots Strawhim dead on the spot.

"At the inquest held the next morning, a verdict of justifiable homicide is quickly returned, exonerating the policeman.

"This same Wild Bill was himself shot in the back and killed while playing a game of cards in Deadwood, Kansas, United States, in 1876. The game was called poker and the cards he held have come to be called the 'Dead Man's Hand.'

"Hickok was considered one of the finer pistoleers of his time and he died young, not having reached his fortieth birthday."

"Fascinating lecture, but I'm not looking for a degree in history. What is your point?" Silk said.

Colburn grinned. "Hickok was the acme of the frontier good guy. Yet he had no compunction against killing a man who irritated him. A drunken cowboy picking up a beer glass is hardly cause for murder, is it? Not quite the dramatic face-off on main street. They were not all thugs, but hardly were they fair-minded heroes, M. Silk. It is quite likely that armed with your pistol in the manner in which you carry it and with no more skills than you currently possess, you could defeat in fair combat most of the gunmen of the old west. Except for a few you've never heard of. But *fair* combats were quite rare. In those days, if you had reason to fear a man might kill you, you either left the area or dispatched him quickly. With as little risk to yourself as possible."

He sighed and looked at Silk. "You didn't worry about what was 'fair,' you worried about your survival. In a 'fair' fight with you, face to face, I would win. I am a professional and should be considerably better than you in virtually any combatsit. You had the advantage on me in that warehouse. You *could* have taken me because I made an error, I underestimated your ability. You had me, but you made a worse error. Which is why you have a headache and an empty holster and I have the gun.

"This is not like stepping up to the line and loosing crossbow bolts at a target, M. Silk. Some of those cowboys could shoot their handguns well enough to hit you every time at a hundred yards—in a target competition. But those same cowboys would miss at close range when their lives were on the line. The game I play isn't sport, either."

"Fine. Fine. I get it. If you wanted me dead, I wouldn't be around now for your old west stories. What *do* you want, Colburn?"

"Why, I thought it was obvious. I want a little time with Zia. And lucky for you, she wants *you* alive."

TWENTY-SIX _____

WHEN SHE WAS ten minutes away from town, Zia put in a com to Silk.

He didn't answer.

The net informed her that the call could not be completed, as the callee was off-line or out of service range. Her belly went cold.

She left instructions for her com to repeat the page until a connection was made. Silk was a pain sometimes, but he was expecting her. While she could think of reasons he wasn't answering—his com could have a dead battery, he could be in a null spot, he'd put the unit down and gone to the fresher—what she believed was that he wasn't answering because he couldn't. That meant somebody had gotten to him, and it meant she was going to have to move fast to save him—if it wasn't already too late.

Which meant there wasn't time for a chain-of-command complaint. She would have to go straight to Mintok and make the complaint one he couldn't ignore.

At this hour of the morning, he would probably be in his own cube, if he hadn't picked up a lover and decided to stay at her place. Zia didn't think that likely—Mintok had always liked being in total control and with her, at least, had preferred his own lair for their sexual sessions. His computer had once contained her vox and print admit codes, and he could have changed them—certainly *should* have changed them—but Mintok was enough of

an egoist to think she'd come back to him someday.
Thought he was God's gift to women. She knew he
was responsible for the attacks, and she might even have
figured that out without the telepathic thing. The people
after her hadn't been seriously trying to kill her until it
got personal, although the others might have been making
more of an effort to take out Silk. Or not. Could the man
really be that simple? Did he think she would fall over on
her back and spread her legs if he had her lover deleted?
Sure, the jabs at her might have confused things for a
little while, but sooner or later she would have figured it
out. Apparently he didn't give her credit for much, given
the time they'd worked together. Or maybe he just didn't
care: Mintok wasn't that stupid, just vain.

She put the flitter into a lower speed corridor and
watched the lanelock grid light up. She could stay in
the air another five minutes, then go to ground mode for
the run to Mintok's cube. If this new mind-reading toy
kept working, she'd find out what she wanted to know
in a few seconds.

If Mintok had hurt Silk, he was a dead man.

"Don't misunderstand," Colburn said. "This isn't *personal*, it's business. Three months is how long it will
take for my biologists to download the entire complex
of the longevity treatment so that we can replicate it."
That might even be true; who could say? Surely it was
complex enough so it wasn't going to be like copying
an entgame infoball into one's personal comp.

Silk said, "You're crazy, you know that? Why the
hell should Zia agree to give you three seconds, much
less three months? All she has to do is make a call, and
the whole intelligence apparatus on this planet will fall
on you like the wrath of God."

"I suppose that's true. That might be difficult for even
me to overcome. Still, did you ever have an infestation
of ants, M. Silk?"

The man looked blank, and Colburn smiled and continued.

"If you step on the one you see, that doesn't eliminate the thousands of others running around, or the nest, now, does it?"

He saw that his point was quickly taken. He continued. "We are speaking here of a major slice of information, possibly the most important bit of business since the secret of the atomic bomb, or maybe the FTL pull. I know that breaking into the top-security complex to steal the records is almost impossible, but if I can collect someone who has undergone the treatment, I can work backward from there. It merely takes longer."

"Three months? I would think Earth's biomed genetic experts could do it a lot faster than that."

Colburn shrugged. "Well. Here is where we run into a slight problem. We are men of the galaxy, you and I, and both somewhat adept at stretching the truth, so I expect you should know it when you hear it."

Silk made a jack-off sign with one hand. "Skip the flattery."

Colburn smiled larger. He said, "If I were to take this extremely valuable secret back to Earth, what do you supposed my reward would be?"

"I have no idea. Two weeks in Rio?"

"Close enough. As a paid agent, I do well. And there would be a substantial bonus. But let's face it—nothing near what the secret to living five hundred or a thousand years is really worth."

He saw Silk process it. A big part of this sting had to rely on allowing the man to come to his own conclusion on his own, without too much prompting.

"I see. You don't plan to go back to Earth. You have another buyer lined up. Somebody with big stads. Maybe another planetary government."

Good. He was right on target. He could see what Zia saw in him. Rough and untrained, but the man had promise. Too bad.

Silk continued. "Somebody who's got good, but not the best, biodocs—that's why the three months. You want to take Zia to another planet, copy the biological info from her, and sell it. You're planning to double-cross your employers."

"Precisely put."

"And if we step on you, Earth sends somebody else. Zia has to sleep with one eye open for the rest of her life—or until they get the secret."

"Give the man another point for accuracy."

"If we agree, you leave Zia alone."

"Much more than that. I leave her alone but I also leave her very, very rich. The amount of money involved here is more than a king's ransom. Her share—and your share—could buy you both a lifetime of luxury."

"Yeah, only with E2 ops looking for us instead of Earth's."

"Well. With the exception of Zia herself, E2's agents aren't nearly as good as Earth's best, there aren't as many of them, and there's no reason at present they should be looking for either of you. A clever bit of deception could easily convince them that you and Zia Rélanj perished in an accident, an explosion or fire, say, a disaster that would leave no bodies to examine. By the time they learn otherwise—if they ever manage to do so—you could be half the galaxy away, with new faces, new IDs, new lives. While I'm sure New Earth's covert agency is every bit as vindictive as any other world's, they wouldn't have a clue about where to look for you. I'd see to it that you also had the longevity treatment, M. Silk. Fifty or a hundred years from now, all of it would be long forgotten."

Thus the cast. Now the fish had to bite and set the hook himself, but Colburn didn't see how it could fail. It was a once-in-a-lifetime offer; how could anybody with half a brain refuse? Zia had pretended to reject it out of hand and she hadn't told Silk of the particulars, that was easy enough to see, but she had been chewing on it, thinking about it, considering it. And now with her lover given the same package to hold, Colburn didn't think for a moment they would turn it down. The risk was minimal, the reward beyond great.

Silk sighed. "Just for the sake of argument and not agreeing to anything here, how would this work?"

Colburn kept his expression serious, but he wanted to laugh. *Got him.*

"I take Zia offworld secretly. We relocate to our destination, begin the process of copying the biologies. When sufficient time has passed, I provide you with transportation to join us. My, ah, patrons get the secret of the longevity treatment, you and I and Zia get our monies, and we go our separate ways. We all live happily ever after. Maybe literally. Nobody comes looking for you or Zia. Simple."

Colburn went to fix himself a drink from the room's cooler while he allowed Silk to think about the offer. Most of the mechanics of it were true, and that central beam should glow sufficiently bright through the darkness of the prevarications to be believable. The trick in successful lying was to grease it with plenty of truth.

Once in a sales psychology course, an instructor had taught Colburn that when pitching a couple, you should always try to do it with them together. One or the other would almost always always find an attractively crafted sales presentation more attractive and would then help you sell the other one. Failing a communal opportunity, pitching each member of the unit was the next best thing. The pitch could be shaded somewhat this way, so that each person heard something a little different. In this case, Silk and Zia cared for each other, and thus offering each of them the chance to protect the other was a big selling point. Don't do it for yourself—do it for him/her . . .

"What happens now?"

Colburn shrugged. "Up to you. In the drawer of that chest are your gun and com and other personal gear. You are free to go. You and Zia make your decision—take a day or two, if you like—and I'll be in contact. If you go for it, good. If not, well, no hard feelings. Nothing personal, just business."

"We could still drop the law on you."

"I don't believe you will. But if you do, I can beat them."

"You think you're that good?"

"I know I am."

Silk gathered his stuff and left the hotel. This wasn't what he'd expected, though he wasn't sure what he'd expected. Zia hadn't told him any of this. Well, at least not the details of the offer Colburn had made. To be rich, healthy, with Zia and hundreds of years ahead of them versus his second-class-citizen status on a world that hated his kind? What kind of choice was that?

He didn't trust this Colburn, but what he said made sense. If power corrupts, so does money, especially big money, and there was no doubt the amount of money involved here would be astronomical. Would he like to be sitting on an account packed with a couple of million stads, with a clean slate on a world where such a sum would buy respect and anything they wanted?

Stupid question.

Would Zia think it was worthwhile? This was her planet; maybe her loyalties went too deep. She hadn't told him the whole story about this, had she?

The money sounded good, as did the live-forever hormone treatment, but what Silk realized was that keeping Zia safe was more important. When it got right down to it, that was what counted. Given how he'd moved out, gotten away from her to find out what he felt about all this, it was a big realization.

Speaking of whom. She would be worried about him. It was almost dawn. His com had been turned off. He powered it up and called her.

Zia buttoned her com off so it wouldn't distract her. She checked the loads in her pistol and headed for the entrance to Mintok's building.

Getting into the building was easy enough. She had a wide-spectrum override card, and the door's electronic keeper rolled over when she ran the card through the scanner. If Mintok hadn't changed the codes, all she had to do would be thumb the plate and tell the door to open and she'd be in his cube. He could have the door rigged to warn him of any admits, but she'd have a few seconds, and that should be enough. In five seconds, she could be standing next to his bed with her gun plugged into his ear. He wouldn't even have to talk, all he'd have to do was to think. It was a little risky but simple.

She took the stairs to Mintok's level, the second, and strolled down the hallway as if she owned it, her pistol holstered and hidden under her shirt. She passed a man on his way out and nodded at him.

At Mintok's door, she paused. Took several deep breaths and looked both ways, then thumbed the admit plate. "Open the door," she said.

The locked *snicked* and rolled silently open.

Son-of-a-bitch.

Zia darted into the cube, ran straight for the open bedroom door, and slid to a stop next to the bed, gun pointed down. The room was dim; the face of an LED clock spilled a red glow on the pillow; from the fresher behind her, a sliver of light gleamed on the bedroom wall.

Empty. The bed was empty—!

She spun and dropped into a two-hand shooting crouch, facing the fresher. He must be on the bidet.

She took short, quick steps toward the fresher and shoved the hinged door wide with her left foot—

Nobody home.

She came up from the crouch, lowered the barrel of her pistol.

Where the hell was he?

There came a quiet hiss. Like somebody blowing air softly through pursed lips. For a second the sound didn't register. Then it did.

Gas!

Zia held her breath and ran toward the cube's entrance.

Too late. Halfway through the front room, she felt herself start to gray out, and the floor called to her. She went down . . .

TWENTY-SEVEN

SILK FROWNED. ZIA wasn't answering her com.

The sun was coming up, another hot day about to be spawned, and she should be in Beagle by now. He'd been unconscious the better part of an hour, and, added to his visit with Colburn, maybe ninety minutes had passed since she had been due to call. Where was she? Even if her transportation had broken down, she'd be able to contact him. That she wasn't on-line didn't feel good, not at all. Something was wrong.

What was he supposed to do about it?

He was tired, having been up all night save for his drugged nap, and what he wanted to do was find a soft spot and sleep for a week.

Something else bothered him as he walked along the morning street, watching the early carts roll past, the day workers going to their jobs, the night workers going home. They were oblivious to his drama, wending their way along on their bikes and trikes, worried about things he no longer had the luxury to worry about: kids, work, taxes. A recycle truck lumbered past like a hungry beast seeking its dawn meal of plastic and paper. If Colburn's offer was legit, then why all the thugs using Zia and himself for target practice? That didn't make any sense; all the spy had to do was lay it out, keep low until they made up their minds. He needed them alive—Zia alive, at least—then the last thing he wanted to do was risk anything happening to her. She was golden. And if Colburn had any sense, he'd realize that killing Silk would piss Zia off, maybe enough so it might skewer the deal if she had any mind to take it.

Well. It wasn't a logical universe, least not in the way that people treated each other. But Colburn struck Silk as a man who kept his knives sharp—killing either of them would be as dull as a drunk's locker-room stories. No, that would be criminally stupid, and it didn't play. This guy was too good to make that kind of error.

So. Somebody else was after them. Who? And why?

Silk looked for a taxi. Maybe there was a way to find out. If the bad guys were still out there looking for him, he knew where he was apt to find some of them.

He spotted a taxi and waved at it. The motorized three-seat yellow-orange trike with a cracked and peeling glasfiber body putt-putted to a stop. "Where to, pal?"

Silk gave the driver his home address. It was time for this rabbit to grow some teeth and find himself a dog to bite.

Zia came to retching. Fortunately she hadn't eaten anything recently, and the heaves were mostly sour-smelling gas and a little foul-tasting liquid. She spat, not caring where it landed.

"Well, well. Look who's awake."

Mintok.

She was on her belly, naked, lying on a bed. She rolled over. He leaned against a wall five meters away, a small pistol held loosely in one hand.

She spat again in his general direction. It didn't go far enough.

"This what you wanted? To knock me out and rape me?"

"One could argue the point about it being rape," Mintok said. "You wouldn't know I was doing it if you were unconscious, so you might or might not be willing." He grinned. "I stripped you to make sure you weren't hiding any weapons. I admit I searched very carefully, but that's all I did."

For now.

Zia kept her face calm. Her gift was still working. She could read him.

Later, I'll wet the old lance, believe that. Everywhere it'll fit.

She sat up on the bed. Her nudity didn't bother her, and if it gave her an edge, she'd use it. She crossed her legs, tailor-fashion. *Stare at that, bastard.*

He did.

He said, "I figured you'd show up at my place sooner or later."

He thought, *I had the fresher door rigged with thump-gas and you walked right into the trap, stupid twat. I'm surprised you made it into the living room before you went down.*

"You had the fresher door rigged with thump-gas," she said. "I should have known you weren't as stupid as I thought you were. You never intended for the clowns you sent to take me out, you just wanted to get my attention."

Smart girl. I knew you'd figure it out.

Zia shook her head. She wished she'd figured it out a little sooner.

"I'd have been real surprised if they'd tagged you," he said. "They weren't what you'd call first-water ops. And they had orders to play soft."

She picked up fast images of the players. Mercs, some private inquiry agents, a few freelance stringers. Nobody on the full-time Nessie payroll. A couple of them had ID saying so, but it wasn't company issue. Mintok had gotten it for them. Whatever game he was playing, it was his and not Nessie's.

"You got my attention." She reached over and scratched under her right breast. Watched him watch her nipple bob.

Great goddamned tits.

"Okay. Why?"

What poured out of his mind at that question did so in a fast jumble, like the spray of a powerful water hose. It splashed against her and she couldn't absorb it all:

Dropped me, me! *because of that fucking terran prick—so much money if the guy can be believed—going to fuck you until you can't walk—haven't heard back from the delete team on Silk yet—Red is out of it, Hildy's dead, they got her—that slick terran bastard op—but all that money, I can retire rich—you could have gone with me, I liked you a lot but now, now—I really liked you a lot—*

"You'll never know," he said.

Wrong. She could pick enough out of that blast to get most of it. That she would prefer another over him was a nasty puncture wound bleeding ego like a cut artery spewing blood.

And he had sold out. That bastard terran op she caught a flash of was Colburn, covering his bets with a backup plan. He wasn't trusting to her decision alone, and probably most of his operating information had come straight from Nessie. She would bet all of the money the terran spy was offering her plus the last demistad in her pocket against a bent nickel that Mintok had pulled most of this shit on his own, without consulting Colburn. He'd been offered a nice piece of the pie, but he wanted more.

She knew she should keep her mouth shut and let it play out. Mintok wanted her, wanted to believe that when push came to shove, or poke came to climax, he was better in bed than Silk. If she played that angle, if she told him in the heat of passion how much better he was, he would buy it. He wanted to believe it. And even though he would think she was lying to save herself, on some level he already believed it. He would keep her around as long as she was willing to play that game, to stroke his ego and his organ to full inflation. She knew men, she knew this man, *and* she could read his mind. He had a gun. She had a bigger weapon, if she used it right.

She should let it lie. But in that moment, she had to push it.

"You're working for Colburn," she said.

How the fuck does she know that? Did he tell her?

"He told me," she said. Might as well sow a few more
seeds of dissension. "And my guess is he also told you
that he wants me alive and healthy or you don't get the
rest of your money."

Bitch! Cunt!

He wanted to fall on her, rape her, strangle her and
burn her corpse; she could feel it like heat from a sudden
flare. But it was a measure of how good he was at the
lying game that it barely showed.

He said, "Well, it's a relative term, isn't it? You could
have a broken arm or a few bruises and still be healthy.
You don't need all your teeth to be healthy."

She might be able to take him in hand-to-hand, but
he had that gun. He could dart her and do whatever he
wanted to her while she was out. She had to negate the
weapon.

She uncrossed her legs and spread her knees wide,
her heels almost on the opposite sides of the bed. Her
labia and downy blonde pubis were open to his view.
"You don't really want to beat me up, do you, Tave?
Isn't there something else you would rather do?"

It was a rhetorical question. She didn't need her telepathic advantage to know the answer.

Colburn came out of his light sleep instantly and
answered the com. It was the broker/thief he thought
of as the Night Crawler.

"You know who this is?"

"Yes."

"I have located the . . . item we discussed. It will be
available in another day."

"Very good. Where shall we meet to arrange payment
and details of the transfer?"

"Same as before. Same time and place."

"Good. I'll see you then."

Colburn shut the com off and lay back on the bed.
Things were coming along as planned. After the transaction, it would be time to begin tidying up loose ends. The

thief would have to disappear, of course. As would the contact inside New Earth Security, Mintok. The agents at the The Scat's front company who'd met him would be in a terrible industrial accident. The person who had sold him the explosives and timers he would use to delete those agents, along with the pesky lover Silk, well, those arms dealers would move to a suite in Davy Jones's locker for a long watery sleep. Or maybe he'd use the big cats in the local zoo. He'd disposed of a body or two that way. A pair of hungry ligers or ündersloongi could really mess up a forensic pathologist looking for cause of death . . .

Sleep. The little details would be easy enough to accomplish if a player was alert, but a tired man could screw up even simple tasks. The endgame approached, and a mistake could always be fatal. He'd stayed alive this long by being careful.

With a skill born of long practice, Colburn put himself back to sleep.

Silk had one slim advantage, or so he thought. He knew somebody would be waiting for him, and they didn't know for sure when or if he was coming home.

He had the taxi drop him three blocks from his cube, and he slowly walked toward his building. Either he was going to get killed or somebody was going to tell him what the hell was going on. In a way, it was almost pleasant to have it reduced to that essential choice. Nothing complicated, either/or.

He spotted the man seated in the delivery van. The guy was parked a hundred meters south of Silk's building. He sat at the van's controls and smoked a flickstick while he pretended to read a hardcopy newspaper. But he wasn't very good, and it was obvious he was watching the entrance. He was a smallish man, dark hair and dark skin, with a white tattoo on his bare forearm.

Silk circled to the passenger side of the van. The man appeared to be alone in the vehicle. There could be somebody in the back. And he didn't have any idea how many others might be sprinkled around the building, or inside his cube itself, waiting. They could be linked on an open com, checking on each other, but Silk reasoned that it was likely that nobody was watching Smoky here, not if they were looking for other prey.

Speed was probably more important than finesse. He knew he wasn't very good at this game but given his experiences thus far, except for Zia and Colburn, neither was anybody else. His experiences on Earth didn't make him think otherwise, except for that one big guy who tracked them to the Amazon. And the people chasing them here hadn't done all that well, given that Silk didn't know squat and he'd managed to stay out of their grasp. Sure, some of it was luck, his was good, theirs bad, but that could only take you so far.

Enough stalling. Do it.

Already it was warm and rising rapidly to hot; the van was parked in the open. The sun had residual help from the muggy night; the smoker had the van's front windows open to get what breeze there was.

Silk approached the van obliquely, keeping out of the mirrors as best he could. He reached the passenger side, tugged at the latch. The door glided back. Luck was not to be counted on, but it was nice to have.

Smoky had time to look around in puzzlement before Silk pulled his pistol and slid onto the seat.

"Good morning. Start it up and let's take a ride. Keep your hands where I can see them or I'll shoot you." He smiled, like a man having a very good time.

Smoky blinked.

Silk waved the pistol. "Any time now."

Smoky started to reach for his safety harness.

"Never mind that. Go."

"My restraints—".

"You won't need them if you drive carefully."

One-handed, Silk buckled his own harness. It was a little awkward sitting sideways but he managed it. Smoky watched him, frowning.

"If you have a sudden urge to stomp on the brake or smash into a light pole or something, you're the only one kissing the windscreen. If I don't like the way you drive, I shoot you."

"Might kill us both," Smoky ventured.

"I'm living on borrowed time, pal. What the hell. *You* ready to die?"

He could almost see Smoky's mouth go dry. He took a big drag on the flickstick, then launched it through his window onto the street. "Why me?" Smoke clouded his face. Silk noted that the white tattoo on his forearm was of a naked man with a big erection.

"Because you were here. You and I are going to go somewhere quiet, and you are going to tell me all your secrets."

"I don't know anything!"

"You know who I am and you know who told you to sit here to watch for me. That'll do for a start."

"Soon as I move the van, people will notice," he tried. "They'll get you."

"So they get me. Ask me if I care. You're going to tell me a story, friend, and if I don't like it, guess who will be holding Hell's Gate open for me when I arrive?"

Silk must have sounded pretty desperate.

Smoky cranked the van's engine and pulled away from the curb. He did so very carefully.

TWENTY-EIGHT

MINTOK PUMPED AWAY, driving himself into her as hard as he could. Zia urged him on, holding his ass with both hands, moaning, calling his name out, acting as if it were the best sex she'd ever had. He still held the gun, the barrel pressed against her temple, but he was moving faster, getting near his climax. He started to quiver, he thrust quicker, harder—

He came. He arched his back, lifted his head—

The gun sagged away from her head. He would never be more vulnerable.

Zia pulled her left hand free and stabbed his eyes with her spread fingertips, felt his right eye give, missed the left by a hair—

He screamed, reached for his eyes—

She twisted to her left and shoved, both hands against his chest. He was a big man but he was hurt and already recoiling. He rolled off her, still climaxing, a jet of milky white spurting into the air between them, then slammed into the wall next to the bed. He still had the gun but she was focused on it and she grabbed his hand and jerked, turned it sharply, heard a bone in his hand or wrist *crack!* wetly. Fortunately he didn't have a finger on the trigger, and she pulled the gun loose. Fumbled and almost lost it as he screamed and blindly reached for her, caught her neck in both hands and squeezed—

Even with the broken bone, his grip was powerful. A few seconds and she'd be choked unconscious—

224

But she had the gun and she turned it, jammed it into his belly and pulled the trigger, once, twice, three, four—!

He let go and fell away from her. Leaned back against the wall in a sitting position, then kind of oozed down to lie on his side. The little holes in his belly welled and bled, but not much.

Jesus.

She leaned back against the bed, suddenly too tired to move. He was only centimeters away, his legs still touched hers, but it took more energy than she had to kick herself free. He wasn't a threat any more. With four stun rounds at contact range, he might be in a coma for hours, maybe all day—

He convulsed suddenly. Moaned. Stopped breathing. What—?

She touched his neck, pressed her fingertips against the carotid. No pulse.

Christ, he must have had a reaction to the chem. It happened. She looked at him. She could call for help. A good medical team might be able to bring him back, if they could get started soon enough. Call an ambulance, get him on life support, he might make it. She stood. Started for where his com lay on the dresser. But as she stumbled the few steps, it suddenly occurred to her to check the loads in the pistol. The medics would want to know that. She pressed the magazine release.

Looked at the three rounds remaining.

Saw the black bands on them.

She stopped and stared back at the corpse. It wasn't some allergic reaction to the stun chem. It was poison. He had been carrying death loads, and he meant to shoot her with them once he was done with her.

They might still bring Mintok back. There'd be some brain damage, they'd probably have to replace major organs—heart, liver, kidneys, maybe lungs—but even a poisoned needle could be beaten, were the doctors fast and sharp enough and did they get to the victim early in the golden hour.

Fuck that.

He was going to kill her? And Silk? Let him stay dead. He deserved it, and she wouldn't have to spend the rest of her life looking over her shoulder for him. He brought it on himself.

She went to the room's fresher, put the gun on the counter next to the shower, and turned the water on. When it ran as hot as she could stand, she stepped inside. This was probably one of Nessie's saferooms, and if Mintok had brought her here, it was because he didn't expect anybody to bother them while he tortured her.

She sprayed herself with the soap cycle, lathered as best she could under the hard water, then rinsed. She repeated the cycle twice. It was time to get out of this business. She didn't have the stomach for it anymore. Once, she could have screwed a room full of yabbos like Mintok, then shot them all as they lay in satisfied stupors, done it without the smallest qualm. Now—?

Now she felt ill, and it wasn't just the aftereffects of the knockout gas she'd inhaled. More, she still didn't feel clean as she stepped out of the stall and activated the dryer. This was no way for a grown woman to spend her days.

Yeah, she didn't know how to do anything else; her last job before joining the agency had been as a teenager working in the tiny Jacktown library. But what was the point of living for hundreds of years if you had to do work like this? A few months ago, the thought would never have occurred to her. Now, it loomed large enough to blot out the years she'd spent as an op darker than a tropical storm blocking the sun.

She fluffed her hair under the blower, looked at herself in the mirror inset into the wall. Probably one-way glass, only Mintok wouldn't have a watcher posted behind it this time.

Silk was willing to work and let her idle, if that was what she wanted; at least he'd said so before he moved out. But she didn't need to rely on that. She might not have any skills other than those of a spy who used sex to pry information from foolish men, but she did have something else she could sell. Something very valuable. Something the terran operative had already made an offer on. And she had certainly paid enough for it.

Dry now, she went to find her clothes and her com. She had to find Silk. Mintok didn't have him and, according to his thoughts, had not been able to delete him, either. Silk was still alive, and he and she had some talking to do.

Prodded with a pistol, the van driver gave his name as Benny, and while Silk didn't believe him, it was as good a name as any. He directed Benny to an industrial area, had him park the van behind a big recycling bin half full of scrap plastic.

"Now, Benny, let's talk. I could describe all the horrible things I can and will do to you, and you can bluster and say you don't know anything, but let's cut to the end. You tell me who sent you and where I can find them, and you get to live. Don't, and you don't. Is that clear enough for you? Any part of it you don't understand?"

Benny put one hand to his mouth and rubbed. His eyes were wide, and Silk could almost hear his heart thumping rapidly in fear. Could he dart this guy, then cut his throat or bash him with something and kill him, just like that? Could he coldly murder the man?

Well, no.

If Benny were to jump out of an alley with a knife and he had time, Silk could certainly shoot him, and if the gun he happened to have was lethal instead of a stunner, yeah, he could live with that. Self-defense. And even when he was mostly nonviolent back on Earth, he could have blasted the man who killed Mac without any hesitation and felt righteous about it. But Benny here was a small fish, a thuglet; he probably deserved some locktime for assorted petty crimes, but not death. Silk had come a long way from the days when watching a violent entcom made him feel sick, but he had not come so far as to be an executioner.

But Benny didn't know that.

"It's all the same to me, Benny. You live, you die, I don't care. People have been following me, shooting at me, and I might not live to see the next sunset. I've got nothing to lose by deleting you; what else can they do to me? Kill me twice?" He grinned and raised the pistol so it pointed right at Benny's left eye.

"Mintok," Benny said. "Mintok is in charge of the operation!"

Zia's boss. They'd met during his debriefing, and the big man had hated Silk on sight, made no bones about it. That explained the agency registration and Nessie security stuff that kept coming up. But—why?

It wasn't likely Benny here would have that part, so he didn't bother to ask.

"Where is he?"

"I don't know."

"How were you supposed to tell him you'd gotten me?"

"I—uh, I got a com number."

"Give it to me."

Benny did.

"And this is all you know?"

"I swear!"

Silk nodded. Then he shot Benny in the chest.

Benny lurched forward, surprised. He slumped.

Silk dragged the unconscious man from the van and managed to heave him into the recycling bin. He saw that the top hinged down and there was a lock on it, so once Benny was inside, he closed the lid and secured it. Anybody who might dump something on the sleeping man would have to unlock the lid first, and they might be curious enough as to why it had been locked to spot old Benny. And if he woke up before anybody came out to dump their trash, then he wouldn't be running to a com to call and warn Mintok. That should give Silk enough time.

He started the van and pulled out of the alley. As he drove, he used the van's com to connect to the number

Benny had given him. He would talk to Mintok, convince the man to meet him. Convince him to leave him and Zia alone. Somehow.

As he waited for the connection, he felt around under the seat until he found Benny's weapon. It was a needler, similar to his own. Good to know he hadn't misjudged the man. But when he popped the magazine to check the loads, the black band around the top round of the caseless said otherwise. Benny's pistol carried poisoned needles.

Damn. These guys were playing for keeps.

"Yeah?" came a female voice from the com.

"Zia?"

"Silk! Where the hell are you?"

What was Zia doing with Mintok's com?

For a moment Silk swam in a hot sea of paranoia, chased by monster sharks hungry for his blood. Could Zia and Mintok be in this together?

"Silk, Jesus, I've been so worried about you! Are you okay?"

He blew out a sigh. If Zia wanted him dead, she could have done it a thousand times, starting back on Earth when he realized he would rather let her shoot him than hurt her. The sea evaporated, the sharks flopped helplessly on the dry bottom. If she was on the other side and against him, fuck it, he didn't want to play any more. He said, "Well, I've been having a fine old time. I've got a van. Where can I pick you up?"

She told him.

"What about Mintok?"

"Not a problem any more."

"I'm on my way."

He hurried to find the woman he loved.

TWENTY-NINE _____

COLBURN AWOKE AT noon, refreshed and alert. He had
a few chores to do before he met the Night Crawler to
collect his ship. A shower first, then lunch, and he would
be off to take care of business.

Zia was never so glad to see anybody as she was to see
Silk in that beat-up van waiting at the curb. She hurried
toward him, and she had time for a moment of wonder:
Would her mind-reading ability work on Silk? And if it
did—did she really *want* it to work? Maybe it was better
if she didn't know how he really felt. If she didn't have
access to his innermost thoughts and feelings.

What if she didn't like what she saw there?

But as she reached the van's door and he slid it open
for her, his emotions enveloped her like a pair of gently
cupped hands holding a flower: Whatever else he was,
however else he felt, the first thing from his mind to
touch her was relief—and love. And the reflected image
she saw of herself in his thoughts staggered her. Nobody
was that gorgeous; no human woman could possibly be
that breathtaking. This was not the woman she saw in
her mirror.

Did Silk really see her as a goddess who practically
glowed even in the bright sunshine? Good Lord. If you
could bottle that, you could put the best plastic surgeon
who ever lived out of business overnight.

Then she was in the van and he hugged her. She thought the intensity of his emotion might burn her, it was so hot. After a few cycles of the universe dying and being reborn, he pulled away from her—not too far—and tried to talk. "Listen, I'm a stupid fool for leaving you, I—"

She put two fingers on his lips. "Shush. You don't need to say it. I know."

Tears ran down his face. If only he could know her as she in that moment knew him. Truly feel what he felt.

Maybe, if things worked out, he could.

Something was different about her, Silk felt; something had changed. For the better, too, because he had to drive one-handed; she wouldn't let go of his other hand, and she beamed at him the way a mother beams at the child she loves.

Well. He could drive one-handed. He could wade across a lake of fire, leap mountains, fight a legion, if that's what she wanted.

She smiled at him. "Where are we going?"

"I don't know about you, but I'm exhausted," he said. "I have to get some rest. We'll find a place where we'll be safe, and sleep for a few hours. After that, we'll figure something out."

"Okay."

He blinked and glanced at her, then back at the road. "Okay? All right," he said, "who are you and what have you done with the real Zia?" He smiled. *She's letting me decide what to do? What's going on?*

She said, "Yeah, you can decide what we need to do. I'm tired of this game, and from what I can see, you're getting into it. Despite all the crap, you've been having fun, haven't you?"

"How did you guess?"

She returned his smile, squeezed his hand. "You wouldn't believe me." There was a short pause. "You ever read *Macbeth*?"

"I saw a production of it when I was in school. Been fifteen years or so; I don't remember much of it. Murder and hand-washing come to mind."

"Well, you and I have done the Macbethian role reversal, Silk. I'm up to here with the spy business and want out. You've been doing pretty well at it and are wondering if you might not be good at it with a little more training."

"Jesus, are you reading my mind?"

She laughed. "Took you less time to realize that than I did."

He stared at her, puzzled.

"Let's go take a nap. I'll tell you about my day—then I'll tell you about yours."

Colburn tried to contact Mintok but was unsuccessful. Supposedly the number he had was a secured line directly to the man's personal unit, but if so, he wasn't answering it. He frowned. The Nessie op had to be eliminated; of all the people on E2, he was the most dangerous to Colburn's future plans, and there was no way he could leave the planet with Mintok walking around. Sooner or later Silverman would send somebody to hunt for him, and when the hunters got here, Colburn didn't want them to find any kind of trail. A loose cannon with the fuse burning was hardly a clever thing to leave careening around behind one's back.

Well. He had time yet. There were other details to arrange. A surprise for the Night Crawler. The man surely knew about spookeyes and boats, not to mention aircraft that operated no louder than a whisper, and still he trusted the darkness and remoteness of the dock to protect him. Probably didn't think he was worth the trouble, but he was wrong about that, too. Colburn didn't even need any of the scopes or craft to do it, precisely because the Night Crawler was so predictable. He would bring help, of course, and maybe he had in mind taking the money and keeping his ship, but that kind of treachery was to be expected.

Meanwhile, the contacts at the pharmaceutical company were also walking dead and didn't know it. There were only three of them, and each had absorbed a slow-acting contact poison when they'd recently shaken his hand, from the carefully hidden clearstik patch on his palm. The amount was small and not enough to be fatal yet, but all three men would be feeling somewhat under the weather by now. Thus they would hurry to examine the bottled water in their office when they got an anonymous tip that the liquid had been spiked. Removal of the water's filter cartridge would be enough to cause a small explosion—well, small by military standards, perhaps, but certainly large enough to flatten a goodly portion of the building around it. If one or the other of them happened to be late to the party, well, the poison would eventually finish its job. It was always good to have a backup plan running in such matters.

As for Silk, well, a timer coupled with a motion sensor would do nicely for another small bomb. A few days after Colburn and Zia left for their destination, the timer would arm the explosive device hidden in an air vent or under a bed or a couch, and the first time Silk walked past it . . .

All the loose ends would be tied into neat knots, he would be away with his prize, and nobody from Earth or E2 would be able to tail him. Even if they could track every ship that landed on every planet for the next few weeks—a task currently impossible—it would do them no good, because wherever he landed his transport wouldn't be where he planned to end up. The best hound couldn't find a rabbit who left no tracks, who had no scent, who could turn virtually invisible or even into something else.

There were chemicals he could and would use to make Zia somewhat more pliable, until she got used to the idea of being with him on a permanent basis. She was a realist, he was sure, a hard and sharp-edged woman who would see that her best interests lay with Colburn, at least for the near future. And he was sure that once she got to know him, she would eventually come to like him. He didn't expect her to love him, wasn't sure that such a thing really existed, save in fantasy stories. And if it did, it was unnecessary in any event. As long as she did what he wanted, served him mentally and physically, what else mattered? He could mold her into exactly what he wanted.

End game, and time to make another few moves. First, king takes a couple of pawns, then a knight, a bishop, and finally, the queen.

When Silk awoke in the hotel room, Zia was still asleep next to him. They had both been exhausted, too much so to make love, but they had slept entwined together. Two or three times he'd floated up from sleep enough to stroke her arm or press against her hip and been comforted enough by her presence to drift back into slumber. They might be in a world of trouble, but it was okay because they were together now.

He was still a little tired, he was hungry, and he needed to go pee, but he kept still so as not to wake her. Let her sleep as long as she needed to.

When they'd met on Earth, he'd been a mental wreck. Mac had just been killed, his safe and secure future shattered, and he hadn't yet realized what a self-centered twerp he'd been. Yes, he and Mac had been contracted; yes, he loved her, or had thought so, but what they'd had more than anything had been a marriage of convenience. They'd both been ambitious, concerned more about their own careers than anything else. Her talking about her job bored him; him talking about his put her to sleep. They'd had good sex—he'd thought it was great until he met Zia—and they cared for each other, at least in the sense that they lived together without major discord. Of course, they'd never had any real stresses to deal with: They both held good jobs, were well paid, and didn't have children, obnoxious relatives or bad debts to intrude on their island paradise. They had been sophisticated, or he'd thought so, attractive, unflappable. Lying here, his groin pressed against Zia's warm backside, he remembered a boxcar crash he'd spun a few days before Mac had died. Odd that should come up now. A malfunction had sent the shuttle tumbling into an uncontrolled entry that had cooked four hundred and some-odd passengers and crew before dumping the crisped ship and well-done corpses into the Pacific off the Big Island. He remembered how blasé he had been about it, how he'd joked about feeding the fish expensive *ausvelters* when he'd fired the spin to Bryce Xong, his old buddy in the newsnet. Hey, shit happens, tough. That a neighborhood's worth of people—living, breathing humans with families, hopes and dreams—had died was less important to him than in so doing they'd made him work an extra twenty minutes on his day off.

Jesus. Had he really been such an asshole?

Yep.

Was he any better than that now?

He hoped so. He hoped that by finding out what it meant to love somebody, to want their love in return, to be willing to give up something of himself for another meant that he wasn't just another self-centered idiot who didn't give a damn about the rest of the universe as long as he got his.

He'd changed. Even from when he'd moved out, it had been his ego that did it, his insecurity. Even then, he'd known it wasn't Zia. Now, whatever it took, he wasn't going to let her get away from him, not even if he had to sell fruit on a sidewalk or live on the damned dole. Whatever he had to do, she was worth it.

She turned over and smiled at him. "Thank you," she said.

He returned the grin. "For what?"

"Wanting me enough to sell fruit on the sidewalk or live on the goddamned dole to keep me. I love you, too."

Holy shit! How could she know—?

"I can read your mind, Silk."

He forgot about being tired and hungry and having to go pee as she told him the story.

• • •

He took it well, Zia thought, as she finished the tale of her recent adventures. She felt him believe it.

Enough so he spun her an erotic picture and she knew for the first time what a man who loved a woman felt for her sexually.

They both hurried to the fresher and when they were done, they ran back to the bed, fell on it, and made love. Before her brain shut down and she lost herself to the passion, Zia knew a wonderful blend of feelings she'd wondered about for a long time. So that's what it's like for a man. Simple, but very powerful. No wonder they liked it so much.

Afterward:

"Is it going to bother you that I can tell what you're thinking?"

He shook his head. "I dunno. Maybe sometimes. I can only control what I do, not what I think. What happens if I look at another woman walking by on the street and have erotic thoughts?"

"I'll probably kick you in the balls."

They both laughed,

"You want to see if you can block me out?"

"What, a mind-shield? How?"

"I don't know. Maybe one of Taníto's meditation exercises?"

"Okay." He closed his eyes and concentrated.

I am a point in the universe, still, alone—God, she looks good after we've just fucked, oops!—my being is calm, I am part of the flow—I want to nibble on her, Jesus! I can't fucking concentrate with her lying here smelling like pussy, come here!

They giggled and rolled together, and she wrapped her legs around his hips and that was the end of the shield experiment.

Later, he asked the question she'd been wondering about.

"If this is a side effect of the Treatment, have any of the others who've undergone it developed this ability?"

"I don't know. But I think we should find out."

"Yeah. Even if only one out of a hundred who gets the Treatment can live to be a thousand *and* read minds, we're in for a big shakeup."

Bigger than fire, the wheel, atomic power, spaceflight. Those were just tools, but this, this could change humanity forever. Talking about the emergence of fucking Homo superior *here, aren't we? A dozen people armed with longevity and telepathy and a like mind-set could take over the galaxy. Can kiss the job of spindoc goodbye. What would it be like to live in a world where nobody could lie to anyone? Are we ready for that?*

Zia kissed the back of his hand, pressed it against her cheek. "Ready or not, it doesn't look like there's a choice, does it?"

He nodded. And he was cynical enough to believe that if any of the current planetary governments found out about this, about Zia and the possibility there might be others like her, then they would do whatever it took to control them. Or, failing that, stop them. And if that included killing everybody they couldn't control, he didn't doubt they'd hesitate for a second.

"We have to be careful," he said.

"Very," she said.

THIRTY

"WHAT TIME IS it?" Zia asked. The room's single high window let in darkness mixed with street light.

Silk glanced at his chronometer where it lay on the bedside table. "Almost 2100," he said.

"God, we've slept and screwed away the whole day and half the night. I don't suppose this place has food service?"

"I doubt it. We picked it because it was a hole in the wall and out of the way. We'll have to go out."

"Yeah. We might as well get to it."

"You still want to try to sneak into the biomed center? I dunno how smart that is."

"It's the fastest way to figure out what we need to know. We don't need to fugue the records or rascal a computer, all we need is a medic involved in the program. What they know, I'll know."

"Against the risk involved, I don't see what good that does us."

"If I'm the only one this has happened to, it makes a big difference. I could be a fluke, and if they don't know about me, it makes it easier for us to run. If there are others, somebody might be watching us a lot closer."

"Yeah, well, they aren't too good if they don't know where we are now."

"Maybe they do know, Silk. Maybe we're carrying some tiny 'caster that tells them exactly where we are.

Earth doesn't have a lock on that kind of technology."

They examined each other as they showered, but found no unusual lumps or bumps. Zia wasn't convinced that meant anything for sure. As much stuff as they had pumped into her, a bioelectric tracker could be hidden deep enough inside her not to show.

"Going to the center would also let us know that," she said. "If I run into one of the medics on the program and they know about it—"

"You'll know," he finished. "I guess. What happened to letting me decide what to do?"

She grinned. "I let you pick this place, didn't I?"

He had to grin and shake his head. He'd gotten better, but she was still better at this biz than he was, and he knew *she* knew *he* knew it.

"Thank you, my darling. Let's do it."

With food and rest and a certain amount of her other tensions relieved, Zia felt considerably better. As she and Silk approached the entrance to the medical center, she hoped her new trick would be enough to get them past the guards. She didn't know if Mintok's body had been found yet. If it had, security might have been tightened all over the city.

She figured they had a chance because, she knew there were always contingencies in the organization in which she worked and likely there would be in this kind of setup, too. In theory, you were supposed to have the proper ID, there was a procedure the guards were locked into, and nobody could scam their way past the safeties. But those safeties hadn't been installed to work against a mind-reader.

A different pair of guards than she'd seen before sat inside the biomed center's entrance, both armed with high-capacity hardslug handguns. One was a short, squat woman with a buzz cut that made her look almost bald. The other was a bodybuilder whose uniform was fighting hard—and losing—to keep his massive muscles in check.

In theory, since she was a patient, they ought to let her into the building. Allowing Silk in was something else, but she had an idea that might work. If not, he could stay outside with the van, it wasn't the end of the world, even though he was adamant that he go with her. He wanted to protect her, and she couldn't fault him because she knew he really meant it. The man loved her. She liked that.

"Evening," she said. "I'm Zia Rélanj. I'm having a little problem, and I need to see the doctor." She put a quaver into her voice and leaned heavily on Silk, who supported her with an arm around her shoulders, as if she were too weak to stand alone.

They checked her name on the computer. "Okay, you can come in. Who is this?"

They nodded at Silk.

"He's my contracted."

"If he's not on the list, he don't come in."

"Listen," Silk said, "something has gone wrong, she can hardly stay on her feet. Let me help her inside."

The two guards glanced at each other. Zia reached for their thoughts.

From the bodybuilder, remembering his instructions about medical emergencies: *Anybody on the list wants in 'cause of a prob, don't stand around with your finger in your butt, get 'em inside, fast.*

From Buzz-cut: *The boyfriend is either on the list or he's got the security password sequence, or else he waits outside.*

Zia kept her face as expressionless as she could. To Silk, she said loud enough for them to hear, "Okay, you'll have to break cover. Tell them the first password, honey."

Silk blinked at her. She didn't look at the guards, but she listened.

The bodybuilder: *The first codeword for today is "rooster." Stupid fucking shit, if you ask me. Then I say "henhouse," then they're supposed to say "fox," then I say . . . what? I forgot the fucking response . . .*

With her head turned so they couldn't see her lips, she whispered, "Rooster," to Silk.

He looked at the guard. "Rooster."

The bodybuilder said, "Henhouse."

Buzz-cut thought: *"Fox," then "weasel," then "egg."* She glanced at the bodybuilder. He looked back at her, shrugged almost imperceptibly.

"Fox," Zia whispered, "then he says 'weasel,' then you say 'egg,' but he doesn't remember it."

Silk grinned. "Fox." He waited two seconds, then said, "What's the matter, forget the damned response? Hey, I know how it is, I think all this cloak-and-dagger junk is a pain in the butt myself. But let's cut to the chase— you say 'weasel' and I say 'egg.' You want to open the fucking door before she collapses?"

Buzz-cut hit the control button, and the door opened.

"Is Dr. Marad in?" Zia asked.

"Yeah, she's working middle shifts this week."

"Tell her I'm on my way up." Zia tendered her ID, and they checked it. They didn't ask Silk for his.

"I'll call an orderly—"

"It's okay, my contracted will help me. He's cleared to be here."

Yeah, that's right, if he knows the codes better than Bilroy here does, he's probably a major player in Security even though I ain't seen him before.

"I'll get the elevator," Buzz-cut said.

The guard on the elevator didn't have a problem with them, and the guards on the fourth floor had been called by the pair on the ground and warned to look sharp, that a patient and her uplevel boyfriend were on the way up. Zia read that, along with the secondary security codes from them, gave them to Silk, and they were admitted quickly.

Marad was waiting for them in her office. She raised an eyebrow at Silk, but Zia didn't let her wonder too long. "I have a big medical problem, Dr. Marad. I'm having—ah, well—these strange hallucinations."

Marad thought: *Ah, another mind reader.*

Zia smiled and knew that the woman knew Zia had "heard" her.

She pulled her pistol. "Please keep your hands where I can see them, Doctor. I would like to keep this conversation private, please."

Marad smiled, unafraid, a saintly visage. "The gun isn't necessary."

Zia saw that was the truth, and she reholstered her weapon.

"Let's talk, shall we?" she said.

"Hardly matters if I say anything, does it?"

"True. How many of us are there? Who've had the Treatment?"

One hundred and forty-seven patients, top-level execs or governmental agency heads or rich or all three, except for you and twelve medics who helped develop it.

Zia shook her head. Only a relative handful. She looked at Silk, then realized he didn't know what she'd just picked up. "Say it aloud, please, Dr. Marad."

The doctor did so.

"Is that all?" Silk said.

"It's a big carrot," Zia said.

"How many have developed my particular side effect?"

"I don't know for certain," Marad said. "Twenty-two people have reported 'hallucinations.' Fifteen percent, so far. A few of them have had sufficient manifestations to understand and recognize what has happened."

"And where are these twenty-two people? Not in custody?"

Marad raised her eyebrows. "The richest, most powerful people on the planet?"

"And none of the other patients have the effect?"

"None who will admit it."

Zia saw where that went. Say you were an intelligent, wealthy, politically powerful senator. Say you suddenly discovered you could read minds. Would you run to the doctor and complain? Maybe not. Maybe you'd keep your mouth shut and thank your lucky talismans and proceed to make yourself richer and stronger. It was a very sharp edge, it would cut and leave no blood, and a victim would never feel it.

"You suspect more." Not a question.

"Could be a hundred percent eventually. We haven't pinned it down; one of the CNS hormones working on the brain is our best guess. Different body chemistries process it faster or slower. A lot of things we don't understand yet."

Zia wondered what happened when two telepaths ran into each other. Would each of them somehow know about the other's ability?

"You've opened a real can of worms here, haven't you, Doctor? Rich and powerful or not, why aren't there alarm buzzers blaring all over the planet? Surely somebody in the government can see how dangerous this is. Nothing less than the stability of the civilized galaxy hangs in the balance."

"They don't know about it," Marad said.

Zia glanced at Silk as the impact of what the doctor said hit her. They don't *know* about this uplevels. Marad is sitting on it. Why?

"Why don't they know? Why haven't you told them?"

It is God's Plan.

That thumped Zia like a fist to the solar plexus. Marad was a Believer. They'd talked about it; it was the reason why the doctor hadn't taken the Treatment herself, even though she qualified.

"I don't pretend to know the Mind of God," Marad said. "No mortal can. And God's Plan was created with the explosion that brought forth the Universe. It cannot be altered, save by God. There is a reason you and the others have been made telepathic. I don't understand why, but I do understand that I am God's instrument in the doing of it. And what God creates, man may not put asunder."

Silk said, "What are we talking about here?"

Zia answered. "Dr. Marad hasn't reported the telepathic side effect of the Treatment to the government. She is helping it along."

"God does not need my help. I am but a tool," Marad said.

"God's Crescent wrench?" Silk said. "You're a doctor, a scientist, how can you believe in such stuff?"

"Science only takes one so far. Science comes to a final wall it cannot leap over or tunnel under or walk around. Only faith can clear that last hurdle to be one with the cosmos."

Silk shook his head.

"No," Zia said. "She's right."

Marad's face lit with that smile. "I knew you were still a Believer, Sister. Buried deep, but still there."

Silk started to say something but Zia shut him down with a wave. "Sooner or later somebody will spill the secret," she said. "You can't keep it hidden forever."

"This is true. But until then, I will be a cog in the Great Machine that spins God's Plan."

To Silk, Zia said, "Okay, we've learned what we came for. Let's go."

Silk frowned. "What about her?"

"She won't report us, will you, Doctor?"

Marad answered with another of her saintly smiles.

Zia and Silk turned to leave.

"Yours is a larger role, Sister. Strive to do it well."

"I'll give it my best shot." Beat. "Sister."

In the hallway, Silk said, "You trust her?"

"Yes."

"What about the other? The faith thing? You believe that?"

"If she thinks I'm a Believer and doing my bit to help God along, they could burn her at the stake and she wouldn't give them a word."

"Ah. Smart."

But as they hurried along the hallway, Zia had to wonder. Was there still a kernel of something down deep in her that wanted to believe there was some sense to it all, that there was some organization obscured by the mundane? She thought she'd put it all away when her uncle had introduced her to his perversion all those years ago, but maybe not. Maybe down in her soul, she still wondered.

"Now what?" Silk asked.

"My guess is that long-lived telepaths are going to be a glut on the market pretty soon, if Marad keeps cranking them out. Sooner or later, one of the Treated on E2 will realize his or her best interests will be served by sneaking offworld to sell the secret elsewhere. If it ever gets to where every other person you meet can read your mind, then my job and yours are history. Maybe we ought to think about getting into another line of work.

"Sales, maybe. I think maybe we should take the deal with the terran spy. Better to be rich and healthy than poor and dead."

"You trust this guy at all?"

"No. But I've got an edge, remember?"

They grinned at each other.

THIRTY-ONE _____

THE NIGHT CRAWLER came, wrapped in midnight. He probably considered himself safely cloaked in the warm and humid darkness.

Colburn waited on the dock, his preparations made. Except for not being able to contact Mintok, all was going according to plan.

At 1500 there had been a terrible explosion at a local pharmaceutical company; five people had been killed.

Three of the dead had been Colburn's targets. The others were, well, unfortunate victims of bad timing. Life was dangerous; it got everybody in the end.

The man who had sold him that bomb, and another one he planned to put into Silk's cube, as well as a third device, had, for all practical purposes, disappeared. Oh, good investigators, did they look in exactly the right place, would find traces of something that had once been human. But identifying *which* human it had been would be . . . difficult. Soak a corpse for some hours in a tank of acid used to etch rubysteel plate—plate only slightly less hard than diamond—and you get a body more murk than goo.

And as for the Night Crawler . . .

"Evening," he said. "You got the money?"

Colburn held up a certified cashier's wafer. The amount was locked in and guaranteed. All the bearer needed was the proper code and this little piece of memolast, and he could download the stads electronically from any Banco Galactica in range into his own account; if he would rather, they would issue him hard curry notes or platinum bars, were he stupid enough to want to carry that kind of cash around.

"You mind if I look at that?"

Colburn passed the wafer to him.

The Night Crawler stuck the wafer into a reader slot on his hand-held. Grinned as the amount flashed onto the little flatscreen. "And the codes?"

Colburn returned the grin. "Wasn't there something you were going to bring to the table?"

"Yeah." He produced a keycard, gave it to Colburn, who inserted it into his comp's reader and called up the ID stats.

According to the keycard's infochip, the ship was the courier vessel *Mystic Smoke*, supposedly undergoing engine repairs at the Iron Leaf Spaceshipworks, near the dropbox port of Maxwell, a hundred and fifty klicks northwest of Beagle, on the seacoast.

"The repairs are a fake," Crawler said. "The ship is ready to lift. You plug in the card, program a destination, and you're gone. Already got Coast Guard clearance good for the next ten days. After that, you have to bribe somebody on your own. You got ship rations, but bring your own liquor."

Colburn pulled the card out, tapped it on the comp, then put the little rectangle of plastic into his tunic pocket and sealed the cro closure. So closed, the pocket was airtight and waterproof.

"The codes?"

"Not so fast," he said. "How do I know the ship is where you say it is, in the condition you say it is in?"

"What—you don't trust me?"

They grinned at each other. Men-of-the-galaxy here.

"Okay, what do you need?"

"I'll put a three-hour delay on the transfer wafer. I've got some resources; I can have the ship checked out. It's green, you download the money before the sun comes up. If you're running a fugue, it gives me time to hunt you down and kill you."

Crawler laughed. "Hey, I'm an honest man, more or less. I can live with that." He passed the wafer back to Colburn, who pretended to punch numbers into his computer. The delay was already programmed and he reckoned that Crawler knew it, but he played it out. He gave the wafer back to Crawler.

"Codes?"

He gave them to him. Crawler input the numbers and letters, then smiled.

Colburn didn't need to look, he knew what it said: "Code Accepted for Valid Transfer, Pending Delay" lit the screen. "Retransmit code 0306 hours this date."

"Three hours, just like you said."

"Pleasure to do business with you," Colburn said.

"You wait here while I leave," Crawler said.

"No problem."

"You're ever onplanet again and you need something, call me."

"I surely will."

The Night Crawler turned and sauntered away. He had two bodyguards hidden in the darkness watching. Colburn knew because they'd tripped the tiny sensors he'd planted at chest-height earlier in the day. He hadn't triggered the detectors until just before midnight, and he'd since picked up three chirps from the wireless receiver stikbutton hidden behind his left ear. He made no sudden moves. Night Crawler might be relatively honest, but the guards could be jumpy, and he didn't want to get shot. Even though he wore softweave armor under his tunic and pants, a high-velocity handgun round would be painful, and they might be good enough to try for a head shot. He turned and walked toward the edge of the dock until he was leaning on the rail, looking out at the wide river.

What the Night Crawler and his guards didn't know was that an inflatable airbag was attached to the pilings directly under Colburn, at the waterline. The same kind of bag that stunt players used to stage falls in

the entcom vids. Colburn put his hand on his hip
and, with what should be an undetectable pressure,
he triggered the remote in his pocket. Twenty meters
below, two large tanks of air under high pressure
began to spew, filling the bag. It would take only
twenty seconds to inflate, and a little green light
would go on inside when it was ready. It was noisy,
the rushing air, he could hear it, but he figured
that even if the guards picked up the sound, they
wouldn't be able to identify it. The bag would col-
lapse when he hit it and he would get wet, but it
was too risky to try a jump directly into the water
from this height in the dark without some kind of
insurance.

The transfer wafer he had given the Crawler was valid,
but it also had embedded in it a hair of thermel. It would
take five minutes the way it was rigged before it ignited
and destroyed the wafer. The Night Crawler wouldn't
be making any calls to download Colburn's money in
three hours.

The little green light on the airbag flashed.

Without hesitating, Colburn flew over the rail. He
started in a swan dive, and did a slow, layout half flip
forward, using the light as a target.

Somebody behind him yelled.

He hit the bag flat on his back, arms and legs extended
wide. The sides blew out as they were designed to, broke
his fall, and he felt the water slosh under the thin fabric
as he scrambled free of it. He achieved the tepid water
and hurriedly swam under the dock.

On the dock, the night turned to day.

The third bomb he'd bought from the man who now
slept in acid went off. The explosion was lateral, from
a shaped charge, and it scoured the dock like the stone
wind from a volcano, sanding everything with white fire.
The thick planking was enough to protect him from the
blast, but the noise vibrated Colburn's chest and tried to
get into his bones. Some debris hit the water as far away
as midriver and continued to burn as it floated.

Even if the wafer hadn't been destroyed, neither the Night Crawler nor his bodyguards would be calling anyone ever again.

Colburn swam to the raft he'd left moored under the dock, flopped into it, and cast off. The tiny electric pulse motor pushed him into the river's current and he started downstream, to the place where he'd parked and hidden his cart.

Above him, the surface of the dock burned brightly.

"Looks like a fire at the docks," Zia said.

Driving the van, Silk nodded. "Yeah. You want to try Colburn's com number again?"

"Sure." She thumbed the recall button on her com. Turned the sound up so he could hear.

"Yes?"

She looked at Silk. He nodded. She said, "M. Colburn."

He recognized her voice. "Ah, M. Rélanj! Zia. Delightful to hear from you."

"Did I interrupt your bath, M. Colburn? I hear water."

"No, I was just finishing. And please, call me Croft."

Zia and Silk exchanged glances. He shook his head. Oily son-of-a-bitch. All that lecturing about gunslingers and mythology while Silk's head was about to explode from the aftereffects of the stun dart. The kind of man who steepled his fingers when he talked, probably had a superiority complex that would shame God.

"Silk and I have discussed your proposal."

"And . . . ?"

"We've decided to take you up on it."

"Excellent!"

"With a few modifications."

"Which are . . . ?"

"We both go with you, and we leave as soon as possible."

"I see. Why?"

Silk shrugged: *Tell him.*

"We've had some trouble. A personal problem with someone I work with."

"You have to do better than that," Colburn said. "If I am going to risk my neck, I want to know details."

"Over a com?"

"Zia, my line is scrambled and shielded, and I'd give you ten-to-one odds for any amount you want to bet that yours is, too. Otherwise we wouldn't be using names, now would we?"

"My supervisor was a very jealous man. He objected to Silk."

"*Was* a jealous man?"

"Yeah, well, in one sense he's no longer a problem; but the solution created another problem, if you understand what I'm saying."

"I understand. Meet me at my cube in the morning, say 0800, with your bags packed. Last night was your final sunset on this world. Discom."

"So?" Zia said, as she clicked the com off.

"I don't trust this guy."

"Neither do I. But we've got something he wants, there are two of us, and I have my little trick. We should have the advantage."

"Maybe."

"Let's find a room and see if we can get a couple hours sleep. You have anything at your cube you have to have?"

"Nothing worth dying for."

"Me neither. Mintok's dogs might have eased off, but maybe not. If this works out, we'll have money to burn and a lot of years ahead of us. Let's not screw it up."

"I hear you."

Colburn opened the valves on his boat and let the air out. The weight of the little motor wasn't enough to sink it, but with a couple of large rocks from the rip-rap on the river side of the levee, the boat went down fast enough. He climbed the slope, then slogged down the city side to his cart. Fire vans screamed in the distance.

So. Mintok was dead. Zia hadn't said those words, but her meaning was clear enough. The fool. He was supposed to take the money and keep them under watch, not try to play his own games. One of the problems in dealing with active sub rosa operatives was that you could never trust them. They always thought they were slicker, sharper, smarter, and they always had their own little games going. Well, it served the man right and it saved him the effort of taking Mintok out, as well as setting a bomb in Silk's place. With their insistence that her boyfriend be allowed to go with them offworld, it would be that much easier. He could have a fatal accident anywhere along the way and get spaced through a lock. Or maybe disappear once they made planetfall at their destination. Colburn didn't know how long the actual downloading of Zia's modern *elixir vitae* would actually take, but surely he could have the medics tell her anything he wanted her to believe. It might even be better that way. Silk has a tragic accident, and who is there to comfort Zia in her time of grief? Yes. He liked it. He should have thought of it earlier.

The cart was parked behind an automated sewer sub-station, nobody around, and Colburn quickly stripped off his wet clothes and the softweave armor. He had a towel and a clean coverall in the cart. He was careful when he removed the ship's keycard from the sodden tunic's pocket. A little water wouldn't hurt it, but there was no point in pushing his luck. He put the card into his dry coverall chest pocket and sealed it shut, wiped his pistol and magazines dry, and packed the wet gear into the cart's trunk. Better and better.

He drove carefully toward his cube. It wouldn't do to get a speeding citation and have to delete the traffic officer who saw his face.

THIRTY-TWO _____

PARKED BEHIND HIS cube was the six-passenger flitter Colburn had rented two days earlier. He had paid for it with cash and used the Claibourne ID for what he expected to be a final time. When he was done with the flier, he intended to disable the built-in tracking device, light the autopilot, and point it out to sea. By the time it ran out of fuel, it ought to be far enough way so the rental company wouldn't find it. And even if somebody logged it on a traffic radar, they wouldn't be able to tell exactly where its flight had originated—certainly not to the vicinity of Iron Leaf Spaceshipworks.

That the ship was where the late Night Crawler said it was had never been in doubt. Colburn had located the courier vessel days before, probably before the Crawler had. It and two other ships were the only ones he'd been able to spot that would fill his order, and he marked them all well enough so he would have been very surprised had the Crawler offered him anything other.

It was best to know the answers before you asked the questions. He'd learned that years ago from a litigator who'd never lost a criminal case in open court. Never ask a man a question you don't already know his answer to and you won't get so many nasty surprises, the lawyer had said. Smart man.

He'd have to make certain Mintok was dead, but he believed that was merely a formality. Zia had killed him, or Silk had, and the man was, like the Crawler and the others, past tense. Everything was neat, clean, tidy.

As he pulled the cart to a halt near his cube, Colburn saw a light on inside.

He slipped from the cart, moved fifty meters back down the street and thought about it for a second. Somebody had breached his security. He knew he had not left a light burning—he never forgot such things—so somebody had turned it on after he left. Who had been there?

Might still be there?

He circled away from the street and toward the back of the cube.

He ran through the possibilities as he catfooted through the lawn next door. Could be Zia, of course. She'd demonstrated before she could come and go undetected. So it could be Zia and Silk, even though he told them to meet him here in the morning. She wouldn't have left the light on if she intended to surprise him; she was too good an op for that kind of piddly mistake. Anybody who knew anything about him at all would know he'd spot it.

Who else? If Mintok was dead, and he believed that, then there wasn't anybody who knew who he was. Unless, of course, Mintok had talked to somebody about him. That was a possibility. Some kind of insurance, maybe, in case the man met with a sudden unexpected end. Ops and their games.

Might it be a common thief? Come to steal what he could from the terran pharmaceuticalist? It would be a stretch of coincidence for that to happen tonight, but that was another possibility he had to consider.

The wise thing to do this close to the end of a caper would be to turn around and leave. He could com Zia and arrange for another meeting place, and let whoever it was who'd come to play wait until hell froze over for him to show up. There wasn't anything in the cube to incriminate him or let somebody figure out where he might have gone. He could rent another flitter in the morning, be light-years away by tomorrow afternoon.

That would be the wise thing, sure enough.

Curiosity, however, was once again more powerful than wisdom. He wanted to know who was in there and why. If he'd made an error somehow and been spotted, maybe he needed to fix it.

They might be watching the doors, but they probably weren't watching the window to the fresher in his bedroom. The alarm system wasn't worth a damn, obviously, but he could use his control to kill any part of it, and he tapped a code into his remote to shut the windows off. The fresher window was electrically locked, and he clicked it open and climbed through easily enough.

He moved quietly, using the house-clearing drill he'd practiced a thousand times over the years. Gun held ready, he checked the fresher, then the bedroom. He slipped into the hall and worked his way to the central living area.

He smelled the flickstick smoke before he saw her. She must have heard him come into the room. She sipped from a glass of bright blue liquor and said, "Hi. That you, Crofty?"

Colburn shook his head in wonder as he walked into the room and found the prostitute Charity Heart seated naked on his couch.

THIRTY-THREE

"YOU READY?" ZIA asked.

"Yeah," Silk answered.

They had just come out of a sporting goods store. They used cash to pay for their purchases, money they had downloaded from a robot teller three klicks away. If anybody was tracking them from credit transactions, they'd be looking there and not here. They each had a new travel bag, several sets of cheap but comfortable polyprop shirts and pants and socks, spare ammo for their pistols, and a few other things Zia thought they might need. Enough to get them through a few days on a less than classy starship in the company of an untrustworthy terran spy, if need be. So they hoped.

An early morning rainstorm piled itself up to the west of the city, mounds of battleship-gray cotton, whiter at the top and shading to purple at the base. The impending rain was near enough so it offered a cool breeze, something Silk welcomed, given the clothes he wore.

"Let's go see Colburn," she said.

They had dumped the van he'd borrowed from Benny the smoker and rented—again for cash—one of the innocuous and ubiquitous two-seat covered electric scooters. It didn't have much range and it wasn't very fast, but they didn't have far to go and they weren't in a hurry.

Zia drove and Silk watched for trouble. He kept his hand near the butt of his pistol as they rolled through the cool morning and the thick traffic. It was only a few minutes to where Colburn was staying, according to Zia. Whatever was going to happen, it would probably happen soon . . .

Colburn didn't like surprises, unless he was the one springing them, and he especially didn't like this one. Still, as he rolled easily from the bed and Charity Heart's warm and naked form under the sheet, he had to admit he had made full use of her availability. As long as she was here, she was a professional and she knew his wants well enough. It never hurt to start a day relaxed and comfortable.

She slept on, or pretended to, as he walked toward the fresher. In another hour, Zia and Silk would be here. He had a few minutes to attend to his morning toilet before he had to do something about the woman in his bed.

She didn't bother to try a cover story, since she had to know he wouldn't believe anything but the truth. He asked, she answered:

"What are you doing here?"

"Leonard sent me."

Colburn had smiled. He put the gun away. The last time he had seen her, his boat was being lifted into dry storage by a massive crane and sling; he and Charity had kissed briefly, and she had taken the large bonus he'd given her and walked to a waiting taxi. He'd watched her go, admired her athletic strides, the flashes of tanned skin as the yellow silk dress had been blown and lifted by a stray breeze off the waters of the sound. Four lovely months with her and thoroughly delightful.

At the time, he'd thought he might be returning to Earth, and he'd kept her com number—another few months or a year or five, well, she was good at her job. Since he'd picked her himself from an exclusive Hong Kong call girl operation, he wouldn't have thought she was one of Silverman's. Probably she hadn't been approached by Silverman until after she'd been with Colburn for a time, but that Leonard, ah, he was a

devious one. She could have been one of his agents
from before Colburn had ever walked into Madame
Chen's establishment. Planted there between the time
Colburn called and made the arrangements, then arrived,
to select his expensive trull. Silverman would know his
tastes. It was possible.

He used the bidet, flushed it, then ran water in the sink,
washed his face and hands, dried them with a clean towel.
Ah, well. It didn't matter. That Silverman had sent her to
check on his progress or keep tabs on him or whatever,
that was the real problem. The man had never done that
before, at least not so blatantly, and maybe it was just
because this was such a big caper that he'd done it this
time. Still and all, it wasn't good. He'd have to get rid
of her.

He checked his face in the mirror. Could use a depil.
He tapped the dispenser next to the sink, squirted a thin
line of the blue-green gel onto his fingertips, rubbed it
on his chin and cheeks, under his nose, down his neck.
The depil smelled of lime and menthol. He waited ten
seconds, then rinsed his face with warm water. Dried,
then rubbed his face. Smooth again.

He sighed. He didn't really want to kill Charity Heart.
It would be such a waste. Of course, if he left her
alive, she'd have to answer some hard questions when
Silverman caught up with her, but she couldn't tell
what she didn't know and she wouldn't know much
of anything—any decent stress analyst or electropophy
operator would figure that out fast enough. He had a new
woman on tap, but this was a pleasant bridge that didn't
really need to be burned, did it?

He had a few odds and ends in his gear, stuff the pharmaceutical company had supplied. There were a couple
of medium-duration hypnotics—an amp of Thetadyne
popped into her lovely buttock, and she'd sleep for another seven or eight hours.

Could he risk it? Should he? Dead women told no
tales, but maybe he was getting soft in his old age.

What the hell.

He found the amp of deep-sleep barbiturate and plugged it into the air hypo. The unit hissed softly as the amp was pressurized. He padded naked back into the bedroom, knelt on the bed, leaned over and kissed Charity Heart on the temple as he slid his hand under the sheet.

She was awake, she smiled, but kept her eyes closed. Arched her back a little and pressed her bare bottom toward his hand . . .

The hypo went off, a sharp *pop!* as the chem blasted through her skin and into her gluteus. She jumped, opened wide her eyes, frowned. "Croft! What the hell are you doing? What kind of game is this?"

"Well, to coin a pun, an end game, sweetie."

She struggled, but he held her and she couldn't move much. "Croft?" He saw the fear in her eyes. "Don't hurt me."

"Shh. Don't worry. Relax, there's nothing to be afraid of. You're going to have a nice nap, that's all. Tell Leonard no hard feelings, okay? And the same goes for you."

Even in the muscle, the stuff was fast. Another minute and her eyes started to close, though she fought to keep them open. Two minutes and she was under. He held her another minute to be sure, then moved, covered her with the sheet, tucked it in around her. Smiled down at the sleeping beauty and her long golden mane.

Then he went to get ready for his new love.

"There's the cube," Zia said. "On the left, with the flitter behind it."

"Got it."

Zia felt Silk's apprehension, but that was natural. She was a little nervous herself.

She pulled the scooter into the cube's driveway and set the brake, switched off the motor. Thunder rumbled in the distance.

Silk said, "You know, the last time we left a planet together it was raining pretty good."

She smiled at him. "I remember. We've come a long way since then, haven't we?"

"Yeah."

"You ready?"

"Yeah."

She took a deep breath, blew part of it out. "Let's go see if he's home."

Silk's mouth was dry, and his pulse was thumping along a lot faster than normal. He forced himself to breathe slower but that adrenaline edge buzzed in him, and he felt like a spring being wound into a tight coil. A sudden move would bounce him off the nearest ceiling. He liked and hated the feeling at the same time.

It wouldn't make any sense for this guy Colburn to put any heavy moves on them, not yet. He needed Zia, needed her cooperation, so doing anything to her or even to Silk now wouldn't be smart. Zia thought the guy was pretty sharp, and Silk had to admit he thought so too, even though he didn't think the spy was as good as *he* thought he was. And there was Zia's new trick. They should have the advantage here. But he'd learned that things didn't always go the way you thought they would, and he didn't want to wind up dead for being overconfident.

"Amen," Zia said.

Silk reached for the announce button.

THIRTY-FOUR

AS SOON AS he was cleared, Colburn put the flitter into the air. He didn't log a flight plan, and the tracking computer was already disabled. He flew on manual, stayed in the normal traffic lanes, kept his speed fast but under the computer-broadcast limit. Zia and Silk were nervous, but they seemed to control it well enough. They sat across and a little behind him, staring out at the countryside below. A lot of farms between Beagle and Maxwell. The water robots had irrigated big circles of organic greens, tans, oranges that dotted the ground far below.

He'd had his travel bag packed and ready when they'd arrived, and neither of them had suspected that Charity Heart slept hard in the arms of Morpheus only a few meters away.

"Where are we going, exactly?" Zia asked.

"Our ship is at the repair works in Maxwell."

"I meant which planet."

Colburn said, "I'd rather not say until we clear atmosphere. Never know who might be listening. Does it matter?"

"I guess not."

They flew in silence after that.

Silk watched the ground far below. They were cruising at maybe eight or ten thousand meters, and the pressurized, recycled air tasted a little metallic. He and Zia sat

side by side on the right side of the flitter, opposite and
a little behind Colburn in the pilot's seat. They hadn't
had much of a chance to talk since they met the spy,
but he figured they'd get a little space when they got
where they were headed. He was feeling pretty good—
until Zia leaned over and pretended to peer through the
window at a particularly colorful patch of farm circles.
She whispered something; it took a second for her meaning to sink in:

"I can't read him."

Uh-oh.

So much for their big advantage.

Zia leaned back and looked through the windscreen.
They were skirting the edges of the rainstorm they'd seen
earlier, but there were other clouds in the distance, at
least three more pods working themselves into thunderstorms. The joy of tropical planets, those fierce squalls.
Maybe where they were going wouldn't have that kind
of weather. She'd miss it, if it didn't.

Once again, she tried to get some kind of mental input
from Colburn. Nothing. He was a blank, not even a buzz.
It wasn't as if the gift had quit—she was still picking up
Silk over there, a low-grade hum of mild worry. Well.
At least it had been mild until she'd whispered to him.
Now it had upgraded itself somewhat.

As for not being able to read Colburn, she had to
wonder what that meant. Was it just him? Was he some
kind of fluke? So far, she'd been able to pick up the
thoughts of most people she'd tried to hear. But maybe
that was because she hadn't run into enough people since
it happened. It wasn't just because he was a terran; Silk
was from Earth, too.

Zia stared into space. Whatever the reason, there it
was. She couldn't see inside Colburn's head.

Okay, so what? She'd been an op for a long time without the ability to read minds; she'd done all right, hadn't
she? Yeah, she'd gotten used to it awful fast, started
depending on it, and that was bad. It was like people

who forgot how to do basic math because they always carried a calculator, or martial artists who depended on weapons and let the barehanded skills atrophy. Her new toy had been so powerful she'd leaned nearly all her weight on it. Not smart. A single prop could be kicked loose, and you'd fall hard if you couldn't regain your balance in a hurry.

So, okay. She couldn't read him. She had years of training in other areas, and even if Colburn was better than she was in some, or even most of those, he wasn't better than she was in *all* of them.

Plus she had Silk.

Colburn was a loner; she knew the type because she had been just like him. Depended on himself, didn't trust anybody else with his neck, picked himself up if he stumbled and fell—which he probably didn't do real often. He had his agenda, and she knew he wasn't laying it all out for them. Fine. She'd been that way, she understood it. She might have stayed that way forever, if not for meeting Silk. It had been physical at first, sensual, sexual, but from that unexpected beginning, they had moved on. It didn't matter at which stop you caught the train, only the trip after that. Even when he'd left, she'd still loved him, and she knew for certain that he had still loved her. That was a big deal, to know somebody would lay himself on the line for you, no questions. That if you yelled for help, he would drop whatever he was doing and come running. Colburn had himself, and he was good, but she had a partner, in the truest sense of the word. The odds were still in their favor. They still had the edge.

"There it is," Colburn said. "The Iron Leaf Spaceship-works."

They were still in the air but in a descending lane on approach to Maxwell. The shipworks were recognizable from the gantries and other giant machines, as well as a dozen or more snouts of atmosphere-vacuum vessels thrust up into the morning. Even klicks away, they could see the bright blue spots of plasma welders working.

One of the fresh-brewed thunderstorms had sent scud to scout the town, and it threw patchy shade over the industrial district as they circled around it.

"Looks like it's going to rain," Silk said.

"Won't bother us," Colburn said. "The Deep ships are buttoned up tight; they can lift through a driving hailstorm against hurricane-force winds. See the rocket boosters? They generate millions of kilos of push."

"Big suckers," Silk said. "Bulky as hell."

"We'll jettison them in high orbit before we slingshot," Zia said. "They're collected by robot ships and reused over and over again."

Colburn smiled at her. "Done a little traveling, eh?"

"Now and then."

The warning beeper for transition to ground travel went off.

"I've got to put the flitter down now," Colburn said. "We'll ground it from here on. Should be there in a few minutes. There's a launch window coming up in about two hours, we should be able to get clearance for it."

They already had clearance for it, actually, but Colburn didn't tell them that. He wanted to keep them busy guessing as much as he could. They didn't trust him—in their places, he wouldn't trust him either—and the more they had to think about, the better. He knew they were going to York, then Fuji, but he didn't tell them that, either. He would program the destination once they were on board, and tell them only after they were well into the Deep.

Odd, the way Zia kept staring at him. She wasn't obvious about it, but now and then he would catch her at it. Sizing him up, somehow. What was she looking for?

What really attracts people to one another? he wondered. Sex, to be sure, and like interests, or sometimes unlike interests; but—what was it that had called to him so quickly and certainly with Zia? The search for equals, he supposed. Silk there might be good in bed, and he had a kind of rough charm, even some rudimentary skills, but he was no match for this woman. What had she seen in him to risk bringing him from Earth to E2? Why would she take a chance on him against maybe losing her career, her status, her professional standing? It must have been something more than just sex. But in every way that counted in their business, Colburn was more of a match for Zia than Silk could ever be. Even with years of training, he was too old to develop the skills Colburn had. He would have had to start ten or fifteen years earlier, and even then, it wouldn't happen. There were other ops who had begun younger than Colburn had, but they weren't better. Nobody was *better*.

If he thought about it logically, Colburn's plans for Zia were far-fetched. Sure, she had the biochem magic that was worth a planet's ransom, and he would be a fool to pass that up. To cap his career with such a caper, leaving The Scat with a mouthful of feathers, that was perfect. They'd used him readily enough over the years, but they'd always had a thinly veiled bias against freelancers. And yes, the New Earther was attractive, so wanting to play with her on that level was not unreasonable. But to feel that she was *the one*, the woman he'd sought more or less unconsciously for years? Well, there was no logic to that, no reason. It was a feeling, and he hated to rely on such things as emotion for guidance.

And yet. And yet. There it was. He couldn't deny it.

Maybe this was what the scribes meant when they talked about the illogic of love. That sudden epiphany of *knowing* that somehow slipped past the brain's control room and established itself deeper, in that amorphous region called the heart.

True, if he were buying a prize breeding animal, he could make a good case for Zia. But that was the intellectual part of him trying to justify his feeling so he could accept it. Rationalization, pure and simple.

He grinned to himself. Ah, well. He was about to retire from the business. He would have time—plenty of time—to explore these new areas of himself. He would bring her along, they would help each other. It would be a matter of how long it took.

He put the flitter down smoothly into the landing lane and drove to the ground lane feeder. They were in the city and rolling toward the shipworks. The computer map gave him the shortest route and he took it—the flitter would tell no tales from the bottom of the sea even if its flight recorder hadn't been killed before it ever lifted from Beagle.

The first big and heavy drops of the thunderstorm began to plash on the plastcrete around them, spattering on the flitter's windscreen and its sensors, kicking the wipers and blowers on. The cabin pressurization gear was long since off, and the filters for the outside air didn't keep the smell of the rain out. Fuji was also a tropical world, if not quite as hot most of the time as E2. Zia would feel at home there.

They must have been on the edge of the storm because the rain slacked, then stopped as Colburn parked the flitter outside the gate to the shipworks. Zia and Silk got out, and the spy played with the controls before he followed them. The flitter sat there for a moment after Colburn closed the door, then rolled slowly away.

"Slaved to the grid," Colburn said. "And going where nobody will find it."

Silk nodded. That made sense. He would have done the same thing if it had been his vehicle and he was trying to hide his trail.

No doubt about it, he was getting better at this. There was a time when such a thought would never have entered his mind.

The gate was automatic. Colburn ran a card through the reader's slot and the gate opened. The three of them walked in. They skirted fresh puddles where the plastcrete had sunk slightly or cracked.

"That seems awful easy," Silk said.

"There'll be a human guard somewhere along the way," Colburn said.

Sure enough, there was an inner perimeter entrance at the end of the lane, and this one was watched by a guard. She was uniformed but unarmed; apparently they didn't have a lot of trouble with people sneaking into the shipworks.

"Morning," she said. "Your IDs, please?"

Colburn smiled and handed the woman three cards. "Morning," he said. His voice was bright, pleasant, almost too much so. "I'm Franz Liszt, these are my assistants, M. McCartney and M. Lennon. We're here to see M. Nemow regarding the menu for the Solstice Banquet."

The guard ran the ID cards and checked them against her computer's appointment list. "Yep, here we are, Apex Catering. You'll want to follow the green line to Admin Two. Nemow's office is on the second level, east end."

"Thank you so much."

The guard smiled. "So, what are we having this year?"

"Well, if we get the bid, we were considering fire-roasted flayed salmon and porklette steaks in cherry wine as the two main entrees."

"Sounds good. Anything's got to be better than that crappy stuff we had last year."

"Apex would never consider serving that . . . vulcanized chicken."

The guard laughed. She didn't seem to consider it strange that the three of them carried travel bags.

Silk was impressed. Colburn had come up with three phony IDs, arranged a fake meeting and he had the patter down clean.

They walked past the guard.

"We won't log out," Zia said, once they were out of the guard's hearing. "They'll notice."

"Eventually," Colburn said. "But the shipworks security won't care as long as nothing blows up. Sooner or later somebody from Nessie or The Scat will figure we have left the planet. After they strain all the commercial passenger lists and run the private vessels that logged flight plans and don't find us, they'll dig deeper and figure we used a stolen ship. They'll show up here, of course, but that will be weeks or maybe months from now. We'll be long gone and the ship we used disposed of. No way to trace us once we're out of the system. They'll guess we left here and likely on which vessel but not where we went. It will be a cold trail and a dead end, too."

"Seems as if you've thought of everything," Zia said.

"That I have."

They followed the green line painted on the plastcrete until they were out of the guard's sight, then turned off. Colburn must have studied a map of the place because he knew right where he was going.

"There it is," he said.

Ahead of them was a ship. It was not as large as most of the ships they'd passed but it was not a lifeboat, either. From his experiences working for the Port of Maui, Silk figured the vessel would probably carry a dozen passengers easily. Even with the booster rockets dropped, it would have as much room inside as three or four big transit buses bundled together, or maybe a twenty-meter luxury watercraft. The three of them would have more than enough space to rattle around in.

"Come on," Colburn said. "Let's get on board and light the fuse."

Zia kept trying to pick up something from Colburn but without success. This telepathy was tricky stuff. When she wasn't in Silk's thoughts, his drone faded considerably. And it seemed to be limited by proximity. The assassin stalking her had been a ways off, but he'd been very angry, and she also realized that big emotions like that also pumped up the volume.

She wondered how much fine control she would eventually be able to manage. If it didn't just go away someday. Maybe it was transient. Maybe that was why she couldn't pick up Colburn.

But she still could hear Silk, couldn't she?

The ability was inconsistent. She had too many questions and not enough answers.

Well. She could worry about it later. Now, as they rode the tiny elevator to the passenger section of the ship—it was called *Mystic Smoke*, she saw from the logo stenciled on it—she needed to stay sharp with her other senses. They weren't out of the woods yet.

THIRTY-FIVE _____

SILK LOOKED AROUND the communal cabin of the *Mystic Smoke*. As big as some cubes he'd lived in, the place was a rounded rectangle, had a relatively high ceiling, and had been decorated in what Silk thought of as nineteenth-century banker's gothic. Three walls were paneled with a good imitation of stained oak, complete with heavy-framed paintings; there were overstuffed chairs and two couches covered in muted, colored fabric; the fourth wall was of fake hardcopy books and inset into it, a shallow ersatz fireplace. The furniture was bolted to the deck—a deck made to look like a wooden floor, complete with glued-down Oriental carpets. All it needed were some white-haired men with pipes and smoking jackets, waving big cigars and drinking brandy. Amazing.

"Good God," Zia said.

Colburn shrugged. "I didn't design it."

Silk walked to the fireplace, found a switch inset into the fake stone, pressed it. A holographic log and fire appeared, complete with the crackling sound effects of burning wood. He shook his head.

A stairwell in the hall took them to the control room. Unlike the central area, this was a no-nonsense place, computer consoles and screens, instrument panels. There weren't any viewports, but there were holographic "windows" inset over large flatscreens. Colburn activated these with a keycard, and the windows showed an overhead view. With the ship moving in space and the microgravity operating, the effect would be as though you were facing forward while sitting in one of the control chairs, even though you'd actually be looking down or up or sideways relative to your destination.

Colburn began to bring various systems on-line. He said, "I can handle this, if you want to take a look around. It'll be half an hour or so before everything is ready."

Silk would have been content to watch Colburn power up the ship, but Zia nudged him. "Good idea," she said. "We'll take a look around."

Back down the stairs—there was an inclined ramp and also a lift next to those—Silk and Zia went past the central room, then lower, to find the sleeping cabins.

"We should have stayed to see where he's taking us," Silk said.

"No point in it. It's all computer-run. Once it's logged in, we can check it later. I can fly this thing if I have to. We need to talk—"

Well, well—

"What?"

"I didn't say anything," he said. "Or think anything."

She stopped. "No. I just got a quick flash of . . . satisfaction. It wasn't your mental voice."

"Finally getting Colburn, then. Maybe it just takes a while with some people."

"Yeah," she said. "I'd feel a lot better if I could peep into his head. I don't hear anything else, though."

They reached the cabin level. The rooms were a little tight, but there were six of them, each with two bunks. "Be a squeeze to sleep together on one of those," he said.

"Not if I slept on top of you," she said. They both grinned.

"This could work out okay," she said. "This whole deal, I mean."

"Any regrets?"

"Not really. Nessie isn't an organization you can feel much loyalty to. They would dump me in a second if

I wasn't up to their standards—I've seen them drop a dozen agents for piddly stuff. And the truth is, I don't feel as if I'm being disloyal to New Earth. The Treatment and the side effect are like a big nuke with the timer running down. The sooner it gets dismantled and spread around, the better. Until it does, it's gonna cause big problems. Once it gets out—and it always does, something this huge—a planet that wants it is apt to do whatever it takes to get it."

"War, you think?"

She nodded. "Maybe. How could the idiots on my homeworld have ever thought they'd keep it a secret?"

"Maybe they'd didn't really think so. Maybe they just wanted to get as much of a head start as they could. Remember history? What happened when they legalized most of the common street drugs on Earth early in the twenty-first century? It was prohibition that made it lucrative. Once you could buy the stuff in any pharmacy, a whole shitload of problems just went away. There were more dopers at first, but fewer thieves, and a lot less drug-related crime. But the dealers who saw it coming made money because they sold out in a hurry."

"Yeah. This is going to shake things up a lot worse than that did." She gestured at herself with both hands. "And I'm the messenger."

"Well, as long as they don't shoot you."

Colburn leaned back in the form-chair and smiled at the computer screen. All systems were up and go, the proper codes and passwords were in place, whoever had been bribed to look the other way was apparently doing so. A few more minutes for the fuel mix to reach proper proportions, and they could lift. Then it would be a short, heavy ride through atmosphere and into orbit, drop the pushers, loop around, and slingshot into Deep. A few days in the warp, and this planet would be a memory.

He allowed himself to visualize an image of a boot-leather tough gunslinger swinging himself on the back of his horse and riding off into the sunset. Pedestrians watched with fear and respect as the tanned and lean shootist rode by, tall in the saddle. Tipped his black hat to the cute and dusty schoolmarm . . .

He shook the fantasy and stood. He stretched a little, twisted until his vertebrae crackled, bent, and touched his toes. Gravity's hand pressed you hard on a rocket liftoff and he didn't want to be shoved into the acceleration couch with a stiff neck or back, that only made you ache worse in the short stretch of zero-gee before the microgravity kicked on. Time to go find Zia and Silk and get them strapped down for the first jump on their journey.

Silk watched Zia cock her head to one side, as if listening. She was hearing something he couldn't pick up.

"There it is again," she said. "A fast impression of somebody feeling a little nervous."

"Could be me," Silk said.

"Nope. You're a lot nervous. I can't quite—"

"Time to get to the takeoff couches," came Colburn's voice. He was on his way down one set of stairs as Silk and Zia were headed up the steps right below those. "We're ready to lift."

Silk nodded. Zia was right. He was more than a little nervous.

They made it into orbit without any problems. Colburn dropped the boosters where he was supposed to, gave the Coast Guard a coded sequence that apparently satisfied them, and appeared to relax as the computer took them on a final so-long parabola around Zia's homeworld.

Did she have regrets? Sure, some. She'd grown up there, lived there most of her life, and it was, for whatever faults it had, the devil she knew. Of course, had she and Silk stayed on E2, she would have had to worry about what she was going to do, now that she was grown up. She couldn't have kept on as a spy. She would have had to do some fast shuffling to explain killing Mintok, and she didn't really have much proof without Colburn to

back her up. In the biz, you were considered guilty until
you could show otherwise. Even if she could manage to
explain why she'd put half a magazine of poison bullets
into her supervisor, they'd worry about her from now on.
Rélanj? Woman who blasted her supervisor? Yeah, you
don't want to trust her too much, no telling what'll happen. Plus when they found out about the mind-reading
side effect of the Treatment, a whole lot of ugly things
were likely to happen.

And then there would be the other part of the job: too
many men—and women—in too many beds, waiting for
her to service them. Yeah, it was business, but having
had to deal with Silk's little adventure with another lover,
she found she could understand how he felt. Were their
positions reversed, she would hate it that he was out fucking people for any reason. He might be having a better
time than he said. She'd discovered she was greedy, she
wanted him all to herself, and if what she had to do to
keep him monogamous was *be* monogamous, then fine,
she could do that. Maybe someday she might run into
somebody else who could do to and for her what Silk
did, but why look when she had it already? Plus the
whole idea of guns and games didn't seem nearly so
much fun as it had been when she'd first started playing.
The idea of a family, children, and not having to gear
up for a life-or-death confrontation on a regular basis
seemed real attractive at the moment. Death got old. The
adrenaline rush began to pale.

Maybe she'd get bored, who could say? Right now a
long vacation with no responsibilities sounded perfect.
They just had to get past Colburn and whatever games
he wanted to play.

She watched him peripherally as the microgravity
began giving them weight again. She would have
thought that proximity would make her reading ability
work better, but it didn't seem to be doing that. He was a
blank again, and save for those two quick hits, she hadn't
heard any more of his thoughts.

Odd, how the ability worked. Or didn't.

The gravity came up to full strength, a hair under normal, and a chime and computer vox announced that it was safe to unclamp and move around.

"What say we go down to the communal room and have a drink to celebrate our departure?" Colburn said.

Zia glanced at Silk. He had unbuckled his safety web and was halfway to his feet.

Okay by me, he thought.

"Why not?" Zia said.

The communal room had, of course, a bar. Silk found the controls for it, and it extruded itself from the wall, a small unit. He looked into the cabinet but there were only three partially filled bottles of liquor inside, one of vodka, one of bourbon, the third of gin. There were a few little packets of drink mix and plenty of plastic tumblers.

"Not much of a choice," he said, waving the plastic bottles.

Colburn said, "Yes, the man who sold me the ship mentioned that I should bring my own liquor."

"We can make do," Silk said. "I've got something called 'Collins' mix and one that says 'gimlet.' " He waved the packets.

"I'll take a little of that bourbon, plain," Colburn said. "No ice."

"Any juice back there?" Zia asked.

Silk opened a latched drawer. "Freeze-dried orange and another one, cranberry concentrate, looks like."

"Mix some of the cranberry with the vodka for me."

Silk did so. Poured a half tumbler of the bourbon for Colburn, then mixed himself a small amount of the dark liquor with half a tumbler of water for himself. He moved to where Zia sat on one of the couches, facing Colburn in one of the overstuffed chairs. Gave them their drinks, then sat next to Zia.

"A toast," Colburn said. He raised his tumbler. "Here's to health, wealth, and . . . long life."

Silk lifted his tumbler in salute, then started to put the drink to his lips.

"Well, there's an entrance line," somebody said behind them.

Silk spun on the couch, spilling his drink.

A lean and sharp-featured man stood there. He wore a silk jumpsuit, had a haircut that probably set him back a hundred stads, and a large-bore pistol in one hand.

Silk didn't have a clue, and his quick glance at Zia told him she didn't recognize the man. Silk looked at Colburn, who smiled at the man with the gun. He knew who he was, all right.

Colburn confirmed it. "Leonard. How nice of you to join us." He took a sip from his drink, did so slowly and deliberately.

"So, let me introduce everybody," Colburn said. "Zia Rélanj, of New Earth Security. Venture Silk, late of Earth, and the wood products industry on E2. Leonard Silverman, head of Special Projects, Terran Security."

The gunman smiled. "Ah, but you forgot yourself. Croft Colburn, freelance operative and master of the double-cross." He inclined his head at Colburn, who nodded in return.

"Want a drink, Leonard?"

"Not just now, no. What I want is for you to tell me a story, Croft."

Colburn was cool, Silk had to give him that. This Silverman character was unexpected and, from the look of him, bad news for Colburn. But the terran spy didn't seem overly perturbed.

"A story? All right. Once upon a time there was an *ausvelt* scientist who discovered a magic potion. Drink it and you could live forever. But the scientist's boss, a greedy soul, didn't want to share the potion with his neighbors. One of the neighbors decided to send a thief to steal the secret of the potion so he could have it, too. But the thief realized that *his* boss was a stingy fellow and that he could do ever so much better if he got the secret and sold it to a *different* neighbor. So he did, and he lived happily ever after. Of course, he was the only one, everybody else being really pissed off."

"Entertaining as always," Silverman said. "I half-expected you to spin some tale about this being a roundabout trip to Earth."

"Leonard. Would I try to lie to you like that?"

"In case you are wondering, this thing shoots ceramic softslugs. Puts a decent hole in a man but flattens against a hard surface without punching through. So if I've a mind to, I can get ten rounds into the air and not worry about blowing our oxy into vac."

"Sensible. The same load I carry on board a starship."

"Shit!" Zia said, under her breath.

Silk didn't think those were the kind of bullets she was using. He doubted that the darts in his weapon would hole a hull.

"Did you kill the woman?" Silverman continued. He looked at Colburn as though Silk and Zia were invisible, but Silk didn't doubt the man knew exactly where they were.

"Charity Heart? No. She's still taking a nice long nap."

Silverman shook his head and grinned but kept the gun pointing at Colburn. "You are getting soft in your old age, Croft."

Colburn shrugged.

Silk flicked a quick look at Zia. Thought: *He can't get us all. I'll go for my gun, jump to the side—*

She shook her head almost imperceptibly. Cut her eyes at Colburn, then back to Silk.

He thought he understood. *Think he might shoot me in the back?*

She closed her eyes, opened them.

What, one blink for yes, two for no?

She blinked slowly again, once.

Okay. I'll wait for your signal.

"Your turn, Leonard. Why don't *you* tell us a story?"

This seemed to amuse Silverman. He chuckled. "Ah. Very well. Once upon a time there was a thief who tried to fool his boss. He was a very clever fellow, but not as clever as his boss, and so he failed at his little subterfuge. His boss was very, very angry and he thought about how he should punish the offender. So he decided to banish the thief from his kingdom and finish the job himself—which he did, and then *he* lived happily ever after."

"Only banish him?"

"The boss was a kindhearted man who had a soft spot for the thief, despite his wicked ways."

"Ah."

Nobody spoke for a second. Silk looked at Zia again and saw her eyes go wide. *Was she getting something, a reading on somebody—?*

Zia blinked once.

It was like a cloudburst. Suddenly Zia was drenched in mental imagery. She'd heard one of the voices before—Silverman's—only then she'd thought it was Colburn. Now, all of a moment, both of them were spewing frantic thoughts that didn't match the cool exteriors. It was hard to separate them—

—shoot him and the boyfriend and space the corpses and take her back to Earth—

—roll to the left and pull my pistol and put him down—

—don't want to risk hitting the woman, string him along until I can get him alone, a clean shot—

—doesn't matter if Silk gets it now, heat of battle, she'll understand, now or later, it doesn't matter, he's dead anyway might as well be here, Leonard won't want to risk hitting Zia, got to distract him, the glass of bourbon in his face, no way he's going to let me go, all right on three, get ready, one—

Zia's hand itched to reach for her pistol, but that was a bad idea. She was loading jacketed ammo, hadn't had a chance to change to the frangible stuff she'd bought. The inner walls were paper-thin; one of the jacketed rounds might be able to breach the outer hull. If she shot at Silverman or Colburn and missed . . .

She looked at Silk and in a conversational tone, said, "Run for the door. Now."

. . . two—what? What did she say—?

"Colburn, don't—!" she yelled.

Silverman pulled his attention from Colburn to her when she screamed, then understood what she said and swung his gun back toward Colburn—

Colburn dived to his left in a twisting motion, reached for his pistol—

Silk launched himself over the back of the couch, hit the deck, rolled up, and ran for the door—

Zia was a quarter second ahead of Silk—

Fuck—! both men behind her thought—

Colburn tried to process it all, but while time had slowed in the classic tachypsychic effect, so had his thinking speed. Silverman was trying to line up on him for a shot—*blam!*—he got one off, missed! Too many years in an office, he wasn't as sharp as he'd once been—

Zia and Silk had somehow anticipated his move from the chair, had started running before he rolled—

He stretched out and came over prone, gun thrust out at Silverman—

Leonard fired again. It didn't seem to have any sound, but Colburn saw the flame of the propellent—he was high, high!—and the softslug zipped over his prone form, splattered through the wall of fake books and then he was lined up and he squeezed the trigger, once, twice to the chest, the recoil lifted the barrel and he helped it, fired the third shot into Leonard's face, saw his head snap back in reaction as the softslug hit him—

Silk went through the door, almost out of the room. Colburn's brain was in targeting mode. He shifted the pistol and fired again, once, twice, then Silk was gone. But he'd hit him. He was sure of that—

"Shit!" Silk said, as he slammed into the corridor wall, bounced off, and stumbled down the hall behind Zia.

"Silk?"

"He hit me in the back," he said. "I'm okay."

He'd thought it was unnecessary when Zia insisted at the store that he put the thick, heavy spidersilk vest on under his shirt. It was itchy, hot, uncomfortable. And in this moment, one of the smartest things he had ever done.

"Thank me later," Zia said. "Come on!"

He didn't know where she was going, but he was going to follow, wherever it was.

Colburn looked down at Silverman's body, bent and picked up the dead man's weapon, and shoved it into his belt. He reloaded his own pistol. "Sorry, Leonard," he said. "It was you or me, and you should have known better." He had surprised him by showing up here. Should have figured he wouldn't trust Charity Heart on her own. Too easy for her to sell out; after all, she was a whore who sold herself regularly, and she and Colburn got along well enough. Should have guessed that she'd have backup. Never would have figured it was you, though, Leonard. Ah, well.

He edged toward the corridor and peeped quickly around the doorjamb. No sign of Zia or Silk. And no blood on the floor. But he must have hit him; there weren't any holes in the walls, and the slugs must have gone *some*where.

He started to step into the hall. He had to find them and calm them down. Silverman was out of the picture; it was an unfortunate incident, but life went on. There wasn't any reason they couldn't move forward. He could help Silk with his wounds, look good for Zia while doing it, and Silk could get some kind of infection if he wasn't hit too bad—

Something crunched under his boot. He frowned, looked down. There were several sparkly bits laying on the floor, little slivers . . .

He squatted and looked at the floor. Recognized the shiny slivers as the fragmented head of a frangible boron-epoxy bullet.

Hmm.

Either Silk had a back made of something a lot harder than flesh and bone, or he was wearing armor under his shirt.

That would explain it. He grinned. That would have been Zia's idea. They didn't trust him, and rightfully so. Ah, well. Next time, he would shoot Silk in the head. But that would be down the line. To keep Zia from hating him, Silk would have to stay alive until he could get rid of him in private. Silverman had been a glitch, nothing more.

He holstered his pistol. He didn't want to look threatening.

He moved down the corridor. He called to them. "Hey, Zia? Silk? It's okay! I took care of Silverman. It's all over!"

They found a pressurized cargo compartment near the rear of the passenger section. It had oxy but it was considerably colder than the sleeping cabins or communal room, cold enough for their breath to fog the air. Must be for personal storage, Zia told Silk. Save for a half dozen large and dogged-down yellow plastic boxes, it was empty.

Silk said, "Anything?"

"Silverman's dead."

"What about Colburn?"

"I'm not reading him again."

Great!

"Hey, it's not my fault, I don't know how or why it works."

"Sorry. What do we do now? If Silverman's dead, why can't we—?"

"No. First chance he gets, Colburn is going to delete you. I heard that much. If he can do it without upsetting me."

"You might tell him you'll be *really* upset," Silk said. He tried a smile. "So I'm out of the scenario, what happens then?"

"I'm not sure. I think he wants to play house with me."

"Can't blame him for that."

"Christ, I'm so tired of this shit—"

"Take it easy. We're okay. We know something he doesn't. We can play along and find our best time, too."

"Zia? Silk?"

"There he is. Come on. Follow my lead," Silk said.

Zia nodded. She *was* tired. She felt like washing her hands and chanting, "Out, out, damned spot!" Let Silk be in charge.

Colburn came down the hall. "In here," Silk called.

His hands were empty when he rounded the corner and stepped into the storage room. "You two okay? I was worried; Silverman popped a couple of shots at you when you took off. I thought maybe he'd hit you."

"No, we're fine," Silk said. "You get him?"

"Yes. He's dead. We'll shove the body through one of the locks before we crank up the Pull. Nobody'll ever find it."

Silk blew out a breath. "Okay. Then it's back to business like before?"

Colburn looked at them both, his smile frozen. "Right."

In that instant, Colburn knew. Something in Silk's voice, something in the way Zia stood there quietly, whatever it was, he knew. Some instinct warned him:

They knew what he planned to do.

There was no logical reason, nothing he could have pinned to a wall and pointed to, but he was sure of it. If he turned his back on them, he would regret it.

What was he going to do about it—?

Once again, Zia heard Colburn's mental flow. It kicked in like a laserplayer with a bad beam:

—they know. What am I going to do about it—? I guess I'll have to take him out now—!

As hard as she could, she shoved Silk out of the way with her left hand and went for her gun—

Primed to live or die, Colburn's honed reactions were too sharp. He saw Zia reach for her gun and he slapped the butt of his own weapon, made a fast and smooth draw, one the best he'd ever done, got the piece out and pivoted his hand up toward her—

Fool! Don't shoot her!

Too late. His finger was already tightening on the trigger. Too late to stop that. But he managed to jerk his arm slightly to the side. The gun went off and the bullet tore her shirt sleeve but went on to smack into one of the yellow boxes, blowing a fist-sized hole through the plastic—

Zia's draw was almost as fast as Colburn's. But he was right in her face, they were almost touching each other, and when his gun went off and burned along her right triceps, she tried to jump and shoot at the same time. They were so close together that her gun came up under his. The top of her gun hit the butt of his pistol, hard, and both weapons went flying—

Silk, surprised by Zia's shove, lost his balance. He turned the fall into a dive, did an open-bodied shoulder roll and regained his feet in a crouch. Saw Colburn shoot—!

Silk screamed and dug for his pistol—

Gone.

It must have been jolted loose during the roll!

Then Zia knocked the gun out of Colburn's hand, and hers went flying after it. The guns bounced from the wall, clattered onto the floor. Colburn started to turn and go for them—

Zia stepped in and drove her right knee at his groin. He pivoted, caught the blow on his thigh, but it knocked him back. He lashed out with his fist even as he stumbled into the wall, caught Zia's head with the awkward punch. It was enough to stagger her. She fell to one knee, shook her head—

Silk couldn't see his pistol, but Zia's was there; it had slid to a stop a couple of meters away. He jumped toward it—

• • •

Shit!

Colburn hit the wall, rebounded, and dropped into a fighting stance, his left leg forward, braced himself. Zia was down on her knees, shaking her head. Good! But Silk was moving—where was he going? The gun—! He'd never get to his before Silk made it to Zia's fallen piece. Fuck—!

Zia was closer—

Silk dropped to his knees in a parody of *seiza*, snatched up the pistol and spun—

In time to see Colburn wrap his arms around Zia's neck and head in some kind of chokehold, lifting her to her feet.

Silk stood, the pistol aimed at Colburn's head. He kept Zia in front of him, blocking a body shot.

"Put it down," Colburn said. His voice was as cold as interstellar vacuum.

Silk didn't move.

"Do it or I'll break her neck."

"And throw away ten million stads?" Silk said. His voice was as calm as he could make it. He kept the pistol steady.

"We're past the money," Colburn said. "We're talking about life and death. The gun goes on the deck or Zia does."

"You hurt her and I'll shoot you. You can't win."

"Maybe. Everybody dies but you, Silk, and you get to spend the rest of your life regretting it. You love her."

"If I put the gun down, you'll kill us both."

"No. We'll keep our bargain. Same as before."

"Let her go. I can hit you this close before you twitch."

"But you won't risk it. And it wouldn't be sporting, would it?" He stood there silent for a moment, then smiled. "Hey, here's a deal. Kick the other pistol over here. Put yours on the deck. I'll let her go, two guns on the floor, whoever can get to his first wins. A fair fight."

Silk didn't move for a second. Then he raised from the slight crouch and pointed the gun toward the ceiling. Edged toward Colburn's pistol where it lay on the deck.

"Don't do it!" Zia managed before Colburn tightened his grip and cut her off.

Silk shoved Colburn's pistol across the deck with his foot. It slid to a stop a meter in front of them. He turned and took a couple of steps. He was three meters away, two and a half—

"Far enough. Put yours on the deck and stand up. I'll let Zia go, she moves aside, and we do it."

Silk nodded. "Okay."

Zia mumbled something. Silk couldn't make it out. Then she fell silent.

Slowly, Silk squatted, the pistol held in his right hand. He turned it sideways, barrel pointed toward Colburn and Zia. Watched Colburn's face as he started to lower the gun to the deck.

Colburn smiled, and Silk didn't need telepathy to know what he was thinking. He was gathering himself to dust this fool. He was a professional, faster, smarter, tougher than Silk could ever be. He'd told him as much after that warehouse incident. And told him other things, too.

The gun was nearly on the floor. Silk saw Colburn's grip on Zia relax a hair as he prepared to drop and recover his own weapon. Probably as Silk started to stand. Silk would be on the way up, Colburn on the way down. Silk wouldn't have a chance. Colburn would have the jump, he was faster, smarter, tougher.

With a motion that was almost casual, Silk relifted the gun, aimed it one-handed at Colburn's right eye, and pressed the trigger.

It was a jacketed slug and dangerous to shoot on a spaceship, but the bone over Colburn's eye, the brain behind it, and the skull behind that slowed the round enough so it didn't do any damage to the hull when it hit it.

Colburn had enough time between's Silk's move and the bullet that killed him to register surprise. Then he fell away from Zia, his muscles robbed of motive, and collapsed onto the deck.

Faster and tougher, maybe. Not as smart as he thought.

Zia's breath made fog in the air as she stared at the body. At the end, she had seen what Silk planned to do. It amazed her, but probably not as much as it had amazed Colburn.

Silk walked over and looked down at the body, the gun dangling in his hand. She stared at him.

"He thought he knew me," Silk said. "He thought I'd play fair."

He looked back at the dead man. "Your own fault," he said. "You shouldn't have told me those cowboy stories."

Then he and Zia were hugging each other, and the cold and the corpse on the floor didn't bother either of them.

THIRTY-SIX

AN HOUR LATER, with both Colburn and Silverman ejected into vac, they sat in the control chairs while Zia checked the computer. "We're on our way to York," she said finally.

"What then?"

"Well. We don't know who Colburn's pet medic was, but between the two of us, I'm sure we can find one of our own."

"You still want to go through with it?"

"We have to."

"Why? The money?"

"No, you lout, not the money. The Treatment. The same as before. We need to break the monopoly before it gets any deadlier. Plus another reason that's more important."

"More important than the future of the galaxy?"

"Yes. I want you to have the Treatment. That's part of the deal."

"I might not get the telepathic part."

"I think you will; you're halfway there now. And it's the other part that's more important."

"Ah. So we can . . . ?"

"You don't need to say it," she said.

He grinned. No, he didn't need to say it, but he did anyway:

"Live happily ever after."

They smiled at each other.